That Is TOO Wrong!

An Anthology of Offbeat Horror Stories Vol II

Edited by Jan-Andrew Henderson

A Black Hart Publication

Scotland. Australia.

Black Hart Publishing. Brisbane. Edinburgh.
www.blackhartentertainment.com

The rights of the authors to be identified as the authors of this work have been ascertained in accordance with the Copyrights, Designs and Patents Act 1988.

Book Layout © 2019 BookDesignTemplates.com

Edited by Jan-Andrew Henderson
Cover design by Jan-Andrew Henderson and Book Design Stars

That is TOO Wrong!
ISBN: 978-0-6452722-3-9
ISBN: 978-0-6452722-4-6 eBook

Nothing is easier than to denounce the evildoer; nothing is more difficult than to understand him."

Fyodor Dostoevsky

I shall not commit the fashionable stupidity of regarding everything I cannot explain as a fraud.

Carl Jung

For Pamela

Introduction

When I asked for submissions for the horror anthology, *That is So Wrong!* I was astonished by the number of excellent entries I received. As a Scotsman, I abhor waste. So, rather than turn down stories that deserved an audience, I decided to kill everyone in the world with a homemade nuclear bomb.

Well, that was Plan A.

Then my six-year-old suggested Plan B. Bring out another anthology. So, here's *That is TOO Wrong! An Anthology of Offbeat Horror Vol II*

People sometimes ask me what 'offbeat horror' actually is. I have two prepared responses.

"Speak again and I will destroy you."

Or the more polite.

"Fucked if *I* know."

I can tell you this second collection is still short on vampires, zombies and idiotic teenagers in woodland cabins - and there's not a sniff of Cthulhu (I'm presuming he smells). I did sneak in one werewolf, however, because I don't want to disappoint traditionalists.

Instead, I've tried to make the second collection as idiosyncratic as the first. Some stories are intended to make you chuckle. Some to make you wince. A few might make you scratch your head. Not because it's suddenly become infested with green pustules, though that would be a bonus, in my opinion.

Because good horror *is* infectious. It plants a small seed in your brain and makes you see normality in a slightly more sinister way.

It can contaminate anyone and I should know.

I wear all black and always have done. It wasn't anything to do with gothic tendencies - it just made me look slimmer. I also used to live in a haunted graveyard. Not because I relished a view of endless headstones but because the rent was cheap and it was like inhabiting a park - only full of dead people.

Then I started a ghost tour company. Why? Cause it was better than working in a bank. After that, I began writing and collecting horror stories. I dressed in black, lived in a graveyard and ran a ghost tour company, so what else could I do? I *have* tried writing romances but nobody will buy them because the main characters always die.

So, I appreciate the slow slide from normalcy to creepiness. The idea that we are never totally in control of what happens to us. The acceptance that fighting the flow often puts you on a different, darker track. I may as well relish what I have become. I don't like convention and I've picked stories that reflect that.

In many ways, horror is the domain of the outsider. Offbeat horror is the domain of the outsider's outsider.

So, there you go. That's my definition.

Welcome to the club.

Jan-Andrew Henderson

Contents

Introduction.. 5

Contents 7

Looking for Soul Food and a Place to Eat 9

Life, Apathy and Extraterrestrials 23

Dread Circus 31

This Ghost Needs To Fuck Off....................................... 39

A Lovely Little Catch Up.. 49

My Mom Ate My Dad and Here's Why 59

If You Go Down To The Zoo Today. 75

Woke Up Like This.. 85

😁🙀😛👻👣😟 99

Ophelia.. 113

The Killing Pen 125

The Swallow 129

Dragon Rufus Interrupts Class 147

The Tit-Haunted Man... 155

How to Read a Woman 173

Moonlighting.. 179

Something to Do on a Rainy Day When You're Dead 191

Never Give Up 195

Pity the Penguins.. 201

Sugar Mice 205

Cherry Bomb.. 213

About the Authors.. 253

Looking for Soul Food and a Place to Eat

Jan-Andrew Henderson

If a tree falls in the forest and no one hears it, does it make a sound?

George Berkeley: Anglican bishop and philosopher (1685-1753).

To die will be an awfully big adventure

J.M. Barrie. *Peter Pan.*

Daler Board Meeting Minutes: 1

"Progress?"

The Chairman of Daler sat at one end of his long boardroom, sunk in a huge leather chair. He was so far away, I wondered if he was going to whip out opera glasses to see the product properly.

Popper was at the receiving end of his comment and the focus of everyone's attention. He stood in front of a magnificent wide-screen monitor used for official presentations, which he completely ignored. Popper was never one for showing off.

9

On a trolley beside him was an unassuming laptop. It was bigger and clumsier than Daler's current best-seller, the *Mamba Striker 7*. That didn't bode well.

"This is the *Weej 13*," Popper said. "It's a quantum leap forward in our technology. Literally."

"He is so fired," Lacy muttered next to me.

"Specifications," the Chairman snapped.

"It incorporates a quantum chip. Very experimental but undeniably promising. There are no raised keys because the keyboard operates using the same principle as those air hockey games you get in an arcade." Popper thought for a moment. "I suppose you'd just call it a board."

"Clunky, isn't it?" I hissed. "That'll make for a hard sell."

"What about connectivity?" Tennyson from Tech raised his hand. "Are there any marked improvements to the HD screen? Don't tell me you brought the headphone jack back?"

"I sacrificed all that stuff to make way for new components."

The board members gasped. Their eyes apprehensively shifted from Popper to the Chairman, as if they were watching a tennis match played with a grenade.

"Why?"

I had to admire the Chairman's economy with words. The astonished gazes swung back towards Popper.

"I was well on my way to producing *The Mamba Striker 8* when I discovered a function for this machine that no company can match." He shrugged. "To be honest, I've no idea how I did it. But it works and we can replicate it."

"You can't throw a design that took years to perfect out the window for one new application." Tennyson had obviously appointed himself Devil's advocate. "Marketing will go apeshit."

"Billy and I are marketing," Lacy snorted. "Tenn is right, though. *Weej 13* looks like it was built by Atari. In 1989."

"Explain." The Chairman raised a liver-spotted hand to silence them.

"This isn't a laptop." Popper smiled for the first time. "It's a Ouija Board."

There was an eruption of stifled laughter and groans of embarrassment from the board members. The Chairman cleared his throat noisily and the hubbub immediately stopped. He wasn't known for his patience.

"You say it works."

"And how." Popper patted the machine. "It doesn't just talk to the dead. It summons them. Permanently, as far as I can tell."

"This is ridiculous," Tennyson scoffed. "If you're stuck with the new model, just man up and say so."

"Tell that to my technical research assistant, Marylin," Popper retorted. "She's in the lobby outside."

"Did she come up with this dumb idea?"

"Marylin died of cancer six months ago."

The board sprang up, toppling over chairs. They trooped out, murmuring to each other. Lacy and I were about to join them but the Chairman waved us back down.

"Marketing ideas," he commanded.

"Because of COVID-19, you're probably feeling a bit lost and lonely." Lacy stroked her chin. "Now you can have your family with you all the time. Even if they've passed away."

"Don't let death spoil your social life," I added.

"*Weej 13* is a terrible name, though," Lacy complained. "Sounds like a shaman from Glasgow. What about *Mortal Coil 1*?"

"I like it." The Chairman nodded.

The others shuffled back in, white and shaking.

"I put my hand right through her," Tennyson said. "I don't. I just…"

It was nice to see him lost for words.

"Simms?" The Chairman turned to his Head of Finance. "Give Popper whatever he needs to put this into full production."

"Yes, sir."

Popper smiled again.

Daler Board Meeting Minutes: 2

"Report."

"We've certainly let a cat among the pigeons." Julius from Public Relations had the floor and the screen was filled with charts and graphs, which nobody understood. "Let me start with the good news. Sales have exceeded our wildest expectations. In fact, we're struggling to produce enough *Mortal Coils* to satisfy demand."

"That is not good news and you have no idea what my expectations are. Put all our resources into building more machines."

Coming from the Chairman, this constituted a major speech and Julius was suitably abashed.

"We're calling these 'ghosts' The Re-united. We wanted The Re-turned but there are a couple of shows on Netflix already using the term and they threatened litigation for copywrite infringement."

"Acceptable," the Chairman grunted.

"Understandably, we've received flak from all major religions. They're less than pleased to find that, no matter which God they believe in, their adherents can bring back loved ones. They're trying to get around it by various counterclaims."

"Such as?"

"Ghosts don't have souls. It's all a mass hallucination." Julius ticked off the excuses on his fingers. "They're not really spirits but beings from another dimension."

"That's an odd claim for religious institutions to make," Tennyson remarked dryly. "A multiverse kind of makes God redundant."

"So does logic," Lacy smirked. "It's all marketing, Tenn."

"My favourite is their idea that the whole thing is a trick by Satan," Julius continued.

All eyes switched to the Chairman but the irony was obviously lost on him. He wasn't known for his sense of humour.

"Officially, we're in the clear," Passmore from Legal broke in. "There's no law against what we're selling."

"Our biggest problem is that the Re-united don't seem to *do* much. They kind of hang about the places they're used to, performing the same actions they always did. Don't show a lot of interest in the people who summoned them, neither."

Julius shrugged

"At the moment, the sheer novelty of having your dead dad around is enough. That may wane with time, I imagine."

"Your loved ones the way you always wanted them." I framed a banner in the air. "No mess. No fuss."

"Billy and I have plenty of advertising ideas, never fear." Lacy exuded confidence, like always.

"As you suggested in your memo," Julius said. "The board has all had a go at resurrecting someone. Now we need some feedback."

A few of the members winced. A suggestion from the Charman was really an order.

"C'mon, folks," Julius urged. "Can't do my job properly if you won't flag any obstacles."

"My mum follows me from room to room," Tennyson said eventually. "She doesn't hassle me or anything, but..."

He lapsed into sullen silence.

"Out with it," the Chairman commanded.

"I've got a Maserati and a penthouse apartment - but how am I supposed to bring a girl home now?" His face reddened. "I can't even... ehm... masturbate with her watching."

"I have the opposite problem," Simms put his head in both hands. "My gran goes at it with a vibrator every day. Four o'clock on the dot."

There was muted sniggering around the table.

"It's not funny," Simms cried. "I've had to go into therapy."

"There is a point I'd like to raise," Lacy said. "My sister and her boyfriend died in a car crash so, naturally, I brought her back."

I raised an eyebrow. I hadn't known about any sister. Then again, Lacy and I were work colleagues rather than friends.

"A few days later, the boyfriend appeared too." Lacy frowned. "They spend all day necking on the couch. And... more."

"There you go," Julius beamed. "Isn't that nice?"

"Lovers Re-united," I gave Lacy a thumbs up. "See what I did there? We could use it as a tagline."

"Only, I didn't bring the boyfriend back," Lacy continued sourly. "I can't imagine who would. He was a violent scumbag, everyone but my sister hated. Even his parents disowned him."

"I'll have the research department look into that." Julius blanched. Then he reluctantly asked the question on all our minds.

"Did... eh... you partake in the experiment, Sir?" He bit his lip nervously. "Perhaps you'd like to share your experience."

"I only look to the future," the Chairman said evenly. "The dead are has-beens."

Daler Board Meeting Minutes: 3

"Where is Simms?" the Chairman demanded.

The board members fidgeted awkwardly in their seats and glanced at an empty chair.

"Simms committed suicide," Tennyson said finally. "I guess he didn't like his grandmother as much as he thought."

"Then why isn't he here?"

"Good point, sir." Bertram from Personnel made a quick note. "I'll draw up his dismissal papers."

Poor old Simms. Now he was dead, stuck with his horny gran and out of a job. He never was one for thinking things through.

"Continue," the Chairman folded bony hands on his chest.

Popper had the floor. The man's face was pale from lack of sleep and his dishevelled hair was sticking up, as if he had seen a ghost. Which was more than likely, under the circumstances. Come to think of it, the entire board was looking worse for wear.

"The Re-united appear to be acclimatising to life among the living," Popper said glumly. "It looks like they've started bringing back their own loved ones, whether the device's owner likes it or not."

"Didn't you include password protection?" The Chairman's face was granite.

"It's hard to hide stuff like that when a dead person is always looking over your shoulder. A lot of customers are trying to return the machines before their warranty expires."

"Got that covered," the Head of Marketing assured us. "*Mortal Coil* does exactly what it's meant to. No refunds."

"Excellent."

"It's getting rather disturbing, though," Popper said. "My dad brought back his dad, who brought back his dad... and so on." He wiped his brow. "I found a Nazi in the garden shed and a Victorian gardener trying to dig up my rose bushes."

"Projections?" The Chairman was not known for his sympathetic nature.

"Roughly 15 times as many people have died in the past as are living now. If this carries on, the world is going to get very crowded. Add in the animals and..."

"Animals?"

"Dogs and cats, mainly. But there have been reports of bison on the streets of Chicago. I presume some expired medicine man is behind that."

"I'm loath to do anything so drastic." Tennyson hesitated. "But I feel we may have to consider a recall."

"I second that," Lacy added belligerently. "I've got a Roman Centurion on my toilet."

"I don't think it matters," Popper said quietly. "I'm pretty sure the Re-united have learned to bring back folk from the other side without the need for technology."

"That's an infringement of our patents." The Chairman's eyes blazed. "How do we get rid of them?"

"I don't know."

"Figure it out!" Tennyson urged. "We're already facing some major class-action lawsuits."

"It's worse than that," Popper replied. "Folk can see what it's like to be dead and they're none too pleased by the revelation. People are turning to atheism in their millions."

"Positives?" The Chairman demanded.

"Well, wars have almost stopped because nobody is willing to die anymore," Julius said. "Except Simms, apparently."

"That's not a positive," the Chairman grunted. "We have an armaments division."

"No, Sir. Sorry, Sir." Julius shot Popper an anguished glance. "Perhaps we could reverse the polarity on the machine?"

"This isn't an episode of fucking *Star Trek*, Julius. I'm working on it."

"Miss McPherson?" It was the first time the Chairman had ever used Lacy's name. He must be desperate.

"I can't see any spin that will work in these circumstances," Lacy admitted. "We're up shit creek without a canoe, never mind a paddle and our stocks are sinking."

"Disappointing." The Chairman pursed his lips, managing to give everyone the evil eye at once. "I don't pay you to fail."

"No," Lacy shot back. "You're paying us to take the blame for *your* failure. I'm not some inverse exorcist and I do my job bloody well."

There was a shocked hush and Julius almost slid under the table.

"Hmmmmm. If you want something done right, do it yourself." The Chairman got slowly to his feet. "All right. I shall be back once I've sorted this."

He walked, ramrod straight, to the window and slid it open.

"In the meantime, Miss McPherson is in charge."

"Me?" Lacy stammered. "Why?"

"You're the only person who ever dared contradict me."

Then he jumped.

We ran to the window and peered out. The Chairman was a crumpled speck on the sidewalk, twenty floors below. He wasn't known for his ability to take criticism.

"Give the man his due," I whistled. "He put his money where his mouth is."

At the moment, his mouth was probably somewhere at the back of his skull, but I felt that would be taking the analogy a tad far.

"Get on the *Mortal Coil* and bring him back," Julius urged Popper. "See if he has any answers."

"What's the point?" Popper was shaking. "He's going to be like the rest of them."

"He's the Chairman," Julius objected. "Nothing stops that bastard getting what he wants."

"We'll wait a few hours." Lacy stopped the argument with a raised finger. "Give him time to find some answers."

"You're the boss." Popper shut the laptop.

"Yes," Lacy grinned. "Yes, I am."

I shuddered.

Daler Board Meeting Minutes: 4

"Report."

Lacy sat in the Chairman's leather seat, wearing an expensive chiffon jacket. It felt strange not having my only confidant next to me.

The other board members seemed bone-weary and dispirited. Bertram was wearing pyjamas with bunny slippers and looked like he'd had them on for several days. There was an egg stain down the front of his dressing gown.

"We found the Chairman." Popper was close to tears. "He's in his mansion out on the West Key. Spends most of his time trying to do a jigsaw puzzle he can't touch and shouting at the staff. Doesn't seem to realise they all quit."

"Sales?"

"Non-existent."

"Legal status?"

"Now we're being sued by the right-to-life mob." Passmore heaved a sigh. "We've got Neanderthals and mammoths running around but no dead foetuses. They claim we're hiding them in Guantanamo Bay."

I noticed Passmore had grown a beard. It might have been a disguise, as the board were getting daily threats on their lives. Or, perhaps, he didn't see the point in shaving anymore.

"We're fighting lawsuits brought about by The Christian League, who are horrified by the fact that they found Jesus and he looks like a Palestinian. Plus the Arab states, the World Health Organisation, the American society for Psychics, The Proud Boys and Donald Trump, to name but a few."

"Donald Trump?"

"He claims the dead voted against him illegally."

"Yeah, but that was after the elect... Aw, never mind." Lacy closed her eyes wearily.

"There's also a jihad out on all board members but, thankfully, not many takers. World religions have well and truly lost their appeal with the populace."

"Summation?"

There was silence from the board. Bertram produced a pair of needles and began to knit.

"We are well and truly fucked?" I volunteered.

"Put out a press release." Lacy patted her cheeks and let out a huge sigh. "Say we are days off finding a way to return the Re-united to whence they came."

"You really want to use the word *whence*?" Tennyson asked. "It's old-fashioned."

"I don't give a shit how you phrase it." Lacy stood up. "We'll find a way around the problem. We always do. And at the next meeting, I want you all groomed and in suits."

She put on her overcoat.

"Meeting adjourned. I need a triple vodka and Coke. Usual place, if anyone cares to join me.

The board began packing away their things.

"You too, Popper," Lacy commanded. "Bring your research. We need to pick your brains."

"I do have some ideas," Popper sighed. "Normally I'm not much of a drinker but tonight I'll make an exception."

We sat in the local bar. A couple of shady characters were playing pool and there was a collection of mountain men skinning beaver in one corner.

"I don't get it," Tennyson complained. "These ghosts are incorporeal. Why don't they sink into the earth or fly off into space?"

"Death, like life, is full of unanswered questions," Bertram said philosophically.

"Whatevs. If we've no idea where these bastards came from, how can we send them back?" Tennyson raised a middle digit to the mountain men. "I'm not sure Popper is up to the task."

"I'm right next to you, dumbass," Popper slurred, waving to the barman. "Another whisky and pineapple, please."

"Settle down, Pops," Lacy grunted. "Let's hear your words of wisdom."

I was tired of the whole thing, so I made my excuses and left. Just like last time.

That's what saved my life.

A car bomb demolished the building five minutes later. About twenty different organisations claimed they were behind it. Except Donald Trump, who denied all responsibility.

Phelps from Homeland Security was waiting for me as I left the bar.

"Any luck, Billy?"

"I didn't learn anything about how to send the Re-united back. But I took minutes like you asked."

"You were part of the team who developed *Mortal Coil*." Phelps' displeasure was palpable. "I thought you might have some insight we missed."

"For the hundredth time, I was in the marketing department. They'll repeat the same actions, over and over, until they die again. Send in a whole squad of agents for the next round, if you want. The board won't notice."

Then I had a thought.

"Didn't you get hold of Popper's research?"

"It's encrypted and his handwritten notes went up in the blast." Phelps sighed. "His ghost carries them around in a folder but, of course, we can't open the damned thing."

He shook my hand.

"I guess you kept your end of the bargain. You're free to go."

He glanced around

"Wow. Is that a velociraptor?"

I walked back to my house, as it was a beautiful night. The streets were packed with partygoers, though I couldn't tell which were dead and which alive. There was a group of ranch hands practising their quick draw on 21st Avenue but they might have been in fancy dress. Not that it mattered. In the city, almost everyone is a stranger.

No cars, though, which was nice. Drivers didn't want to plough through a bunch of phantoms and discover they'd mown down a real pedestrian in the process. The air smelt clean for a change.

When I got home, I made myself some dinner and sat between my parents.

"Did you know?" I said. "The Aztecs made swords embedded with prismatic obsidian that are far sharper than present-day razor blades? Or Ancient Egypt had proctologists called 'shepherds of the anus'? That Mayans cultivated stingless bees in Central America and the Indus Valley Civilization had the world's earliest known flush toilets?"

They didn't seem interested in my revelations but no surprise there. They never had. Also, they died in 1996.

"It's amazing what you can learn these days, just by observing."

Because I *had* been observing. Well... snooping. It's a trait of mine. For instance, when Popper was still alive, I'd snuck into his office and had a peek at his notes.

But I'd no intention of telling Phelps from Homeland Security what Popper had written on the last page.

One of the most bizarre premises of quantum theory states that, by the very act of watching, the observer affects observed reality.

"The board were looking at this all wrong," I told mum and dad. "The Re-united haven't come from anywhere. They were always here. We just couldn't see them."

"Would you like some melted cheese on toast?" Mum asked dad.

"Yes, dear, I would."

"It's simple quantum physics," I continued. "*The Mortal Coil 1* didn't summon anyone. It just made them visible to those who are alive."

I patted my mother's knee affectionately and my hand slid through to the couch. Still, it was nice having them around again. My wife would be home soon, too. She'd ignore me, of course. The fact that she was still alive wouldn't change that.

It's about acceptance, in the end. All in all, I was quite satisfied with how the world was turning out and saw no need to alter it. That was the problem with corporate types and government departments. They couldn't stand change unless they were controlling it.

"You want the problem to stop existing?" I shrugged. "Shut your fucking eyes."

I got up, fetched myself a glass of wine and sat down again.

"I can't believe nobody gets that. After all, it's what we always do."

Then again, people are not known for their common sense.

Life, Apathy and Extraterrestrials

Justin Zipprich

No shit, there I was. Sitting at work, gazing out the window, when I first saw the spaceships. There were three of them, up in the sky. And, to be honest, they were a little boring. No bells or whistles. No fancy lights. Just plain Jane, run-of-the-mill, metallic flying saucers. They simply sat there, high in the air, for at least three hours. I know for sure it was that long because that's the amount of time I spent at my workstation staring out the window.

I find work to be overrated.

I have a pretty boring job, so I never really feel like doing any actual work. It's a rather mundane position. I specialize in life insurance but, no, I'm not an insurance salesman. I don't go door-to-door and bug you while you're eating dinner or anything like that. I work in an office, supporting those that bug you during dinner. I complete checklists, verify licenses, scan documents and blah, blah, blah. I don't get paid very much and the management doesn't appreciate me, so I basically walk in every day with the intention of slacking off.

At the age of thirty-one, I thought for sure I'd be making more than thirty thousand dollars per year. They say we're still feeling the effects of recession and, some months, people have to decide between buying food for their families and paying rent. I've read all the stories but don't always believe them. Most people I hear about are making plenty of money. That's how they afford all those fancy cars.

Take my friend Pat, for instance. He works at a retail store and makes almost one hundred thousand dollars a year. I see annual incomes for our clients on their life insurance applications and I've rarely come across any of them making less than fifty grand per year. All I'm trying to say is, there's money to be made. Finding a way to get it is the hard part. But I digress.

After clocking out five minutes early, I walked to my car and noticed the spaceships had multiplied by the hundreds. Soon the sky was filled with these flying, silvery orbs. It was so saturated by polished silver the setting sun had been completely blotted out, leaving nothing but near darkness.

By the time I arrived home and flicked on the television set, they had descended. A fun-loving MTV type news personality, with too many tattoos and a hipster hairstyle, described the scene.

A cluster of ships had landed in every city across the globe. The footage was pretty rad, aliens descending and introducing themselves to the people of planet Earth. Walking down the metallic ramps, they resembled beings from those invasion flicks of the nineteen fifties. Small grey bodies, large oblong heads and black oval eyes. They utilized a small slit of a mouth to talk and, to absolutely no one's surprise, did not speak English.

As they spouted their gibberish to the world, the rest of us sat at home, glued to our television sets watching the live feed. Apparently, the aliens had a lot on their minds because they spoke for hours. I'm sure they opened with the classic request. "Take me to your leader."

How cliché would that be? I mean, whom are they even referring to when they say that? Did they mean the President? The Prime Minister? Is there such a thing as a leader of the world? If so, who is he? What does he do? How can anyone possibly deal with all of that power? But, of course, I digress.

Sitting back on the couch, bored to tears, while trying to rationalize the very idea of a world leader - I found myself falling asleep.

I woke up, a few hours later, to the sound of static. The television seemed to be on the fritz again. It did that from time to time. I must have lost the signal.

Suddenly I remembered the whole alien ordeal and began wondering what new developments had occurred while I'd been snoozing. I tried to flip through the channels but every button I pressed presented me with more snowy static. No huge deal. I'd just call my friend Big Mike later on to get the details. Big Mike was usually up on these things. He was the best small appliance repair guy on the west coast and a self-appointed expert on black-market information regarding the threats of technology.

Back in 1999, Big Mike was the first person to tell me about that Y2K bug and all the panic and chaos that would come along with it. When the year 2000 rolled around, I asked him what happened with all the bad Y2K stuff that was supposed to happen.

He just shrugged his shoulders and told me it wasn't their time.

He also told me all the stuff that went down in the *Terminator* movies could really happen too! He said he takes care of small appliances because, when the machine revolution happens, he wants to find himself on the right side. I'll have to think about that next time I decide to pick a fight with my refrigerator.

I figured I'd call him in the morning. For now, I decided it was time to make myself some dinner.

As soon as I walked into my small kitchen, I almost had a heart attack. In front of me, holding a box of generic breakfast cereal, stood one of the alien beings. Up close, I could clearly see the details of the interstellar traveler. Its gray skin was greasy and oilier than it had appeared on television. The creature also had two short antennae atop its head and what appeared to be a deep pouch on its belly, which housed God knew what. It cocked its head to the side as it looked at me.

While the alien and I engaged in a staring contest, I couldn't help but think about the ways that people on our planet were divided when it came to space invaders. They could be split into two groups and it all depended on what type of movies they enjoyed more.

Group one were fans of the 'mean alien' films like *Independence Day*, *War of the Worlds* and *Signs*. In those, the aliens came down to cause hell and murder everyone and everything in sight. These movies made this group absolutely terrified at the prospect of extraterrestrial life. They knew there were monsters in space whose only intention was to exterminate all life on Earth. They were here to slurp out our brains and rip us from limb to limb, while they used advanced tools to suck away all of Earth's natural resources, like the innards of a milkshake. After which they would go back to their planet while leaving ours in ruin. That is, unless actor Will Smith defeated them. Then we would all be saved.

I personally felt I was a member of the second group, who liked 'friendly alien' movies. We were fans of Spielberg's *E.T. the Extraterrestrial*, *Earth to Echo* and *Super 8*. We believed aliens would come to our planet simply to explore and, ultimately, be our best friends.

Sure, the members of group one would misunderstand them. But us few believers would soon create a friendship with the creatures. Hell, they might even give us special powers we could use to help those in need. I had always wanted an E.T. of my own and now I had the golden opportunity.

The plan was to slowly saunter towards the being, as if approaching a cat. I would outstretch one hand, so it could sniff a few fingers and realize that I meant no harm. Once it was used to me, we would become the greatest of pals. We'd hang out all the time, play video games and create a special language that only we could understand. Then we'd tour the country under the stage name UFO - or Ultimate Fun Organization! We would perform magic tricks for all those young at heart.

I quickly realized I had included myself in the wrong group. I was ripped from my fantasy by a squid-like projectile that emerged from the alien's greasy front pouch. The mini beast hurled itself at my head, at what must have been one hundred miles an hour. With no chance to duck, the squid made contact and used its tentacles to latch onto my skull in an uncompromising death grip. A long umbilical type cord connected the squid to its host.

In a panic, I shook my head as hard as I could in every possible direction. I slammed it against the refrigerator, the cabinets, anything to dislodge the grotesque creature. Finally, I exhausted myself and sat down cross-legged, letting the creature do its bidding.

I heard a slurping sound and felt a searing pain as a sharp appendage shoved through my skull. In complete misery, I felt the attachment drill deeper, forcing itself into my brain.

Devoid of all free will, my body and mind were now under the alien's control. It forced me to stand, turn around and walk towards the front door. Once outside, I realized I was not alone. As I was escorted down my street, I was joined by hundreds of my fellow human beings. All of us walking around like zombies, each with our own personal alien-squid combination. The creatures spoke through us as they communicated with one another. What came out of our mouths was gibberish, sounds that our vocal cords could never have achieved without the aliens' aid.

In the distance, I could see the skyscrapers that made up the famed city of Los Angeles. I had a feeling the city was our destination and I was apathetic about the whole situation. On one hand, L.A. was a fun place to visit when friends came to town. There was a bunch of different bars, museums and other sights to see, that were of some interest. On the other hand, I didn't like how dirty the place had gotten over the last couple of years. The mayor had made all these campaign promises about clean streets and pollution laws. Unfortunately, that had gone out the window after he was elected into office.

These days the streets were covered in trash, while the homeless ran rampant and violent gangs controlled most of the neighborhoods. If you didn't watch your step, a brief friendly visit could easily end in death.

Now that I thought about it, perhaps the aliens were here to clean up this crumbling city. They had, no doubt, been around for centuries.

They probably sat by the wayside as all the negative changes occurred to our beloved home. They'd have seen it all. From the glory days when Los Angeles was a beacon of hope, to a steep decline into the awful place it had become.

I bet that must be it! I was now very optimistic the aliens had descended on our planet in order to use us humans. To whip this city back up into the wonderful place it once was!

What else could it be? I bet they were also going to teach that rotten mayor a thing or two about how to treat his citizens. This was why they'd come, I was convinced of it.

I was thrilled to be a part of the revolution!

It has been two months since the aliens landed on Earth and life, as we know it, has come to an end. Giant robots were brought in for the sole purpose of reducing Los Angeles to a pile of rubble. Any buildings that resembled our modern architecture have been destroyed and replaced with thousand-foot statues, in the shapes of the alien leaders' heads. On top of that, they've made that rotten mayor an honorary member of their race. The guy is like a king to them.

Almost every human being has been eradicated from the planet and only a small group have been left alive. We spend most of our time building statues and praying for sweet, merciful death. They whip everyone constantly, often forcing us to fall asleep in a pool of our own blood. Of course, I don't construct the statues. I work in the fields, supporting those who construct those statues. I carry heavy stones, slave for sixteen hours a day and blah, blah, blah.

I don't get paid much and alien management doesn't appreciate me, so I try to slack off. When I do, I'm beaten within an inch of my life.

It's a hard slog but I guess somebody has to do it. Maybe, someday, I'll make my escape from these alien oppressors. If I can, I'll run off to France, where I heard there's a safe house for escaped humans -

a colony of sorts. Speaking of France, whatever happened to those striped shirts they used to wear? Do they still do that?

But I digress.

Dread Circus

Pamela Jeffs

Sabine

This circus hungers for sorrow and souls and our ringmaster is the butcher who feeds it. His footsteps fall heavy as he circles me, brocade gleaming gold against the blood-red of his jacket. His whip trails in the sawdust, braided brown leather, serpent thin and the knotted end, wicked.

"You will fly, Sabine," he says.

My muscles tremble. My heart raps against my ribs. I look to the audience stands for help but they are empty, cleared since this night's performance finished five hours ago. Only midnight's cruel darkness watches now. I clench my fists, clawing at the newly-raked sawdust floor of the main ring. The dry scent of wood curls around me.

"I will not," I say.

Another step. The ringmaster's whip slithers.

"The terms of your contract are clear. One soul for thirty years of health. I kept my side of the bargain. Now, you must keep yours."

It was a contract signed with the devil's henchman. I was young and dying, cancer in my bones. Who would not give their soul in return for thirty more years of life?

The cost seemed worth the gain at the time.

The single spotlight pins me to the floor, its beam ephemeral but as strong as any prison. My fear crowds closer. Beyond, half-hidden in the shadows, I glimpse the red-white of the big top's canvas walls - brilliant colours. Colours that consume.

31

The fabric billows but not in the friendly way a breeze moves canvas. Something seethes behind the surface, dwelling in the space between the fabric and the outside world. Something with claws.

My chin dips to my chest. A sob sits locked behind my teeth. If I fly, my daughter, Belle, will be left with him. She is only sixteen years old.

The ringmaster's voice is smoke and coloured with the promise of death.

"Shall your child be made to go in your place?"

"NO!" the word tears out of my throat before I think. "You cannot."

The ringmaster smiles. His long, silver moustache gleams like chrome.

"Then you will fly."

A shadow catches my attention. A small, thin shape slithers in beneath the arena seats. A flash of white-blond hair. Belle. My stomach drops.

I told her not to come.

Belle

I was born to the circus, bred to fly the trapeze above the main ring, like my mother. But I have other gifts too. I see what normal people can't - that which is hidden from the souls contracted to this circus's dreadful purposes. I've met the terrible being that truly owns this arena, he who the ringmaster fears. Seen the other bone-white, ragged-winged monsters that preside over intimate midnight shows where performers, following their thirty-year contracts, disappear.

Those creatures live in the shadows between the panel seams of the big top. They call the ringmaster to them when they are hungry, when their bodies are drained of colour and become weak. White-eyed, they crawl out of the walls, ruined wings dragging and forked tongues licking at the air.

And he feeds to them his sacrificial lambs.

Tonight, the monsters already line the arena, clinging to the shadows. Their voices mutter in sibilant hisses as they bicker between themselves, each anticipating the consumption of the trapeze artist named Sabine.

My beloved mother.

"I want the blue of her eyes," whispers one monster.

"The warm gold of her hair is mine," says another.

"That's good," lisps a third, "It leaves the pink flush of her cheeks to me."

The ringmaster circles. His whip slithers up and over my mother's back. Her shoulders tremble and the spotlight refracts, like shattered rainbows, off the sequins of her costume.

The monsters salivate, drinking in the watered-down pigment.

But it doesn't sate them.

I know, because I've watched this show before.

Sabine

How you die, is up to you. Like those before me, I choose to go with dignity.

I rise to my feet, thankful to stretch the cramps from my legs. I lift my chin and imagine the stars are gleaming bright outside. That those heavenly bodies will gather me into their company.

I refuse to look at Belle, lingering in the shadows. How I wish she hadn't come. She sees things the rest of us don't, often talking to gods, angels and demons. She knows the truth.

Yet I fear what she will witness now - worry that she will see and never sleep again. For I know what it is to witness a loved one flying and that dreadful, final moment when their life-light winks out. I set my shoulders and send Belle a silent thought of love and strength.

She will need it.

The ringmaster coils his whip away and grins, shark-like. He clicks his fingers and, from the ceiling, falls a climbing rope. But it is not the one I use in the show for the townsfolk. This one is different, made from the spines of those who have flown and fed the circus before me.

I grasp it, shuddering at the cold that seeps into my skin. The yellowed bones and dried connective tissues whisper of lengthened lives and unnatural deaths. My husband Manfred, Belle's father, numbers amongst them. We met here in the circus and fell in love. Ten years we had together before his contract was due. He flew and his spine was added to the rope, long ago.

I begin the climb, the bone edges jagged against my palms.

I will be brave like Manfred was.

Courage in the face of fear will be the last lesson I give my Belle.

Belle

My mother climbs, a butterfly pinned by the light. The bone rope clatters with each movement. The monsters around her still, their anticipation rendering them silent.

Despicable, they wait.

She reaches the swinging hoop. For an instant the light catches her cheeks and the ghost of the unshed tears that slick them. A deep breath and then she soars.

Sabine flies like an eagle, sequined in gold and silver, and oh so brave. She tumbles and twists, the perfection of her art stunning to behold. She floats past the red-white, red-white panels of the big top, graceful as a swan. Then her face changes.

Her hands turn to stone. A cry escapes her lips. But she doesn't fall. She keeps flying.

Tendrils of colour - the yellow of her hair and the red from her lips - peel away from her, whisper thin. From the shadows the monsters lumber to their feet, dead eyes rapturous and gnarled arms held toward the light. Their tongues uncurl, eager to capture the essence that is my mother.

As the hues of her body fall like smoke through the air, the creatures devour them. With ingestion comes a flush of new life and health to their broken bodies. Their forms smooth out and, in moments, they are no longer the pitiful creatures they were. Instead, they are silver-haired and pale-skinned angels, glistening wings of gold held regal above their shoulders.

But their eyes still look dead. These are fallen angels, regaining only a measure of the splendor they owned before their fall from grace.

My mother flies but for a moment more. Her colour having faded, she is a chalk-white statue clinging to the hoop. Then she dissolves into a fall of dust and a tumble of bones.

The ringmaster's whip cracks out. The end catches my mother's spine before it hits the ground. With a flick of his wrist, the bones twist and click into place at the end of the rope.

Sabine has taken her place in the dread circus.

I promise myself I will not cry. I am as my mother was…

Brave.

The golden-winged angels step out of the darkness and into the arena. The light does not hurt them now. They circle the ringmaster and each places a hand on his shoulder.

"Payment," says the largest of the angels and he breathes a measure of his own new life into my mother's killer. The ringmaster's white hair darkens and his withered face grows smooth.

The angels disappear, melting back into the bright-paneled canvas walls. The ringleader stands for a moment in the centre of the empty arena. His long beard, now black, sweeps down his chest.

"Belle," he says. "Come out."

I crawl back against the frame of the seat and huddle my knees to my chest. My hands are still small. There is not much colour in them yet.

I press my eyes closed.

I will not fly. Not yet.

Footsteps then black boots appear, covered in the dust of my mother's demise.

The ringmaster stops by the seat.

"Go back to bed, child," he orders.

I draw my courage close and crawl free from my hiding spot. I straighten my shirt and stand facing the ringmaster. He is much taller than me.

"I know what you are," I say.

"And what is that?"

"A butcher. A demon."

"What will you do about it?"

I clench my fists. Hatred burns, a hot coal in my heart.

"I will see your bones added to the rope."

The ringmaster chuckles. His eyebrows rise in mock fear.

"Then perhaps I should make you fly now!"

"You have no power over me."

"Your mother should have read the small print," he grins. "What was hers is now mine. That includes her daughter."

"Perhaps once," I correct. "However, I have signed a contract with another."

"Who might that be?" The ringmaster laughs. "I am God in this arena."

"A poor choice of words. My agreement is with the *owner* of the circus."

His eyes widen. The canvas around us ripples.

"I will be the star attraction. You are merely a middleman. Expendable. Replaceable."

"What have you done?" he whispers.

"In exchange for offering my soul," I say. "I have demanded yours."

The ghosts surge forward. More than I can count. My mother among them. They sweep by me, reaching for their enemy and mine.

Their touch is poison to his flesh.

Dark hair turns silver, then white. His hands solidify to stone. A dreadful scream and he crumbles into a pile of dust and scattered bones.

The troupe steps back. Sabine looks at me with tears in her eyes.

"I was never going to be free, mother. But I have avenged you and, for a short time, I will soar."

From the ruin of his corpse, I claim the ringmaster's whip and put his hat on my head.

The monsters in the big top's seams begin to mutter.

This Ghost Needs To Fuck Off

B.O.B. Jenkin

Being bullied by a ghost is the pits. Makes me envious of all those families who go through normal hauntings in those supposedly-true movies. I want to be jumping at shadows, afraid of every creaking floorboard in the wee hours. That scene in *Poltergeist* where the dude peels his own face off after seeing crawling meat? That sounds like a lovely change of pace from my current existence.

"James! Slow down, James."

Great, here she comes now. At least she's not insulting me yet.

"I said to wait, you shitty incel."

Are you kidding me? Concrete echoes the impatient tapping of my polished dress shoes as I mumble, "I'm waiting."

Meet Ania, the flailing ball of arms currently heading in my direction. Did nobody teach her how to run before she died? Sucks she's a corpse - she'd be a looker, if not for the deep indentation along the side of her face that leaves one eye popped out and dangling along her cheek. We were classmates three different times over the years and she never once talked to me. Yet, now that she's deceased, she proves impossible to shake.

"How come you always start walking home without me?" Ania whines when she reaches my side.

"Because, half the days, you never even show up. Is that a ghost rule, like you can't always control when you appear, or are you just an airhead?"

"Maybe I only come when I know you have a new short story you want me to read."

"I don't *want* you to read them, but you always seem so interested that showing you is easier than describing them. And you could give some constructive feedback, you know?"

The clouds part and the city is revealed in its shining glory. The sun always illuminates Ania's see-through aspects. The skyscraper behind her looks like something she ate for breakfast which now threatens to burst from her body.

"I do give constructive feedback, you picky hack!"

"Telling me I'm projecting my virginity on every character is hardly what I consider helpful."

"You idiot, it's the most useful advice you'll ever get. All those losers in your writing group are virgins, too, so they won't know how to help. Lemme see your new one. I want to read what lonely losers you wrote about this time."

She's somehow able to unzip my bag to steal my notebook, yet when I try to catch her by the arm to retrieve it, she's incorporeal as smoke. When she plops on a stoop to read, I'm left with no choice but to wait around or risk losing my handwritten first draft. Guess I can kill time on my phone. Hello email, Reddit, and Discord. I wonder if any Amazon packages arrived today.

Does she actually like my stories? Maybe she only follows me because my tales often involve ghosts and she thinks I'm an expert on the topic. I'm less shocked she likes M.R. James style stuff and more impressed that she's willing to wade through my miles-long paragraphs of James Joyce inspired postmodernist tomfoolery.

When she finishes my newest yarn, about an elderly man with dementia who thinks he's still a high school student and doesn't understand where his parents went, I'm fascinated to learn that ghosts can cry.

"You liked it?" I say as she rises to approach me. Her only reply is an angry shoving of the notebook into my hands before storming off.

"What? If the story said something insensitive, that's what editing is for. I didn't mean to upset you."

I think she's not going to answer, but after a minute of silence, she says...

"Stories like this are the only reason I put up with you." And, before I can say *thanks*, she adds. *"You shitty loner."*

This girl! Now I'm glad my story made her cry. I'm starting to think whoever killed her did it for a good reason.

"You know, I've been talking to my therapist about you."

Now, *this* captures her attention.

"You told them you're talking to a ghost? Dude, you're gonna be institutionalized."

"No. I said a girl is bullying me every day when I walk home from school and asked for advice. I'm starting to think he's a quack, though, because he said it sounded less like bullying and more like flirting. And that obviously isn't the case. Right?"

The fact that her cheeks are now beet red makes me think I finally found a sore spot. How does a dead person even have blood rush to their face? I obviously don't believe Ania likes me, but some girls get more self-conscious about this accusation than others. Hence the following overreaction.

"You shitty incel. I know you're jacking off thinking about me. Next time it happens, I'll put a ghost curse on your dick so it withers and falls off."

"Eh? That's not a real thing, is it?" A minute passes without answer. "If anything happens to my Johnson, I'm calling the Warrens to exorcise you."

"Count your blessings a girl is even talking to you. And, by the way, I'm totally expecting you to figure out who murdered me. Hope that's not a big deal."

Yeah, I trip over my own feet. Who wouldn't be thrown for a loop by such a sudden segue?

"Wait, what? How am I supposed to find that out? Aren't there, I don't know, real detectives on the case?"

"They already gave up. Plus, they can't see me, so you're the only person I can pass relevant evidence onto."

"You mean you don't hang out with me for my winning personality?"

"If I could pick and choose, you'd be the last person I'd reveal myself to. Now listen, it all started with…"

And so begins a tale told in brief glimpses and way-too-close-up visuals, the plot lost in tiny details which will, hopefully, paint a picture I can use: Nike shoes polka-dotted with blood. A metal baseball bat, dented as her head. Soaring beneath a blazing sun into glittering Stark's Pond. A man's face, grown distorted as some Lynchian demon, the light's angle leaving him a writhing wall of black.

"What am I supposed to do with that?" I demand. "The only thing I learned that the cops don't know is the killer wears Nikes. Hell, half the city does. I'm wearing some right now."

"Oh yeah, I also forgot to tell you the list of suspects."

One. Mr. Tompkins, the math teacher.

"Dude was always having me stay after class to talk about my feelings. Major creep."

Two. Shitty Asshole - AKA her new stepdad whose name she never bothered to learn.

"Always lurking near the bathroom after I shower to see me walking to my room in a towel. There's also a third suspect I've been considering. He was this total weirdo loner in class, who never talked to anyone, yet all us girls could feel him undressing us with his eyes. It was super creepy and - hey, why are you running away?"

"Take me off the suspect list or I'm not helping!"

"But you admitted you wear Nikes! If you confess, I'll be kind and forgive you. I know you virgins can't control your violent outbursts."

This girl! One thing leads to another and now we're lurking outside her family home, waiting for the supposedly perverted stepdad to enter the scene and hopefully mutter something to himself about the time he killed Ania loud enough so my phone can tape it.

"Seriously," I snap. "What are you expecting me to accomplish here?"

Ignoring me.

"It's nice to see the old neighborhood."

It's a neighborhood I could do without seeing again for as long as I live. Children run in packs, some riding stray dogs and every adult lurks behind a veil of cigarette smoke. No way I'm getting home without being mugged. Ania is lucky she has such a depressing backstory or I'd never put up with this.

When a car pulls into her driveway and a laughing, smiling family pours out, Ania hides her face from mine so I can't see her expression. How can one girl have so many sisters? Hopefully, the stepdad isn't really as creepy as she says, because the kids seem to really look up to him, giggling and hanging from his pant legs as he hauls groceries up the front steps.

"Are you sure this dude was trying to spy on you outside the shower?" I ask.

"Oh, that was a lie."

My fist clenches so hard that knuckles pop,

"I wanted an excuse to see my family again. I can't go too far from my death site without you escorting me, but it's nice to see they're holding up okay."

"Give me back all the sympathy I felt for you a minute ago! Let me guess, the math teacher is actually a nice guy too?"

"No way, he's a creepy creeper! We need to investigate him next."

"The girl whose eye looks like melting ice cream doesn't get to decide who's creepy."

Back to school we go, me asking how she knows he'll be there and her insisting he's almost as big a loner loser as me. That he uses work to cover up the gaping hole where his social life should be. The janitor gives me a funny look and it's only when I'm two halls down that I realize he thinks I'm talking to myself.

"Now you're making me look like a crazy person."

"You do a good job of that on your own."

We tiptoe towards the math room, our four eyes peeking over the rim of the class window. And, of course, Mr. Tompkins looks back at that exact moment - damn the human ability to sense when people are watching them.

"James, come on in. Does someone need help with their calculus homework? I hope my students know they can stay after class anytime. Not just for math help, but to talk about whatever is on their mind."

Okay, I may be a tad socially autistic, but even I can tell this dude's a weirdo. Guess I never noticed before now, saw him as no different from any other math teacher. But, on reflection, isn't he always standing over the shoulders of the female students, far more often than the male ones?

"I told you," Ania whispers in my ear.

"The second thing," I say to Mr. Tompkins. "I mean, I came here for life advice, not a math lesson."

"That's what I like to hear." Throwing himself into a backwards chair so he can wrap his legs around it like a boa constrictor. "Math is for nerds, anyway."

"I wanted to talk about Ania. She was a student of yours, right?"

And, boy, does that throw cold water on his good mood. Only, rather than appearing guilty, he's... dear God... is this weirdo really crying?

"I'm so happy you came to me about this. Please, have a seat."

I do, although I have the feeling I'll regret it.

"Ania used to stay after class once a week. Not to talk about her life, like some students, but because she couldn't do math for shit. Sorry for swearing, but heck, I think we can be candid with one another. Well, she tried and tried, bless her heart. Even if it only came to C's and D's, it was better than the F's she'd be getting, if not for the extra effort."

Boy, oh boy, does Ania look embarrassed at this. And here I thought she was some bimbo who cared more about boys than grades.

"Just ask him if he killed me already," she hisses. But Mr. Tompkins carries on with his story.

"She never discussed friends or family, nor her hobbies and other classes. No, the one thing she sometimes brought up with me... "Well, to be honest, Jack, it was you."

Gulp.

"Me? I don't understand."

"The poor girl would never admit it to me - I don't know if she admitted it to herself - but she was utterly smitten with you. She would always ask me questions like *what kind of stories do you think he's writing?* and *I wonder if he's happy not having friends?* I hope that last one doesn't sound insensitive - but I think she was genuinely curious. Some girls get so popular that their fantasy becomes the concept of cutting everyone off, escaping societal pressures and, well, becoming a loner. I think she was envious of you. Part of her wanted to get better acquainted but the other part thought it would be an imposition on your chosen solitary lifestyle. I really wish she could have told you this, because the look she'd get in her eyes seemed entirely different from the one most girls get when discussing boys. There was something... I don't know... something pure about it. Oh jeez, I'm sorry Jack. I didn't mean to make you cry, too."

"I'm not crying."

Except, shit, I apparently am. Damn this guy. I try to hide my face from Ania but it winds up easy because she's already gone, secretly having bailed during the teacher's humiliating monologue. I thank him for the conversation and stumble away in a daze.

The janitor keeps his distance as I pass.

"If you think that story was true, you're a dumber dumbass than I guessed."

From Ania, waiting by the front gate and annoying as ever.

"Yeah, yeah." As we begin the slow walk home. "So, that's all our suspects. Is there anyone else you might have overlooked? Maybe a jock who got triggered that you turned him down too often?"

"Like I ever turn down football players." Another minute passes before she adds, "We didn't investigate everyone on the suspect list."

Major groan.

"Enough stupid jokes that the pervy virgin can't control himself." I stop walking when I realize she's falling behind. "Oh, come on. You can't really think it might have been me."

"I don't think it," she whispers. I'm sighing with relief when she adds. "I know it."

"Get fucked."

I storm off home, ready to bury myself in books and homework, video games and porn. Only, she gives chase, shouts at my backside.

"It was the day I finally told you how I felt. I knew you liked to take walks near Stark's Pond, so I spent the whole day waiting there, hoping you'd stroll past. And you did! I felt so happy when you appeared from behind the trees, like the universe was answering my prayers. That you were here to give me permission to stop being 'on' all the time. That you'd be the person to finally tell me I can just be myself, instead of my best impression of what everyone wants me to be."

I'm biting my lip now.

"I started blurting everything out so fast that I didn't notice the warning signs," she continues. "It was like you weren't even hearing me, staring at something behind me that wasn't even there. Your skin was clammy and your hands were shaking, so I guided you towards the benches, had you lay down. I only turned my back for a few seconds. I was heading to grab my sweater from beside a tree, going to have you use it as a blanket.

The metal bat was simply lying around. Kids go there to play. There's all sorts of toys lurking in the sands of Stark's Pond. Dammit, why couldn't it have been a wiffle ball bat? You seemed so out of it, I doubt you'd notice the difference, although my skull sure would have.

I really wish I could hate you. Wish your stupid stories didn't paint a portrait of someone clearly struggling to control what shreds of sanity they have left. Would be so much easier if you were a creepy pervert. But, dammit, that doesn't change the fact that you're still a monster."

Her voice follows me all the way home. Or, I thought I was going home, but it looks like my feet took me to Stark's Pond. Feels like something happened here. Something I don't want to know, committed by the type of individual I could do without meeting.

The water glitters, its surface a blanket of diamonds. Somewhere beneath it is a metal bat. Or not, if the cops are remotely competent.

Ania is lying, I couldn't hurt anyone. But I like the idea of hanging here a while, lying in wait to see who comes along. They always say the killer returns to the scene of the crime.

I walk into the pond, dress shoes filling with muck and pressed pants turning soggy to the balls. I wade deeper, until all that remains above water is my nose, eyes and hair.

Maybe I'll hang here a while, survey what there is to see. If someone comes along, I'll know they are the murderer. And I will strike with a righteous vengeance.

I wait to find out where the day will take me, enjoying the warm hug of the pond's dark depths.

I don't have to wait for long.

A Lovely Little Catch Up

Russell Carlton

"The state of you last night."

I needed a moment to assess my situation before I opened my eyes and addressed whoever that was. The taste of whisky was still thick in my mouth and the only certainty I could hold onto was that I absolutely did not want to be conscious. So, that was about standard. My bed, or whatever I'd forced the role of bed onto, was damp. No, clammy. No, slimy. Somewhere between those. It was harder than I'd have normally expected. And it was cold. Actually, everything was cold.

I blinked open my eyes, bracing myself. The sky was grey, empty, and... moving. The illusion of motion caused a swell in my stomach that I suppressed by lowering my eyelids and turning the world off again.

"Jesus, the state of you now."

The voice arresting my retreat was irksome, the smell that followed an absolute violation.

I sucked in enough air to hold the vomit down, reopened my eyes, and looked for the source.

Immediately, I wished I hadn't. Instinctively, I tried to raise myself up in the bed, something made surprisingly easier by the revelation it had four walls, like a baby's crib. The thing looming over me smiled, and it was grotesque.

"What the..." was the best I could do. I wasn't proud.

"I'm gonna assume you have no idea where you are?" it asked.

I did not. I confirmed this by doing nothing at all.

"Or how you got here?"

The thing continued to be correct. I remained mute. The thing sighed.

"Honestly, you're gonna have to join in here or this isn't going to work."

"What's..." I started but quickly ran out of fuel.

"Good. What's..." the thing nodded encouragement. "What's go..."

"Who..."

"No, that's no good. You need to finish one question before you move on to the next - and you need to let me answer in between. That's how this whole thing works. At least, that's how it always used to work. I can't imagine it would have changed all that much."

It paused and let me take a breath.

"Start again, eh?"

"Where am I?"

"Good!" It seemed genuinely satisfied. "You're in the graveyard. Next?"

"The graveyard?"

"Yes, the graveyard. Are we going to get stuck on that?"

"Why am I in the graveyard?"

"Well, I assume the smell on your breath is as much explanation as we're going to get for now. Though you did seem to have a clear idea last night."

"Last night?"

"The dark bit before that came up." The thing pointed towards the sun, or the greyness that suggested there might be a sun somewhere.

"What was I doing last night?"

"Now we get to the crux of it." The thing clapped its hands, or what I supposed were hands, dust scattering from the point of impact. "You woke me up. That's what you did last night."

Suddenly there was a familiar air about my situation. I was in trouble. I was in trouble for something I'd done after whisky. Experience had taught me there was only one way to handle such a moment.

"I'm sorry," I said, with as contrite a tone as I could muster.

"Sorry for what?"

"For waking you up?" I ventured.

"Is that all?"

"Is there more?" I'd learned honesty was usually the best policy when you'd been caught out.

"I'd say," the thing laughed. It sounded like a death rattle.

A connection fired in my brain. It hurt like hell.

"Why were you sleeping in a graveyard?" I asked.

The thing made a face at me, which suggested I should figure that out for myself. I had very little confidence this was true but I lifted a hand slightly and closed my eyes to show I was going to take a minute and try.

I reopened my eyes and looked at the thing. It was mostly human in shape but gaunter than any person I'd ever seen. It was draped in thin tattered cloth and was grey in the same way as the sky. Patches of its legs were darker and slightly liquified, like the bruises on a banana. There was an unusual movement about the creature's surface.

I blinked to try and get a better focus. It was… jeez.

Insects and worms moved in and out of its body. Immediately, I lost control and vomit swelled through me. I turned my head looking for somewhere to send it but there wasn't enough time. A thick acidic soup shot through my throat and out into the morning. It hit the wall beside me, hung for a fraction of a second, then tumbled back down - soaking the side of my shirt and one thigh of my trousers.

I coughed, wiped my mouth clean with my dry arm and looked at the chunder-covered surface beside me. It wasn't a wall. It was earth, and it continued two feet above my head. My eyes followed a globulus fragment of my former insides, as it slid down the vertical plane of dirt and over the lip, where it turned to wood to join the gathering pool of vomitus resting against my hip. I looked up at the thing, my mouth open. For the first time, I noticed its eyes. One faded to a single colour. The other had burst, folded slightly in on itself.

"I'm in a grave," I said.

"You do tend to find them in graveyards."

"I'm in a coffin."

"Yes." The tone was terser now. "More accurately, you're in *my* coffin."

"You're... dead."

"What gave it away?"

I opened my mouth and lifted my arms to gesture. A lump of rejected stomach contents fell off my left forearm and onto my crotch. The thing, the dead thing, raised its hands to tell me not to bother and my brain finally acknowledged the sarcasm. As my hands hung impotently in the air, I noticed thick dirt on my fingers and embedded into my nails.

"Why was your grave open for me to fall into?" I asked, hopefully.

"It wasn't."

"Wh... what happened?"

"You really don't remember?" it asked. "Try. See what you can recall."

I closed my eyes again. I began to take a deep memory jogging breath but terminated my inhalation abruptly when the combined odours of my grim surroundings hit the back of my throat. Another intestinal eruption gurgled inside me.

I remembered we started drinking in the middle of the afternoon. The sun was out and it was a beautiful day for this time of year. We sent a few texts and actually managed to get a decent crowd. Another rarity. We'd planned a pub crawl and maybe some food at the end but, with a big group, it's hard to synchronise empty glasses, ready for a move. We were all having such a good time we ended up staying in the same beer garden all day.

Eventually, people started to filter off. We called the first leavers all sorts of names and they took it on the chin. The later goodbyes had slightly more friction, as we realised the good times were being forcibly ended. Soon, it was just the three of us, drunk and fighting the emerging melancholy of a fine day sliding into an empty night.

We started on the whisky. I knew that from the thin coat of medicinal smoke still fighting with the acid on the back of my tongue. That's when things got blurry, as they tended to. I knew myself, though. Whisky meant I'd become two things, maudlin and amorous. Or, more accurately, if we're honest, lonely.

And now I was in a... oh god.

I assumed the thing couldn't read my mind, but it could read the fear and pain in my eyes. I looked again at the dirt on my hands.

"What did I do?"

"Well, I can't account for what you did before you ripped off my coffin lid and screamed *there you are!* with a manic look in your eyes. But I can certainly tell you about afterwards."

I paused.

"I'm not sure I want to know."

"You probably don't," it said. "But you're going to."

A cold horror shot through my body.

"Did we...? Did I...? Could we have...? Is it...?" I trembled.

"Yes," it replied, matter-of-factly. "And now we have to get married."

My face blanked in absolute lack of comprehension.

"Don't be bloody stupid," it barked. "I'm literally compost and fungus."

The thing held its shroud apart at the waist to demonstrate what we both already knew.

"In credit to you," it continued. "I don't think that was ever your intention. Not that you'd have been capable if it was."

A bony finger was held in the air and then drooped over to illustrate the point, or lack of point, I supposed.

My eyes dropped from the open shroud to the floor. I saw a dirty spade propped against the dirt wall by my feet. Where the hell had I got a spade from?

"Please," I sounded pathetic. "Just tell me."

"Ok," the thing said. It looked as though it was moving to rub its hands together, then bailed out. It was enjoying this.

"Can you pretend I rubbed my hands together just then?" it said. "I don't actually like to attempt it too often, in case something breaks off."

I nodded. What else could I do?

"So." It sat up slightly, into what I could only assume was a storytelling pose. Something wet fell from the back of its head. "First, there was the *Here's Johnny!* moment."

"Sorry if I scared you."

"You didn't scare me. I'm a corpse. The only thing that would scare me is if the bottom dropped out of that coffin and I started falling towards sulphurous flames, while a hoven and horned man cackled in maniacal delight. Your squinty-eyed face and slurred greeting was a shock but not a fright."

"What did I do next?"

"Well, first you stood there and stared at me for a bit. That was creepy. Then you perched on the bottom edge of the coffin and stared some more. I don't think you'd really thought anything through beyond the point of opening the coffin lid. So, you didn't have much of a plan."

That seemed like me.

"Then there was a lot of apologising and some pretty ugly crying. Then you offered me whisky. When I obviously didn't respond, you poured it onto my face anyway. Thanks for that. After, you rolled me on my side so you could lie down and spoon me. Though I suppose I was more of a fork than a spoon. Then, you laid there, mumbling nonsense into the back of my head, until you passed out. I eased myself away when you started snoring and sat here figuring out what to do. I decided I'd wait until you woke up, so we could have this lovely little catch-up."

As the thing talked, I realised there was something familiar about it. I dismissed the thought in an innate act of self-protection.

"Catch up?" I prayed to whatever had reanimated the talking carcass, that it was referring to the getting-to-know-each-other people like to happen the morning after an intoxicated one-night stand.

"You don't recognize me, Owen?"

It knew my name. There was no way that could be a good thing.

I shook my head with muted caution.

"Did you think you'd drunkenly stumbled into a random graveyard and shoved your spade... where did you get a spade, by the way? Never mind. You'd just picked a random grave and climbed in and laid down next to the dead body inside for a cuddle? Is that something you do, Owen? Is this not a really strange way to wake up? How weird are you, Owen?"

I had no answers to any of these questions.

"Do you often apologise to freshly exhumed corpses?"

"No."

"I didn't think so," it pressed. "Though I'm not sure I'd put it past you. I thought you were a nice, normal guy, until... y'know."

"Until what?"

I *was* a nice, normal guy. Well, mostly. I mean, we've all made mistakes. You just have to move on from them, right? Or drown them in whisky. A clamp tightened around my stomach.

I only knew two people in local graveyards. Grandma, and...

"Is that the penny dropping?" it asked. *She* asked.

"I'm," I stuttered. "I'm sorry. I'm so sorry."

I need to pause this for a moment. I need to be clear. I didn't kill anyone. I didn't. I just. Well... I just didn't help.

We'd been fighting. We were always fighting. I don't know how she got me so riled up. I was never like that with anyone else. There was just… something. An argument would come from nowhere and I'd get sucked in, feel trapped. I'd just do anything to stop it. I'd scream. I'd shout. I'd slam the door and march down the street. I'd go nuclear.

I didn't hit her. I never hit her. Well… no. You slap someone when they're hysterical, right? That doesn't count.

No. I know. It does.

I looked around to see if the bottle of whisky still had anything in it. It was wedged in the far corner of the coffin. Upside down. Empty.

God knows how a fight started when she was in the bath. We weren't even in the same room when the first cross words were hurled around the flat. I was in the corridor when she stood up in a rush, so she could attack me from a better position. I watched as the colour drained from her face, when the blood struggled to deal with her sudden rise from the hot water.

I watched as her eyes rolled back and she fainted. I watched the back of her head glance off the taps as she plummeted back into the tub. I moved to the doorway as her head slipped under the water.

Then I stopped. I watched as the surface resettled and became still over her. I watched as she pulled water into her lungs and her body tensed. I watched as bubbles flowed, large and slow from her mouth, small and fast from her nose. I watched as her eyelids opened in the moving water. I looked her straight in the eyes, as everything went still. Once more. I watched. I waited. I closed the lid of the toilet and sat down. I closed my eyes and took solace in the silence. Then, I called 999.

A cluster of dirt hit my chest.

"I didn't… I'm sorry."

Another hit my shins. I watched the spade slice into the pile of soil beside the open grave. More earth hit my shoulder.

"Can we talk about this?"

More dirt. More slicing, lifting, falling. I forced strength into my arms and legs and started to stand. Soil cascaded from my rising body. Something hit my head and I sank back. A rock thumped onto the wood beneath my feet. Another, larger rock landed on my right knee and pain shot through my brain, as the crack of thick bone echoed off the walls of the grave.

More soil followed. Spade after spade. I opened my mouth and a clump rammed itself down my throat. My legs were covered now and the tide of earth crept further up my chest with each new collection of dirt and worms.

"You can't just?" I tried to say with my expression.

She could. She did.

She looked me straight in the eyes as she threw the spadeful that covered them.

From then on it was just darkness. Darkness and the rhythmic thump of soil on soil, and the tightening, as it compacted around my body. Around my face. After I could wait no longer, I pulled soil into my lungs and my body tensed. Bubbles had nowhere to flow. Gravel and dirt scratched the surface of my open eyes.

A short time later, the corpse cast aside her dirty spade and rested on a squat headstone.

"Well," she said to the sleeping bodies all around, as the morning sun finally pushed through the clouds, painting the graveyard in colour. "What now?"

She looked at the freshly refilled grave beside her.

"I guess it's scare for hire, ghost tour guide, or *Loose Women* panelist…

My Mom Ate My Dad and Here's Why

Casey Campbell

"My father used to hit my mom."

Kevin's bottom lip dropped, his puppy dog eyes filling with just enough moisture not to spill over. Sinead wondered if his name was Kevin at all. Perhaps he was Karl, or maybe Kanye? It was easy to forget.

His face set, sad or embarrassed and Sinead felt she should explain how much worse things could be, to make him feel better.

"I don't remember much but I think something similar happened to my mom."

"Really? Wow, we've got so much in common. Did your mother leave like mine?"

"No. She ate him. She's been locked up for the past five years but she's getting out any day now. I can't wait. A girl needs her mother, right?"

Kevin/Kanye's eyes flashed with annoyance, like Sinead had just stolen his punchline.

"Five years? Cute story but you're missing a few decades of prison time. Society frowns on murdering and eating someone."

He chuckled, amused now, playing along.

"It was technically self-defense and it's not illegal to eat someone. It's just illegal to kill them to eat them. It remains unproven my mom murdered my dad before she ate him or if he just died. You know what I'm saying?"

At Kevin/Kanye's stunned silence she assured him.

"It had been a misunderstanding. Don't worry, she's not a flesh-eating zombie or anything. She's just a mom who got in a bad situation. Happens every day. Those lawyers have a lot to answer for and I think she's going to sue when she gets out."

"So, she didn't do it?"

"Oh, she definitely ate him but what else could she do? She had watched all these shows about disposing of a body and was confident she could manage it. Blame a society who puts so much information out there. But my father had been rather large and neither of us had a taste for fat. It breaks down strangely in the pressure cooker. Fat was our downfall."

Kevin gaped and Sinead figured he was absorbing her bravery at having endured such a childhood. Her therapist had been categorical that nothing was her fault. Sinead failed to see where the problem lay, other than unwarranted squeamishness. Humans, they all shot and stabbed each other, ate anything that moved, sucked the ocean dry of anything remotely edible then squealed at eating meat, as if they weren't all animals. Really, when you thought about it logically, so much meat was going to waste, while people starved to death.

But Kevin was not ready for such a debate. In fact, he appeared ready to barf.

Her therapist had talk, talk, talked about everything, yet her face screwed up like she had sucked a lemon when Sinead tried to discuss her own ideas about meat. She had been warned against admitting certain thoughts out loud. Society frowned at the way her mother had raised her only child but Sinead's therapist also said she needed to be honest with those who meant something to her. And she really liked people and felt honesty should be met with honesty.

"As I said, she's getting out soon. If you want to meet her, she'd love it. She's a real people person, like me. I'd like to go back to school and study hospitality or nursing."

He picked up his phone then peered at his watch. He stared around the busy bar and jiggled his leg on the stool.

"I'm just going to the bathroom. Back in a few minutes."

"Great. Should I order another round or ask when our table will be ready?"

"Yeah, another round would be good."

She smiled then reached out to grasp his forearm, his warm freckled skin giving her a tingling sensation deep down in her belly - one her mom said meant she was ready for kids. She wasn't sure. Sometimes her mom said weird things and Sinead wanted to talk to the therapist about it, which felt disloyal.

She took a long smell of Kevin/Kanye's lingering scent, wanting him a little more, since he had gone to the effort of wearing it for her.

This one, he was her future. Her mother said someone would be out there. Her therapist said she had to be open to new people, to feel worthy of love which didn't involve hiding body parts in the freezer. Love should never compromise your morals.

But Sinead found morals flexible. She remained happy if those around her were happy and, like her morals, her thoughts and expectations were flexible too.

She had finished her wine by the time she thought to worry about her date. They had met on Tinder. It had been Sinead's mom who suggested it might be a good place to find love. The women in prison used it to find people who liked to chat, some even forging long-term relationships. So why shouldn't it work for Sinead, who wasn't locked up? She remained free to roam and meet whoever she wanted. Her mom refused to use dating sites herself, claiming she was still recovering from her husband.

Until recently, Sinead barely used social media. Freaks and weirdos wanted to contact her, some for their own notoriety, like those nosy reporters (and the more exciting reality shows who assured she could be famous in her own right). Family members who thought money could be involved or, weirder, those men who went after notorious female killers. They had contacted her via letters, phone calls, emails and now Tinder.

Following her nose in this smelly bar, Sinead waited outside the fetid male bathroom for a few minutes, before bursting inside. Being a Thursday night, the place wasn't as busy as the weekend - but the bathroom was completely empty.

Did an alien take him?

She returned to her seat, peering out the fake saloon-style doors, wondering what to do. Perhaps she should call the cops.

One of the barmen came over and lifted her empty wine glass.

"I'm sorry, sugar. Some men sure are idiots. You want me to get you another or are you going to drink his beer? You look familiar. Have you been on a reality show?"

Sinead frowned.

"Do you think he ran away from me?"

The handsome barman nodded slowly, like he was making up his mind as he went.

"He headed toward the bathroom then ran for the door. Sorry, I should've come over earlier, but sometimes they come back. Your guy is a Tinder whore. He's in here every other night with a different girl. Half of them leave with him after one glass. Horny girls are his thing. A few drinks are cheaper than a hooker, I suppose."

"So, I'm not even good enough to sleep with like a cheap whore?" Sinead felt her entire insides going cold, freezing to solid ice. Who did he think he was? And after she had told him so much about herself. She was wild, embarrassed, sad and still very, very lonely.

"He's a douche, sweetheart. Look, I get off soon. How about I buy you a drink?"

"Really? You want a drink with me?"

"Sure, I help out plenty of girls who get left in the lurch. Tinder is a magnet for desperate chicks like you."

He wandered away to serve someone else and it took Sinead a few minutes to consume this statement fully. She let his words settle in her mouth. Then she slid them to the back of her throat, where they caught, causing her to cough, the statement turning to imagery which she spat back in rage.

"You dirty fucking asshole."

She could think of nothing else to say, so left. It wasn't until much later she realized she had not paid the bill. She logged onto Tinder but had been blocked from Kevin (Kevin, like duh! Kanye was the singer/rapper/president of America).

Uncertain what else to do, she called her mother. It wasn't the allocated time but she told the prison this constituted an emergency. After too much hold music, where Sinead cried, her mother came on the line, voice concerned.

"Baby? Are you all right?"

"No, Mom. I've had the worst night of my life. I went on a date like you said and the guy was a creep. As soon as I mentioned you, he ran off. He didn't even say goodnight."

"Oh, honey. You had me really worried."

"But mom. He told me all sorts of things when we were chatting online and then, when I met him, he was nothing but a dirty liar."

"Well, my little honey-child. That is just people through and through. You think they would say what they really mean but they never do. They tell you what you want to hear for their own selfish reasons. I'm sorry you had to figure this out on your own but it's like I warned you, people are disgusting. Not one person helped me with your daddy. Then, when I took matters into my own hands, they behaved like I was an animal. I tell you, honey, the world makes no sense, so you need to go get what you want. Do you understand me?"

"Sure, I guess."

"You're twenty soon, baby-girl. Time to put away the little kid. I sure am sorry you got caught in the middle of what happened. But I don't for a minute regret what I did."

"Mom, you know they're listening."

"I never once said I hadn't done what I did to your daddy. I've got nothing to hide, just like any other hard-working mom who saw a problem and found a solution. What do all these pious dogs know about suffering.? They don't know, and don't care, what I went through. All anyone remembers is how I got rid of his fat ass. Thank God for those shows or I'd have no idea what to do."

"Getting rid of the blood first *was* super smart."

"Thank you, my angel. It is exactly what reality television is made for. To teach us a different way of living. One of notoriety and free of servitude."

Fearing her mother was about to launch into another of her long-winded speeches, Sinead cut her off.

"So, what do I do about a boyfriend? I'm so lonely."

"I had a call from the lawyer today. I might be getting out sooner than we thought."

"Really?" Sinead sung, her heart soaring. "It'll be great to not worry about things."

"Honey, you're an adult now. I won't be getting out of here and returning to serving you. You have your own life. I intend to slip back into the real world quietly. I'll get a job somewhere and carry on with life."

"You don't want me anymore?"

"Don't be silly. You're my baby-child. I just won't be doing everything for you again. And I suggest you wait a little while before getting a boyfriend. This messy date was probably for the best, although if I was out, I'd track that dirty hose-bag down and shove his rotten thingy down his neck. Make him eat it instead of treating you like trailer trash."

"I *am* living in a trailer, Mom."

"It's just short-term. Hold tight. Don't go rushing off with some loser. When I'm free, we'll sort everything out. Sound good?"

"Sounds great. Thanks, mom. I knew you'd make me feel better."

"It's what I'm here for. I'll do anything to make sure you are fed and cared for in a manner befitting my child. You understand?"

"Sure, mom. I'll stay off the Tinder."

"Great. I'm suspicious it's not as wholesome as I've been led to believe. When I'm out we'll go through it together."

Sinead slept soundly after that. Her mother always knew what to say to make her forget her cares. Mom would be out soon, which would be great.

Sinead had no plans to go back on Tinder but she received a message the very next day after her disastrous date with Kevin. It was a man called Richard and he wanted to chat. With no work at the supermarket, Sinead settled onto the old lay-z-boy chair she had found on the side of the road and began a virtual conversation. This time she was more guarded with what she admitted. Yet Richard still wanted to meet her.

She remained hesitant but he picked a fancy restaurant and gushingly told her he would book and pay for everything. She explained her recent terrible experience and he asked to speak to her on Skype. They chatted face to face until the sun came up next morning and, by then, Sinead knew it was real love.

The date was different too. He had been waiting for her when she arrived. Had pulled her chair out, held her hand until she shook him away, his gaze penetrating. Eventually, she had said, "I've told you so much about me, about my mom and what happened."

"Thank you for trusting me with your story. Some people might feel different but you're just so special. I can't wait to meet your mother. I've never heard of a stronger or more determined woman in my life. To go to such extremes keeping you safe, it makes me profoundly grateful to her. She left you here for me to find."

"Richard…"

"Please, I've asked you to call me Dicky."

Truth was, Sinead felt uncomfortable calling him Dicky. With the last name of Byrd, it took all her effort not to laugh whenever she thought about it. She could imagine perching him on her finger and setting him free. She doubted he'd leave. He already appeared so attached and Sinead pushed aside her uncertainty, letting the words of her therapist sink deep. She *would* let someone in to love her. She deserved it and so did Dicky Byrd. He was right, everything had happened to bring them closer together.

"Dicky, I'd rather my mom doesn't know about us yet. She doesn't want me meeting someone right now. She might be getting out soon and we need to be together, to heal."

"But I can help. I can protect you both. I want to."

Sinead's heart melted a little more and she thought of the foster home she had stayed in from the age of fifteen, when her mother had gone to prison. They had been nice enough people but Sinead always got the impression the government money was more important than the several children. If Sinead behaved, did her homework and a few chores, they fed and housed her without fuss. No one came into her room at night or beat her. No one hid her in a cellar or forced her into anything she didn't want to do. They also never asked for her real name and never once hugged her. On July 4th, at the age of eighteen, Sinead had been moved into a home with adults and told to get a job, since she was in no way smart enough for a scholarship to any university.

That house had been different. With booze and drugs offered to her daily, Sinead's mother had demanded she move. The only thing she could afford was the trailer park and, after an initial settling-in period, she had become accustomed to calling her own shots. Had even begun to enjoy it. She chuckled now at how frightened she had been only a few months ago. Every noise in the night terrifying. The loneliness threatening to overwhelm her.

Her mother had always been free to talk. Every evening at 6.15 p.m. Sinead called the prison, grateful to be back in her own state and not having to pay collect charges.

Dicky bought expensive wine, paid for her delicious meal and, before she understood how it had happened, had taken up residence in her bed. He stayed there for two whole days and Sinead had never felt closer to another human in her life.

She missed calling her mother twice and was dreading their next conversation - but with Dicky at her side she pushed through her concerns.

"Sorry I didn't call, mom. I've been a little busy."

"Busy? What do you mean, busy?"

"I've met someone. He's amazing and we're getting married as soon as you get out."

Her mother remained silent for a long time. With Dicky's prompting, Sinead finally said, "Are you still there?"

"Dump him," her mother spat. "We don't have time for boyfriends now. I'm being let out next week. We need time to heal. I need you more than some guy."

"But I love him."

"Bullshit!" Her mother yelled. She never raised her voice and Sinead froze, stunned. By the time she hung up Sinead had agreed to get rid of Dicky, who remained watching with wide eyes, unaware of what her mom had demanded.

"She's getting out next week." Sinead burst into tears.

"What great news," Dicky enthused, holding Sinead and kissing the side of her head. "I can't wait to meet her."

"You don't understand. We can't see each other anymore. Not now she's about to get out. She said there are plans and we need to heal after what happened with my father. Which *can't* happen with anyone else around."

"I'm not leaving you. Come here," He wrapped his arms around her and Sinead wondered why she felt this torn. It wasn't fair. She had never asked for anything. Lived like a hermit while her mother did her time.

"Mom ate dad, not me. Well, not much. And I didn't even know it was him."

Dicky licked his lips, eyes bright.

"You have to be with your mother. She's right, she needs you now, more than ever. Come to bed. We'll sort this out later."

She nodded solemnly.

"But I'm not letting you go," he reiterated. "I've worked so hard to find someone like you. There is no way I'm going anywhere. I'll move to be near you and your mom. We're all in this together. Deal?"

Sinead nodded, tears streaming down her face. Dicky unbuttoned her pajama top then peeled away the thin underwear slowly, like unwrapping an expensive chocolate.

"I never imagined this would happen to me. That you would be all mine."

Sometimes, when he said those things, Sinead had the sense Dicky had known her for a long time. Yet they had only just met.

Sinead collected her mother from prison. There had never been enough money to get her driver's license so she had taken the bus, jumping with excitement when her mother exited the dirty grey building. Her mom had cried enough to break Sinead's heart and she wondered how she could keep Dicky a secret. Through all the years of upheaval her mother had remained her best friend, her only friend. Now Sinead was lying to her by omission.

Yet she couldn't find the words to explain who Dicky was and how much he meant to her. Instead, they returned to the trailer park, nattering the whole way on the bus. There were so many plans. Mom had used her time in prison to work out the rest of their lives.

Mom wanted her to get back to school. Their strategies hinged on Sinead being educated - and her mother would continue the certificates she had been working on in prison.

"They wouldn't let me do food science," she grumbled. "Like I can't have an affinity with a good-sized pressure cooker because of your father."

They were still chatting when Sinead unlocked the trailer, hoping Dicky hadn't left anything inside - or his scent didn't still linger. His smell caused her mouth to water and her stomach flutter. His deep voice made her weak with pleasure, planning their future, assuring Sinead endlessly how her mother must be part of the deal. How he wanted to meet her, talk with her, be near them both. He wasn't like those immature boys who ran away at the hint of a slow cooker. Dicky Byrd might be the first real man she had ever met.

He was sitting inside, waiting, when the door creaked open and Sinead thought she might be sick. This was not what they had discussed at all.

Dicky raised his hands in surrender, a big shit-eating grin on his face.

"Before you say anything," he placated. "I love your daughter and I want us to be a family of three. You're not alone anymore. I'll protect you both."

Sinead froze in fear, not sure what her mother would say. Or what she would do if mom denied them.

"What's your name?"

"Dicky Byrd." He continued to smile bright, his crooked teeth and lazy left eye making Sinead nervous her mother would judge him before getting to know him.

"Dicky. Isn't that short for Richard?"

His smile faltered, sweat breaking out on his upper lip. His skin paled further, ginger beard clashing painfully with the thinning black mop on his head.

"No one has ever called me Richard. I'm just Dicky."

"You're Richard Byrd, the creep who sends me endless letters and emails."

"What?" Sinead gasped, "No, mom. You've got the wrong person. Please don't ruin this for me. Dicky and me, we're in love. Real love."

"I'm not ruining anything. Would you like to see the emails? I kept the ones the prison didn't delete. He's a jailbird junkie. He likes women who have been in prison or have some link to violent crime. He needs to leave, baby-girl. He's screwed in the head."

Sinead was breathing hard.

"Don't make me choose. We thought you might behave like this. I want to look after you, mom, but I have a life to get on with. I'm sorry I never told you we were still a thing but I'm scared. You have to accept I'm with Dicky now."

She lifted her chin, stunned to be defending herself, defending Dicky. Yet her heart was breaking at the thought of losing her amazing, strong mother.

"Have I ever been disloyal to you?" her mother asked.

"Never." Sinead said instantly.

"Yet I get this." She shook her head.

Then, like a switch had been thrown, her face lit up and she smiled. Stepped closer to Dicky and wrapped her arms around him, eyes remaining on her daughter,

"I'm sorry, both of you. I'm being selfish. I'd been dreaming of this day for so long. You have no idea what it's like in there and I just wanted to be with my daughter. Could you give us a few days, Dicky? I promise I won't steal her away."

She stepped back, peering into Dicky's wonky eyes, her smile now sad.

"I'd love to." Dicky sniffled, swiping at tears, embarrassed by his emotion. "But I don't have anywhere else to go. My folks kicked me out of the house when I started dating Sinead. You're both kind of famous."

"Yes. We would be of interest to all kinds of losers. How old are you, Dicky?"

"Thirty-six."

"And still living at home." This wasn't a question but a statement tinged with disappointment. "Sinead isn't even twenty. You're old enough to be her father, only a year younger than me. I doubt you work. How would you support my daughter, give her the life she deserves?"

"Love is beyond age, race, gender, barriers and social stigmas."

Sinead's mother thought for a moment then smiled brightly again.

"Then, let's make the most of it. Welcome to my family, Dicky Byrd."

"Thank you so much, mom!" Sinead cried, hugging her close.

"Will we all fit?"

"We'll make it work," Dicky assured her, wrapping bony arms around both women. "This is the greatest thing to ever happen to me. You don't know how much I've wanted this. I actually made it a reality."

He began to sob and Sinead reached out a hand to him. Her mother hid her distaste behind a bland smile which Sinead remembered well from her childhood. She had used that smile with Sinead's father all the time. When he drank too much, yelled for food and meat, meat, meat. Constantly moaning how fruit and vegetables were for rabbits and not a hardworking man with a family of two lazy females. But this was different. Father had gone to heaven and Dicky was nothing like him.

Days later her mother wanted to visit town.

"I need to access my bank accounts."

"Oh, sure. I didn't realize you had bank accounts." Sinead ran her fingers through Dicky's stringy hair, noting the ginger roots.

"I hid them in your name." Her mother smiled at Dicky, as if he made her proud. He leaned forward, enthused.

"Of course, you're smart enough to hide money. I'll take you. We never spend time alone together and I want to get to know you better."

Sinead's mother's nose screwed up.

"What a strange thing to say."

"You're my family now." Dicky shook his head, as if waking from a dream. "I love you both so much and won't ever let anything happen to you."

"Could you take mom to town?" Sinead let out a breath, rubbing his knee.

"I can think of nothing I'd rather do."

He was so honoured.

Sinead never saw Dicky again.

Her mother said he hopped a Greyhound bus headed for Vegas. She handed over a scrawled letter of apology from him, which soon disappeared.

"He dumped me on the side of the road." Mom sounded indignant. "With this huge box to carry all the way home. I'm sorry to say this, Sinead, but Dicky Byrd is queer in the head. He wanted me to tell him what happened with your father and went into a rage when I refused. He thought there was some big secret, maybe a stash of money, and he wanted in. I warned you he was one of those killer groupies. I've seen them on the telly. Or, perhaps, he wanted to sell our story to those vulture reporters."

Her mother stood in the tiny kitchen and unpacked a huge pressure cooker. Sinead rolled her eyes.

"I thought you weren't allowed to have these." She dropped a hand on the big box, tears tracking her face, her heart broken. "Your parole officer could be here at any time and you'll be locked up again."

"It'll be our little secret, honey-child."

"My therapist said I had to be open to new people."

"Life lesson, sweet-cheeks. Therapists are not psychic and some of them are just plain assholes. Believe me, I've had a few and found most of them were trying to fix their own problems. They love tricky cases like ours because it makes them feel so normal." She held her palms to Sinead's cheeks, smiling. "Most people just try to fit in and be normal, then they worry about what the world thinks of them. Truth is, the world thinks nothing of nobody. Even the famous ones are lightening in the sky, blips on the blackness."

Still staring at the box, Sinead asked the question which had hounded her since the day the police came and took her mother away. Why not? Her life felt over without Dicky.

"Why *did* you do it? I know Dad was difficult but I thought he was just a grumpy old man."

Her mother peered out the window. She rubbed a thumb nail along her bottom lip in a way which, strangely, turned Sinead's stomach.

"His blandness was unforgivable," she said.

"Did he cheat?"

"Lord no. The man remained loyal to the end."

"Did he hurt you, like… sexually?"

"Not at all. Complete gentleman in that way."

"Did he touch me? Maybe I can't remember it?" She grabbed at anything now, understanding slipping from her reach.

"Oh, dear. Nothing like that. He was a decent husband and father. Just lazy and a little shouty when he was hungry, like most people."

"So why'd you do it?" Her heart hammered.

"The generation today, they understand being famous, being seen, having the world look at you. Social media does it all, if you're smart enough, pretty enough or lucky enough. I was none of those things." She shrugged, "So, I worked with what I had."

"Are you saying you murdered my father to be *famous*?"

"Well my story *is* worth a fortune and I knew we'd need a nest egg. But I'm not that shallow." Her mother laughed, her red frizzy hair and double chin wobbling,

"I killed your fat, lazy, moaning father and ate him because I wanted to."

If You Go Down To The Zoo Today.

Mark Locke

It began as a dare.

There were four of us. Myself, Deen, Howie and Miles. Four fifteen-year-old boys, sprawled out in Miles' bedroom with nothing better to do than screen swipe the day away and smoke his home grown weed.

"One toke of this and you'll feel like you've crashed through a brick wall and come out in Russia." Miles passed a newly rolled joint to Howie.

None of us knew what crashing through a brick wall into Russia felt like. However, if it could numb our brains and remove us from our day-to-day existence, then that was good enough for us. We were supposed to be looking for a way to sell Miles' Triple X brand (which he had named after a Vin Diesel movie he said had the best car crashes) on the black web. But, within minutes of our lighting up, we had spiraled into an endless loop of internet memes and random video titles.

"Dude, grandma falls off bus."

"Seen it. Bro… disco sheep."

"Seen it. Yo, check this."

Howie held up his phone and we lent forward, as a man opened his car door and an unsuspecting passenger fell out onto the sidewalk.

"Man," said Howie. "All you got to do is open a door in an amusing way and you get massive likes."

We nodded. Multiple likes could set you apart from the digital masses, make you feel massively important and, more importantly, make you massive millions.

"This guy's already got 100,000 views. For just falling out of a car. He is gonna be so loaded."

"Whoa, check this out."

We looked across the room at Deen, who sat with his back against the wall, exhaling smoke from his nose like an overworked chimney.

"Check this out, man."

Deen turned the laptop on his knees so the screen's dull light illuminated our pasty faces. We watched as a bearded man dressed in camouflage pointed to a pile of food at the base of a tree and gestured for the camera to follow him up.

"Big deal," I said. "It's just another survival nut. There's loads of them."

"Wait," said Deen. "Wait."

The man, now on a tree branch, put a finger to his lips. We watched as a black bear stumbled into shot and began to eat the food. The camera panned up. The man held up a long, pointed pole. He leapt out of the tree onto the back of the bear and with one thrust impaled the animal. The man gazed into the camera lens, raised his thumb and said.

"Jonson's spears tame the beast. Order yours today."

"Man." said Howie. "That is caveman cold."

"That's nature, dude." Miles shrugged.

"That ain't nature," I corrected. "That's gross commercialism. That's some guy killing an animal to sell something."

"That guy," Miles said. "is gonna be selling bear spears by the truckload. That's exactly what we need to do."

"Sell spears?"

"No, man, not spears. Bears. We need a USP."

"A what?" asked Howie.

"A unique selling point. Everyone got stuff to sell but we need something that makes us different. So people know it's us. We get that, we get the green."

"Have you been watching *The Wire* again?"

Howls of approval from the others flew across the room.

"I love that show."

"Darnell's my man."

Darnell, the show's lead character and drug runner, had convinced Miles that a good marketing strategy and personal touch was all that a drug dealer needed to increase sales revenue.

"So, you want to kill a bear?"

"No man." said Miles "I don't want to kill it. I wanna dope it."

Hoots of laughter echoed around the room.

"Cos bears' lives matter, man."

"You can't drug a bear. They too big and besides they don't smoke."

"How'd you know? Maybe they like to kick back and hang out with all their animal friends, once in a while."

"That bear there." Deen tapped the screen. "Ain't Winnie the Pooh and you ain't Christopher Robin. Believe me, a thing like that does not wanna be your friend."

"How you gonna dope a bear?" I asked. "They run, like, 40 miles an hour."

Miles held in an extra-long toke of his dope and smoke plumed as he spoke

"Shit, I use a strain so strong that he won't be a bear no more. He be a puppy."

More laughter from the rest of us.

"I'm serious. We do this right, people will be buying our stuff from dawn to dusk. Everyone gonna wanna smoke the shit that tamed the bear."

The funny thing was, the more we smoked and joked, the more real it became. Why shouldn't we trap a bear? It seemed so simple, we couldn't figure out why any fool hadn't done it before. Sure, there was risk but the rewards from success - fame, money, pussy - were so much greater.

"Yo, my stuff be stronger than anything nature has to offer. Mike Tyson take a whiff of this? He be knocked out before he hit the floor."

We laughed again but Miles stood up.

"I'll show you some magic even Merlin couldn't pull off."

He left the room and returned laden with an assortment of bottles, pills, liquids and potions.

Miles went to work with the mania of a Michelin-starred chef. He gathered up all the supplies he could find and started mixing and matching tastes and sensations that the greatest food scientists wouldn't have thought of. He took acid, weed, Benzedrine, cough medicine. He crushed up paracetamol, mixed in some Russian vodka, valium, vervain, chlorzoxazone, catnip and tablets used by his parents for their back problems. Anything that had any drug value was crushed and blended, folded and mixed, until he had something he claimed would put a man into space without a rocket.

"How we know if this is going to be strong enough?" I asked.

"We need an astronaut to test this on. Who wants to try?"

We glanced over at Howie.

"No way man. What about Mr. Tiddles?"

We glanced over at Miles' cat, lying lazily on the window ledge, who looked up from cleaning itself with bored brown eyes and yawned.

"Y'all watch this I'm going to send this cat into orbit."

Miles lit up the joint, inhaled and breathed out a long plume of smoke. The moggy lifted its nose, sniffed the air, then rolled off the ledge and right out the window. A dull thud told us its nine lives were up.

"Oh shit, Mr. Tiddles. I killed my fucking cat, man."

"I think he's in a better place." I said.

"He's dead, man, and I killed him. I stoned him to death."

"Well, at least we know it works," said Deen. "We better get some bear bait, Howie."

While Miles was mourning the loss of his pet, we dispatched Howie to the local store to get munchies we could feed to the monster. Thirty minutes later he returned with a jar of honey and fifteen dollars' worth of scratch cards.

"Figure we could do some scratch-offs while were waiting."

"Bears don't play lottery." I laughed.

"I got honey." Howie held up the unopened jar. "And some Pringles."

"Great. How's it supposed to open the jar?" Deen snorted. "You know bears don't got fingers. And Pringles, Howie? You think the bear's gonna eat Pringles?"

"Why not? I do."

"Cos, they only eat stuff that comes out the ground," I said.

"It's roast vegetable flavour."

"What the fuck is this?" Deen pointed to some plastic, orange webbing.

"It's a net to trap the bear. I got it from the grocers. He uses it to hold his vegetables."

"You're gonna be a vegetable if you use that," I said. "Bear will tear through it like tissue paper. We need a rope. A big one."

"Shit. Once it tastes that weed it'll be so chill we oughtta give it pillows and a blanket."

"We should play it some sounds."

"OMG. This not, like, date night," Miles groaned. "We want to catch it, not go out with it."

"Hey, music chills the savage beast," Howie said.

"Where we even going to find a bear?" I asked.

There was only one place to find a bear in our town and that was the zoo. We went down that night and, when we thought no one was looking, hopped the fence.

Our plan was to place the net over the cave, lure the bear into it, drug it, film it and go viral. All had gone smoothly at first. We approached the bear cave with extreme caution. Vegetable net raised high, Barry White on the stereo, joints at the ready, we eased toward the cave. The east side posse had arrived in full effect.

What we had failed to realise was that, unlike the internet, where everything is a mouse click away, nature isn't on the clock. You had to wait for her to decide if she was going to give it up or not. A fact that we were unprepared for. But never let it be said that the east side crew was not adaptable. If we were going to wait, then we were going to do it in style. Just like a Willie Nelson song, we laid our blanket on the ground and like models from a Degas painting, stretched out, lit up and chillaxed while we waited for the arrival of the bear.

"Hey, I matched two symbols," Howie said.

"How much you win?"

"Five dollars."

"How much you pay for the cards?"

"Fifteen."

"So, you lost ten dollars."

"Nah, man. I won five, look."

"You ain't counting the cost of materials."

"What materials? I won. Lookit. I matched two symbols."

As Deen and Howie argued over scratch cards, Miles lit up a joint and passed it over.

"This animal don't know what he's missing," he grinned.

Time passed slowly. We were laid out on blankets, backs to the cave, happily buzzed, eating snacks and swiping screens. We were bored, wasted and had forgotten all about trapping bears.

I reached behind to help myself to another chip, only to feel something warm and wet. I turned and saw that I had placed my hand on, the nose of the most dangerous predator on earth.

A curious baby bear cub.

"Guys," I whispered. "Guys!"

The cub licked my palm then snuffled and sneezed.

"Where'd it come from?"

"I dunno. He just showed up."

"Well, it ain't like he wasn't invited. He's the guest of honour, yo."

"Let me get a selfie."

The cub ambled over, stuck his snout into the Pringles tube and began to munch.

"That is so cute man. This is gonna go viral for sure."

Howie picked up a bread stick and held it in front of him like a spear.

"Put that down, man. You gonna scare it."

"I thought we were gonna kill it."

"You can't kill a cub, man."

"Why not? It's small enough."

"We supposed to get it stoned, remember?"

The cub removed his mouth from the tube and looked over at Howie. As soon as he saw those big brown bouncing eyes, all thoughts of death and destruction melted away.

"Oh my god," Howie said. "You know who he looks like? He looks like Snoop."

"What!" Deen laughed. "You tripping?"

"For real. Check out those baby brown eyes."

"Oh yeah, man. I see it."

"It's baby Snoop."

The tiny bear gurgled and its eyes swirled round. Suddenly it opened its arms wide.

"That is adorable man. Kick it up."

Miles turned up the music and the cub started swaying back and forth, like a boxer moving to its own rhythm. It opened its bear cub paws wide and we placed a joint in its claw. We got up and started dancing, passing the joint around and singing.

"Snoop cubby cub," sang Deen. "What's his name?"

"Snoop," we chorused. "Snoop. Snoop. Snoop."

We danced round the cub, as it stood on its paws and jigged in time to our sounds.

"We did it, guys." Deen pulled out his camera. "This is gonna go viral for sure."

"We gonna be rich and famous."

"Playboy mansion, we are on our way."

We were swept up in the dance, the music, the giddiness at having achieved success against impossible odds. We realized we had actually done something with our lives. No longer were we nameless dopers. Our existence and accomplishments would be affirmed by the number of likes and subscribers we'd achieve. Finally, people would know who we were and what we were about. We would be regarded with awe and pride by people the world over.

As Deen lifted the cub into his arms I tried to hold my phone steady. At that moment of high reverie, a dark, sobering thought suddenly occurred to me.

"Hey guys. If this is the baby then where's the momma?"

I looked down to see crumbs of dark, earth bouncing across the ground and felt the heavy surge of an approaching mass. I glanced at the screen and saw a huge black creature, jaws agape, thundering towards us.

"Bear!" I yelled.

"I know." Deen was still holding the cub. "Don't get excited, man. Take the picture.

I swear the cub had the same expression of disbelief as Deen, when the momma bear swiped its giant paw across his face and took his head off at the neck.

"Jesus Christ," I said.

Deen's body collapsed to its knees, a fountain of blood spurting like lava from his neck. The bear's yellow teeth tore into Howie's arm, ripping it from its socket and hurling it into the air.

"Jesus! My arm, my arm!"

Howie spun round sending a jet of arterial blood into Miles' shocked open mouth.

"Oh my god!" screamed Miles. "I think I got Aids."

"Blow some smoke into his face," I shrieked.

Miles attempted to breathe out but, in a panic, inhaled, and swallowed the joint whole. Coughing hard, he lent forward trying to breathe.

The bear jumped onto his back and pushed him deeper into the earth. It tore into Miles, flaying him. It shook the bedraggled body from side to side until the skin ripped from Miles' back and he was sent flying. The bear roared and its cub looked on adoringly. In my stoned state, I ran into the cave to hide. As the bear followed me, darkness was the last thing I saw.

Our mauled bodies were discovered by the zookeeper next day. The footage I had recorded on Deen's phone went viral within the hour and we appeared on every news and social media channel throughout the world. Shame, we weren't alive to see it. Unfortunately, since the State couldn't afford to have a maneater hanging around the zoo, they shot the momma. The cub became the zoo's star attraction and even starred in a Snoop Dog music video.

The moral of the story is, keep your dreams on your screens, your ego in your jeans and don't ever raise yourself up against Mother Nature.

Cos that Mother? She will fuck your ass up.

Woke Up Like This

Donald McCarthy

For the first time in a long while, I wake up and don't feel a sense of dread pushing against my chest. Even though the first words I hear are *they're all dead,* the misery stays away. No. I've awoken more at peace than I have been since I was a child.

I also realize I've been asleep a very long time. There are some truths that become immediately known.

"Did you hear me?" Malerie Stivens asks. "All the soldiers are dead, Elizabeth. It's just us and Purcell."

I stare at the steel ceiling above, my sight coming into focus. The quiet hum of the *Valentia*'s engines gives music to the otherwise silent ship. I prop myself onto my elbows, lifting my upper body out of the cryogenic bed. The air tastes fresher than when I went to sleep.

"The troops are all dead?" I ask. I had no attachment to any of the soldiers. Why would I? I'm a doctor. Our purposes are opposite.

"Yes, that's what I said. Weren't you listening?"

Malerie comes to the edge of the bed. She's bulky with muscle. A military physician, like me, she takes her place in the armed forces with a dedication I lack. Her red hair is cropped short, much shorter than regulations, and her face knows only seriousness.

"I'm not sure what happened. I woke up an hour ago, felt like something was wrong and found them all dead. Not in one part of the ship. They're scattered."

For a brief second, I see that panic tries to take control of her - but she stifles it.

"They appear to have died of old age."

I swing out of the bed, bare feet meeting a cold steel floor. Standing feels different, too, like there's been a shift in the gravity. Is it the ship? Or something else?

"How long have we been out?"

"As far as I can tell, it's been one hundred years," says Malerie. "I'm hoping it's a mistake, some sort of computer error, yet..."

It sounds like foolish hope but I keep that opinion to myself. I put a hand through my hair and stretch my neck. I feel like I'm reacquainting myself with my body. No matter what Malerie claims, there's no computer mistake. It's been a long time. My instincts were right and it takes all I can muster to repress my glee. Different existence now. Much can change in a century. Perhaps more than people realize.

This is terrible for the soldiers, I suppose, all lying dead somewhere in this flying coffin. Physicians like me get the red-carpet treatment, as we've been in short supply since the war with the Council began. The war that stopped humanity from slaughtering one another, so we could slaughter something new. Doctors and nurses get plopped into cryosleep when traveling throughout the galaxy for military purposes. Some of these distances are considerable, taking a few months. Since physicians travel the most, the Aligned Colonies agreed to put us in cryosleep so we didn't lose precious parts of life to endless space journeys. The physicians' unions had the Aligned Colonies over a barrel on that one.

That luxury may have saved my life. Malerie and James Purcell's, too. I'd send thanks, but whoever approved the decision is probably long gone. Maybe the Aligned Colonies themselves are long gone, too. The makeup of the universe could be as different as the pre-Exodus civilization, when we all still lived on a habitable Earth. When worlds, now ruined, were yet to be touched by us.

Christ, I really am quite happy to be awake so far into the future. Wouldn't you be? After all, between you and me, you'd have to admit it really was quite awful during the war with the Council. Before then, too.

Maybe through all of humanity's history.

But... perhaps not now. There's hope in the air.

James Purcell looks so young sleeping. His eyes are like a baby's when he awakens, full of confusion and awe.

"We're here?" he asks. I loom over him, doing my best to look comforting and almost certainly failing.

"I'm not sure," I tell him. "Something went wrong."

"Where's Malerie?" he asks. He pushes himself up, brushing aside blond hair from his forehead. "And *what* went wrong?"

"She's investigating some of our systems. They're not all working." I hold up a hand to stop him from shouting questions. "You're safe, don't worry. But we've been asleep longer than expected."

"How long?" He's up and about now, almost hopping with anxiety, ready to bounce off the walls of the small room. He wants me to have all the answers, I can tell.

"Probably one hundred years." I wonder if he'll take it the way I do, as a gift. Or how Malerie seems to see it, as a curse.

He says nothing. In fact, his scrawny body remains still, as if he cannot process my words.

"That's not possible," he whispers, almost slurs.

"It seems to be," I say. "The soldiers died of old age. Their corpses are in half the hallways."

I toss the last comment out a little too casually. He grimaces at the tone. What can I say? I've never felt comfortable that my job requires me to heal people only so they can continue to kill. Now, I won't have to think about doing that anymore. There's so much I won't have to think about again. No more of the old worries about war, about income, about family, about lovers. No more, no more, no more.

"How long ago did they die?" he asks.

"I don't know."

"Did we win the war?"

"I don't know that either."

I hadn't considered the question before, come to think of it. That, too, seems like an anxiety which will no longer gnaw at our minds.

"I'm not sure it even matters," I add. "Think of the politics that existed one hundred years before us. Now think of what another hundred years could have gifted."

"Gifted?" he whispers. "Everyone I know will be gone."

He really is young, too young to be here. Too young to see what we were being sent to see. They were having us reinforce a large battalion on Jorjandi, previously a planet known for its esteemed hotel that catered to the rich and influential. Its owners graciously turned the hotel over to the military for the duration of the war. The press fawned.

"Don't think like that," I tell him. "We have no idea what it's like elsewhere. We're just making assumptions."

He knows, though. He's not happy about it but, unlike Malerie, he's not in denial. He realizes the years have given way to something new.

"How can I not think about it?" he insists.

"Let's go see Malerie," I reply. "She should be in the Sensors' Room and might have more information. Let's not panic until we know everything."

"You're certainly not panicking," he states. There's accusation in his voice.

"That's right," I reply. "What would be the point?"

The Sensors' Room offers a wall-to-wall view of space. The view of that vast abyss is interrupted by the blood on the center of the window. Malerie's body is slumped below it, the gun a few feet from her right hand. The way the blood is splattered gives the impression red wings are growing from her back.

I don't say anything. Neither does James. We know why she did it. We know what this confirms. Some people cannot handle change. Some people are comfortable only in what they are used to, no matter how awful it may be.

After standing silent watch, James breaks away, walking to the one computer that's active. It's built into the left wall of the room and it scans his face. His features are lit with red and yellow. I watch, waiting for him to break down, wondering if he'll follow in Malerie's footsteps.

He doesn't.

"I don't know how long it's been," he reports. "But we slowed way down from interstellar speed and have been on impulse since then. The computer seems to think we may have been attacked. Possibly by the Council."

He has no emotion in his voice. That's for the best.

"Lots of systems crashed and I guess rescue never came. Maybe we lost the war. The ship continued its trajectory to Jorjandi, though."

"Why'd we wake up?" I ask.

The computer turned our cryogenics off. His face remains a mask of dispassion. He's completely shut down.

"Because we're almost there."

Out the window, just above the blood, I can make out a gray planet, waiting. For the first time since waking, I feel a tinge of anxiety. I have a suspicion that, down there, I'll find out exactly what type of world I've woken up in.

I don't know what Jorjandi looked like before but, now, it's mainly gray ash. I gaze down on it from above, James beside me, Malerie's corpse beside him. We've broken through the atmosphere, the ship on autopilot, as it takes us to where it's programmed to land. On the horizon, I can make out the Grand Hotel's shape, but it's nothing more than a black form this far out.

"Look." James points. A figure stands in the wasteland, as the *Valentia* begins to decline. It seems like the figure waits for us.

"I guess we won the war," he says.

"No one knows what the Council looked like," I reply, not quite able to resist needling him for being so obsessed with that topic. Ash rises into the air as the *Valentia* settles on the ground. "Could be them."

"They weren't human," he protests.

"Believing that makes blowing up their ships easier." I squint, trying to make out the figure. It stands still, just far away enough that I cannot discern details. The fading light does not help, although the ground seems to shine, illuminating, despite the oncoming night.

"You think the Council were human?"

"I'm not that much of a conspiracy theorist," I laugh. "I think the Council was, or is, an extraterrestrial force that we never saw the face of. Because the moment we see a face, even an alien one, it makes the killing just a little harder."

"So, then, you do think we won?" he asks again, a note of impatience in his voice.

"Your thinking needs to change. Maybe our friend out there will tell you, if you're so curious."

"You're acting like you already know everything," he snaps.

He's not wrong.

"I've never been one to wallow in denial, James. Something happened while we were asleep. And not just the normal passing of history. Something changed. You know it, too. All the bullshit... it just doesn't matter anymore."

"Maybe," James grimaces. He's almost processed the situation but I know he still holds on to some hope that something of what he left behind remains. I can see that hope dragging him down as he walks across the room and through the hallways to the exit. I stay just a few feet behind him, sometimes stepping over corpses of soldiers who never got the chance to kill.

The figure turns out to be a woman in a three-piece suit. She has a mocking smile on her face and leans to the right as she stands. Her face is gaunt, bones almost protruding through skin. When she turns, she appears unnaturally thin, like she does not have quite enough body to fill the suit.

The ground crunches beneath my feet as James and I walk to her. He slows a little, but I keep a steady pace.

"You're not going to believe our story," I tell the woman, once we're in speaking distance. My voice carries well across the rocky plain.

"You came out of cryogenic sleep to discover a lot more time had passed than you thought," the woman replies. Her voice has an echo to it, like it rises from somewhere deep.

"Well, in that case," I say. "You're going to believe our story. This is James. I'm Elizabeth."

She declines to introduce herself and, instead, waves towards the *Valencia*.

"I recognized your ship. Rather out of date. That clued me in. Old warships have appeared on a somewhat regular basis. They just glide out of the blackness of space, left adrift during one of the wars."

Her eyes are bright blue, contrasting with her dull, pale skin.

"But they rarely have people alive aboard them."

"But there *are* some others from our time?" James asks hopefully.

"No." She shakes her head. "They didn't, ah, how should I put it? They didn't adapt."

James glances at me but I don't acknowledge it. He's still in the past. If he does not catch up soon, he'll be stuck there.

"Where are you from?" I ask.

"I live in the hotel," she says. "You probably spotted that. If you'd arrived when you were supposed to, you would've found a makeshift military spaceport right here."

She shrugs.

"But you know how things go. Here one day, gone the next. I was thinking of walking you to the hotel, in fact. You must be eager to see someplace new. You've been in that ship a rather long time."

Before I can agree, James interrupts.

"We need to know what happened."

She turns her gaze on him and I notice how black her hair is, as a few strands tap her forehead.

"What do you mean? Lots of things have happened. You should be specific."

"The soldiers that were here. And the Council. The war." He trips over his words. They sound almost unnatural on this world.

"I'm not an expert on politics," she admits, pulling on her suit jacket. "Before I took this on, I was just a maid at the hotel. I started there after the war with the Council ended, though, so I suppose that's part of your answer. I'm not familiar with the details but the Council was annihilated in one way or another, which, let's be frank, is probably all that matters. Why does one need details when the end is so clear?"

She shrugs

"After that, came the war with the Faceless. How it resolved is, ah, difficult to fully explain. It was, well… interrupted, I suppose. By another war. A war of some kind, at least. A slaughter you may even say. I am one of its survivors, although the use of that word is not perfect. It's the best I can do for now. You might understand more down the road."

"You're not human, are you?" James asks. "Is humanity gone?"

There's a mix of horror and awe in his voice. I want to tell him to shut up, that he doesn't get it. Can't he feel the air? Can't he feel it in his own body? Malerie could. For all her faults, she knew. She understood what happened while we slept and then she acted on that knowledge.

The woman shakes her head.

"That word. Humanity. That's not a word we use anymore." She pockets her hands and turns her gaze on me. "Your friend understands, I think."

I can't help but smile.

"I could tell it was different right away. It's like when you wake up and you know you're not in your own bed, even though you haven't opened your eyes yet."

"How interesting," says the woman. "I suppose it is a bit like that."

She claps her hands together.

"Well, shall we go? I think you'll find you'll, ah, adapt better in the hotel."

"I'm not going to the hotel." James' voice is firm, almost rebellious.

"Then where are you going?"

He doesn't have an immediate answer. The fool.

"Back to the ship," he finally says.

"You'll die there," the woman warns.

"There's enough resources on it for decades."

"That may be true," says the woman. "But you'll still age. And then you'll die there, all the same. Once you go back in it, you won't come out. Sure, you might tell yourself, some days, that you will. But you won't. I've seen your type before. Many times before. If you go back in, you'll never have the courage to adapt."

James takes a step forward before taking two back. Then he breaks into a run, heading for the *Valentia*. I watch him recede. The night of Jorjandi envelops him before long. I wonder if he would've been better off taking the same route Malerie did, instead of wasting away in a new reality he will never understand, never appreciate.

"You're right that he won't come back," I tell the woman. "A shame."

"Yes," she agrees. "So many people made his choice, back in the day."

We keep silence for the first half of our walk. The behemoth that is the hotel becomes clear on the horizon, both a welcome and a threat. I understand how it held so many soldiers during the war with the Council and why they desperately wanted us to reinforce it. I was told it housed twenty thousand guests and was adapted to hold thirty thousand soldiers.

The hotel is only seven stories tall but has long wings that sprawl out like tendrils. It has an air of indestructibility, something that can withstand the violence of history. Countless windows look down at me. I think I see a figure in one or two of them, watching me, evaluating. I welcome their gaze. I'm more ready for this world than they know.

"You've mentioned people having to adapt," I say to the woman. "Did this adaptation or evolution, or whatever you want to call it, happen all at once?"

"You have me stumped there," she replies. "It felt like it happened all at once but I'm not so sure. Maybe it's more correct to say things boiled over. The dam can only hold so long. One day the universe had enough of what we were, I guess. Too much conflict, you could say. Maybe it was our fault. We left Earth and caused havoc in the heavens. I don't know. But it was clear what had to happen: adapt or die. I adapted."

"Is that when you got the suit?"

"It was a guest's. He did not adapt." She reaches out and brushes her index finger across my face. Her touch is cold. "You adapted well. Much better than anyone would expect, considering you weren't even around when things, ah, changed."

"I guess I'm one of those people who always wanted different."

In my mind, I see a field of the dead, grass turned scarlet. All the corpses are mutilated. It was business as usual once.

"I didn't much like the place I was in, or the time. Or the person I had to be."

The hotel shadows us. The steps to its entrance near.

"I'm sure you'll continue to feel different," the woman says. "Continue to change until you're one with this world. Were you always unhappy in your prior life?"

"Weren't you?"

"I very much was," the woman admits. "And then I very much wasn't. Being a maid here was unpleasant. What I do now, what I am now, I like a lot more. What were you?"

"A doctor," I reply. "A hypocritical one, I felt."

It feels nice to say that out loud.

"My job was to heal killers."

"My job was to fluff killers' sheets," the woman responds. "Although, I'm talking about killers of a different sort. Yours only took orders. I dealt with the ones who gave them, in one fashion or another."

There's a bitterness in her tone that takes me by surprise.

"You're still angry about it," I remark.

"No," she says. "I've forgotten the past. It's only a fading nightmare now."

We ascend the steps and I am free of fear. That, in itself, makes me feel like a new being. No war, no hospitals, no Council, no surgeon's organization, not even rent to pay. Everything that once caused me anxiety has faded.

"Did people on other worlds participate in this adaptation?"

"Oh yes," the woman nods. "It's the same story everywhere. Those who adjust survive. Those who don't perish. I suppose it's always been that way. I suppose some have always liked it that way, too. This time, though, those who were usually happy with forcing adaptations realized it wasn't quite for them."

I think I see a smile.

She opens the door, revealing the hotel's lobby. At first, I'm let down. The lobby is large and gold, the couches appear comfortable, the furniture a style that must've come about after I went to sleep. The check-in desk is a sleek silver that promises competence and servitude. Exactly what one would expect in a luxury hotel. A hint of that old depression creeps up my spine and misery starts to push against my chest. This world does not seem so changed.

At least, not until I look up.

The ceiling is higher than should be possible. Far higher than seven stories. That alone would whisper of a new and interesting reality.

But, from the ceiling, hang long, sharp nails, infinite in number. On each nail is a human being wearing a now tattered suit, the end of each nail protruding through their chest. Rotted flesh hangs off the corpses, swaying in an invisible breeze. From here, the bodies are indistinguishable, like they're decorations for the hotel's new owners, as opposed to anything that once lived.

"Beautiful, isn't it?" says the woman. "I love seeing them like that. This was the grand slaughter. The last slaughter. The one that allowed us to adapt."

"Quite a display of the dead."

"All war memorials are, whether people wish to admit it or not. Humanity, whatever it was, turned out to be a mistake. Now, we've thrown away the errors and embraced what we always should've been. You don't find a thrill in seeing them like that? In knowing we've prevailed?"

There's a hint of desperation in her voice. She needs me to share her glee. I look away from the extinct and directly at the woman.

"I think it's in the past."

Whatever she is, human or not, she has not fully given herself to this beautiful new world. She's not like James but she's not like me, either. She's helped discard what humanity once was, but her hate for those fading days still burns. I understand why she greets newcomers. She understands them still. I bet she wishes she doesn't.

I walk by her, heading further into the hotel. If she has it in her to adapt, then she will follow my lead. But I don't need hers anymore. Perhaps she will just reside in this hall, guiding newcomers past the obscene spectacle above but never truly becoming one with this reality.

Not like I have.

I offer one last look at the sight overhead. The extinct gaze at me with their dead eyes. Let them. Let them see how they didn't have to perish. How they could've embraced something new, if they weren't so blinded by humanity's basest instincts.

Let them see humanity's final victory, which is its final defeat.

Wade Hunter

Jeff hit the send button. The computer made a whoosh as the email flew off into cyberspace. He sighed and stared at his screen, questioning himself. Questioning a lot of things.

Wilson from the next cubicle poked his head around the side barrier. Jeff liked Wilson. Wilson was one of the true friends he had in the Bureau of Paranormal Affairs and pretty much the top field agent on his team.

Wilson offered up a smile.

"Jeffrey, bro. Ready for your big meeting with the Director?"

Jeff raised an eyebrow, looked at his computer and back at Wilson.

"Yeah. As best as I can be. But, you know..."

Wilson gave a short barking chuckle.

"You're ready, but your competition for the big promotion is plowing the boss's daughter. The things some people will do to get ahead."

Jeff's face screwed up and he gave a short nod.

"Got it in one, buddy. Thanks for the reminder."

Wilson shrugged.

"Well, let's be honest, anyone sticking it that battleax deserves some kind of promotion."

"I love you man but I'm seriously considering ramming this Bic through your eye." Jeff twirled a pen between his fingers. "However, I have enough issues right now and don't need to go to this meeting with blood all over my shirt."

99

Wilson was used to his dry humor but still caught the sour look on Jeff's face.

"Yo, you know most of us are backing you. You're the best squad leader we have."

"Thanks, buddy. I appreciate it. Unfortunately, Thomas has plenty of sycophants in the division."

"Sheep and kiss-asses," Wilson said. "Send them out on one or two missions and they'll get culled off."

Jeff looked at his computer and checked the sent file. He turned back to Wilson, who was leaning so far back in his chair Jeff wasn't sure how the guy didn't topple over.

"You deserve the position," Wilson went on. "I mean, that thing with the garden gnome plague over on the South Side - that was genius. Then the vampire infestation in our own building. You've earned this promotion. I know Thomas is using the inside lane on the boss's daughter - *wink, wink* - but there's always hope."

Jeff looked at his computer.

"Hope or other things," he muttered.

"What was that?"

Jeff smiled.

"I said, maybe you could get him to bugger you in the bathroom before the meeting and let me take pictures?"

"Jeff, bro," Wilson chuckled. "We're buds and all that. But no. I mean, you've seen Duffy's daughter. Anything that has been in that glob of nasty isn't coming anywhere near me. I won't even take a piss if Thomas is in there with his wang out. I can, however, buy you a beer after - either celebratory or consoling."

Jeff sighed. "Yeah. I'll probably need more than one."

"Seriously, dude. I'm pulling for you. Just not on Thomas."

"Fair enough."

Jeff's computer dinged. He reached around the back and unplugged the portable hard drive.

"How do you think the defense proposal thingy will go?" Wilson asked.

"We'll find out."

"Shit is brilliant, man. Planting mental seeds in documents then triggering them with emoji text messages. I mean, who doesn't automatically look at their phone when it lights up. How has the testing gone?"

"Small scale stuff. The magic thing limits anything more. Plus, I don't want one of our guys working on it and leaking information before it gets approved."

"Right," Wilson said. "How are you testing it then? How do you know it works, bro?"

Jeff looked around and leaned in.

"I haven't said anything but I tested positive for Void control awhile back. I've been training outside of work."

Wilson's eyes went round.

"Dude! Void control? You mean you can..." he wiggled his fingers.

Jeff looked around again, nodded.

"Yeah, I'm getting there. I've concentrated on battle magic mainly. You know, to help in the field."

"Righteous."

"Just don't say anything."

Wilson made an act of zipping his lips. Lisa from 4C walked past, glaring at the two men.

"Hey, Lisa," Wilson grinned. "Looking like sunshine today, as always. Is that a new shirt you picked up at Goodwill? Reminds me of my grandma."

Lisa snarled. Wilson smiled back. Lisa turned her glare on Jeff and held up her phone.

"Why are you calling a meeting? You know Thomas is getting that promotion, not you. Who do you think you are to rearrange my day?"

"Do you have that report on the haunting at 32nd Street ready?"

"You aren't the boss of me," Lisa snapped.

"Actually, I am. You are on my squad of researchers. You send all your reports to me. That makes me your immediate supervisor. That makes me your boss. It's how these things work."

"Well, not for long. I hear Thomas is canning you once he gets the promotion to manager."

"How many times has Thomas canned you, Lisa?" Wilson asked.

Lisa turned blazing eyes on him. He blew her a kiss. She stormed off. Wilson laughed, leaned forward and tapped at his computer.

"Dude, what meeting? I didn't get anything?"

"Just something to tie up loose ends. You don't have to be there. As a matter of fact, you should go get us a table at Garfield's before it gets too crowded with the after-work crew."

"Leave work and start drinking early?" Wilson said incredulously. "Jeffrey, as my immediate superior, how dare you suggest such a thing?"

He turned off his computer, stood and slid the chair under his desk.

"See you there." He extended a fist for a bump. "Good luck, bro."

"Thanks, man."

Harold B. Duffy, Director of the BPA, was a three-hundred-pound ass bladder stuffed into a suit two sizes too small. It pushed his neck fat up into a halo that rested on his collar and bounced when he talked. The man never met a good idea he wasn't ready to take credit for. Jeff knew that all too well. It was a lesson he learned time and again.

Mr. Duffy smiled and opened his arms as Jeff entered the room.

"Simmons, come in, have a seat. I believe you know Thomas well enough."

"Thomas." Jeff gave him an obligatory nod.

"Jim!" Thomas yelled. "How're they hanging?"

"It's Jeff."

Thomas's mouth made an 'O' of contemplation. He stole a quick glance at Mr. Duffy, as if to confirm Jeff wasn't trying to play some trick on him.

"You sure?" he asked stupidly.

Jeff made a show of checking his badge.

"Yep. We've worked on like three projects together. How do you not remember that?"

Thomas stole another look at Mr. Duffy, who nodded confirmation. Thomas brightened.

"Right, Jeff. Got it. Guess I better remember that. Always thought it was Jim. You look like a Jim."

Jeff stared a hole through him, contemplating if he should take the stapler off Mr. Duffy's desk and ram it into Thomas's nose.

There was a creak as Mr. Duffy settled in his chair.

"Uhm… Yes. Well, gentlemen, we all know why we have gathered here today."

"Damn right, pops." Thomas offered up a fist to Mr. Duffy for bumping. Mr. Duffy let it hang. Thomas waggled it a bit. Mr. Duffy's lip drew into a tight line and he shook his head in short sharp movements. Thomas shrugged, leaned back, and tried to dig something out of his teeth with his tongue.

Jeff stared at him in amazement. He glanced at Mr. Duffy and spread his palms.

Mr. Duffy hesitated. He closed his eyes, rubbed a hand over his face, took a cleansing breath.

"Right. As you both know, the Division Manager spot has opened up, after George got himself turned into a vampire during that infestation thing in the basement."

Thomas scoffed. "Stupid move."

Mr. Duffy, apparently finding balance, nodded.

"Yes, stupid move."

Jeff turned to Thomas.

"Weren't you supposed to have his six when he went down there?"

Thomas shrugged. "He went in without me."

"Body cams show you left him."

"Same thing. Listen, I had to hit the head. My belly gets a little shaky when I'm nervous and we were going down into a nest of vampires. He didn't follow me."

"He was in front of you. You turned and left him without a word. You locked the door to the basement and trapped him."

Thomas tapped his temple.

"Trapped those bloodsuckers too. Good thinking by me."

"Gentleman," Mr. Duffy cut in. "The loss of George was a blow to us all, but we must move on."

"Move on?" Jeff goggled. "I had to *stake* George."

"We all have to make sacrifices in this department," Mr. Duffy said.

Jeff's eyebrows raised so high they almost became part of his hairline.

"George was my uncle." He stared back and forth between the two men. "I had to tell my mother that I drove a giant stake through her brother's chest then cut his head off."

"Oh, that's why it was a closed casket," Thomas said in a moment of enlightenment. "Totally makes sense now."

Mr. Duffy straightened his tie and took three slow breaths.

"Moving on. With George gone, the manager position is vacant. And it has come down to the two of you as final applicants."

Jeff tried to relax his shoulders. He'd been working his entire career for this. He deserved it. He'd done everything right to make it happen. The Director wouldn't be so stupid as to put Thomas in a place of any more power.

"After reviewing your proposals for the military defense contract, the position is going to Thomas. I'm sorry Jeffrey."

Thomas jumped up on his chair, clapping his hands.

"Yes!" There was fist-pumping. There was a finger in Jeff's face. "Suck it, Jimbo! I'm totally your boss now."

Jeff stared. His eye twitched. It took everything in him not to punch Thomas in the groin. He turned back to Mr. Duffy.

"No offense, sir, but are you f'n kidding me right now?"

Mr. Duffy straightened as if steeling himself against a storm.

"No, Jeffrey. That was the decision we made."

"You made."

"Dial it back, Jimbo," Thomas said. "Or I'll have you tossed."

Mr. Duffy slapped the desk. The sound of a beefy palm whacking wood bounced off the walls of his office.

"Sit down, Thomas."

Thomas sat. Mr. Duffy gathered himself.

Jeff leaned forward, tapping the desktop with a finger as he punctuated his words.

"You're telling me the defense department liked the concept of mice with tiny bombs strapped to them over my proposal?"

Mr. Duffy shrugged. "Well, they didn't *hate* it."

Jeff bit the side of his mouth in an attempt to control himself.

"They liked it more than my proposal?" He repeated through clenched jaws.

"The magic thing?"

Jeff threw up his hands.

"Magic is just a small portion of it and you know that. It's the key that makes it work. The concept, the application, the infield use are almost without limits. You're trying to tell me they liked the randomness of training small rodents over the precision of my plan?"

"Mice are cheap," Thomas chimed in.

"The idea doesn't even fit with our division."

Thomas shrugged.

"That doesn't make the mice cost any more."

Jeff rounded on him.

"And how many furry little grenades would it take to overtake a city?"

"Lots probably. But those little buggers breed like mad."

Jeff shook his head in disbelief.

"Lots probably? This was your proposal. You don't know the answer?"

"Who knows these things?" Thomas gave Mr. Duffy an exasperated look.

"You should. It was your proposal. What about breeding and training feeding and storing them. And the time involved to strap bombs to them. The manpower just stacks up."

"Yeah, well, you need a wizard for yours to work. Those bastards charge an arm and a leg."

"Yes. Yes, they do. And they are on *our* payroll, which means *we* would be charging an arm and a leg for the defense department to use them. We profit greatly from it."

Jeff turned to Mr. Duffy.

"Really. They went with his proposal?"

Mr. Duffy shrugged.

"Well, honestly, no. In truth, they liked yours."

"I'm sorry, *what*?" Jeff looked from Mr. Duffy to Thomas and back. "Then how?"

He pointed at Thomas.

"How is he getting the manager position? Despite everything else in our records, which clearly shows I am more qualified, you said it would be based on the defense department's response to our proposals."

"Probably because your stupid thing wasn't even tested," Thomas said. He'd found a toothpick somewhere and was now using it to try and dig out whatever was in his teeth.

"It *has* been tested."

"Small scale stuff. Mice are everywhere."

"The defense department was worried about the small scale of your test results," Mr. Duffy broke in. "Also, Thomas has displayed other attributes that you just haven't, Simmons."

It was too much for Jeff to take.

"Oh. As in the ability to bend your daughter over a desk and ride her like the county fair bronco?"

"I beg your pardon," Mr. Duffy bristled. "Thomas, do you have nothing to say in defense of your fiancé?"

Jeff threw up his hands.

"Fiancé? Well, that explains it."

Mr. Duffy leaned across the desk. His voice was suddenly cold.

"It's the way of the world, Simmons. Best you learn that real fast before you say anything else that may damage your career here in this department."

"That's just great, juussst great." Jeff leaned back into his seat. "You know what?"

He pulled out his mobile, pounded away on it for a few seconds, then slapped it down on the desk. The other men's phone dinged. They both reached for their devices. A look of surprise spread across Thomas's face.

"Wow, dude, did you just quit? You already have this written up or something?"

"No, Thomas, I typed that entire massive letter in the few seconds I had my phone out."

"Really? Damn."

"No, not really, Thomas!" Mr. Duffy yelled. His face was red and getting redder. He pointed a quivering finger at Jeff but, before he could start his tirade, there was a knock on the door. Mrs. Quinn, the secretary, poked her head in.

"Here are the papers you just printed, Mr. Duffy, sir."

"I didn't print any papers."

Jeff stood and took them.

"Thank you, Mrs. Quinn. You can leave for the day."

"No, she can't. Who are you to give my secretary orders?"

Jeff smacked the papers down on the desk. Mr. Duffy grabbed them, read the top page and began to laugh.

"I don't think so. You damn well know that any concept or piece of work produced for the BPA while you work for them is, and remains, the property of the BPA - whether the employee quits or is fired."

"Just let him take his stupid magic, mind control, electronic thing with him," Thomas sneered. "Probably doesn't work anyway. Good riddance to dead weight."

Jeff turned and held up a finger.

"One, it does work." He held up a second finger, made a finger gun, and pointed at Thomas. "Second, I couldn't agree more about the dead weight."

"Whatever. Should have proved your stupid idea worked instead of quitting."

Jeff picked up his phone and typed. The other men's phone dinged again. They both looked at the screen.

"Why did you send me a bunch of emojis?" Thomas asked.

"Simmons?" There was a tinge of fear in Mr. Duffy's voice.

Jeff grinned at Thomas then turned his smile on Mr. Duffy. He stared the man right in the face.

"Thomas, what do you really think about Mr. Duffy's warthog of a daughter?"

Thomas rolled his eyes and made a show of sticking his finger down his throat and gagging.

"It's kind of like banging a rotten bag of hot garbage."

Thomas's eyes went big. Hands shot up to cover his mouth.

"Excuse me, young man?" Mr. Duffy glared.

Thomas moved his hands to apologize.

"She squeaks like a dog toy when I pound that shit."

He ducked to avoid the stapler that came flying at him. Mr. Duffy turned back to Jeff.

"You," he accused.

"Simple truth command," Jeff smiled. "If you read my proposal, you know how it works. And look at that! It works *fantastically*!"

He spread his hands.

"Tada. Magic."

"You embedded your resignation letter."

Jeff raised an eyebrow. Mr. Duffy nervously looked at his phone then back to Jeff.

"What did you do to me?"

"Be a good little dog and sign the papers that Mrs. Quinn just brought you. I'll wait." Jeff returned his attention to the phone, typed in a message and hit 'send'. Mr. Duffy was straining with his left hand, trying to stop his right hand signing the papers.

"I will not do it," he growled as he fought himself. Sweat broke out on his brow.

Jeff sat back down.

"Oh, scratch your head with your left hand for me."

Mr. Duffy's left hand started scratching his head while his right scribbled a signature. Jeff snagged the papers once Mr. Duffy was done and put them in his portfolio.

"Thank you."

A fist collided with Jeff's face. The blow sent him sprawling out of his chair and onto the floor. He looked up to find Thomas standing over him, shaking with rage. Jeff shook his head in an attempt to clear it. Blood ran from his nose. Thomas dragged him up by the collar.

"I watch hardcore animal porn to feel clean after bagging her," he yelled in Jeff's face.

Punch

"I practically drink Listerine now."

Punch.

"I have nightmares where she's Jabba the Hut and I'm Princess Lea."

Punch.

"Get the portfolio!" Mr. Duffy yelled from behind his desk. "Get the portfolio. The papers."

Thomas dropped Jeff and reached for the portfolio. Fortunately, Jeff fell on top of it. He typed a fury of emojis into his phone and held it up in front of Thomas as he bent down.

"Don't look," Mr. Duffy called.

The warning came too late. Thomas's eyes went glassy. He snarled and turned towards His boss.

"Oh shit, what did you do to him?"

Mr. Duffy's phone dinged. He reflexively looked down at it.

"Damn it!" he snarled. Thomas and he circled each other around the desk as Jeff pulled himself up, grabbed his portfolio and slipped out the door, closing it behind him.

Mrs. Quinn was standing by her desk, doe-eyed and clutching at her fluffy labels.

"Mr. Simmons, what's going on? Half the office got up and left a few minutes ago. And, oh, Mr. Simmons, you're bleeding."

"Am I?" Jeff spit blood into a garbage can. "Mrs. Quinn, please fax these over to HR immediately."

He handed the signed papers to her. Something crashed inside Duffy's office. There was a lot of yelling and screaming, followed by another loud bang. Mrs. Quinn jumped.

"Mrs. Quinn," Jeffrey gently turned the older secretary's attention back to him. "Fax these. Then leave. I will expect you back here on Monday. I think we'll have a lot of paperwork to fill out."

Mrs. Quinn took the papers, jumped at another resounding crunch from inside the office and started scanning the papers into her computer. She worked with the speed of a pro and sent everything to HR. Her brow narrowed.

"Mr. Simmons. This says if anything happens to Mr. Duffy, you're the new Director."

"Does it? Interesting."

There was a cry of pain from inside the room.

"But?" Mrs. Quinn started.

Thomas came flying through the door and fell in a heap. Jeff wrapped his arm around Mrs. Quinn and led her towards the elevator.

"Time to go."

He typed into his phone and sent a group text. Dings rang out around the office. Jeff slid Mrs. Quinn into the elevator and followed her, as Mr. Duffy, bloody and mad-eyed, stepped out of his office. He raised his chair and slammed it down into Thomas's head. There was a pop and a lot of blood.

"Oh, my lord," Mrs. Quinn cried.

Mr. Duffy looked up and saw Mrs. Quinn and Jeff getting on the elevator. Jeff smiled and waved.

Mr. Duffy bellowed and charged. He made three steps before Lisa from 4C intercepted him and drove a pair of scissors into his neck. Screams and the sounds of destruction filled the office floor, as the elevator doors slid shut.

"Mr. Simmons?" Mrs. Quinn asked in a shaking voice. "What was all that?"

"That?" he pointed at the closed doors with his phone. "Just an office meeting I invited some people to earlier. I think it's time that we cleared out dead weight. No worries. Everyone who left has been instructed on what to tell the police."

Jeff put his arm round the secretary.

"Mrs. Quinn, do you like beer? I'm meeting Wilson at Garfield's to celebrate. You're welcome to join us."

Ophelia

Rob McClure Smith

[Excerpts from a work journal kept by the late Professor Frank Thurston of Boston University, the document partially recovered from a damaged flash drive found near Watertown, following his drowning in the Charles River]

January 5:

Not a stellar day in the lab. Malfunctions in the fugitive plugs of the soft controller led to a complete shutdown of the molded hyper-elastic actuator matrix. Trace widths of the catalytic inks printed at 450 kPa and 345 kPa and error bars indicated far more than standard deviation for n=3 measurements. Informed Erica that the plateau moduli of the inks are an order of magnitude higher than those of the matrix materials. Smirking, she suggested we consider deploying a lobster as the base model. Made that infuriating snorting noise she cultivates when feeling superior also. Later, graduate assistant with the teeth (Soo-Jin?) discovered mouse droppings in the 3D printer. Unbelievable.

January 7

Arrived late at lab due to frenzied preparations for conference presentation. Malfunction of the printed platinum reaction chamber resulted in Ophelia's collision with a wall and damage to vent orifices. Further infuriating delay now inevitable. Did use inappropriate language in workplace setting but apologized immediately. No need to involve HR. Erica said best not mention mishap at conference. Obviously still annoyed at not being invited.

January 8

Travel day uneventful but tiring. Briefly explained research to the hefty woman occupying the majority of my seat-rest on plane. Looked disconcerted and, afterward, became bafflingly engrossed in film about hearing-impaired cleaning lady falling in love with fish man. Implausible premise. Tonight, strolled to highly recommended Italian restaurant. Excellent lasagna but bread questionable. Waiter unnecessarily obsequious so left 17.5% tip. Entered Yelp review (average) then back to hotel to polish presentation till 10.30. Rewrote introductory paragraph thus:

As we know, soft robotics aims to provide safer, more robust robots that interact with humans and adapt to natural environments better than their rigid counterparts. The longstanding goal in our field is the creation of robots entirely soft, replacing components such as batteries and electronic controls with analogous soft systems. Our recent project at The Center for Biologically Inspired Engineering succinctly demonstrates how easily to manufacture key components of a basic soft robot. Today, I want you to meet.
[Pause for effect]:
Ophelia the Octobot.
(video 1)

As you can see, Ophelia is not only soft and cute, being a fully autonomous robotic device resembling a small octopus - but is made completely of silicone rubber and controlled by microfluidic logic, autonomously regulating fluid flow and catalytic decomposition of her on-board monopropellant fuel supply. Gas generated from the fuel inflates fluidic networks downstream of the reaction sites, resulting in actuation. [Pause]. But let's have another look at our girl in action.

(video 2)

Revision just this minute interrupted by text from Elvira (not her real name), my own hearing-impaired cleaning lady, regarding the discovery of bat droppings in bathroom. Unsure what expectation is, with me being 600 miles distant. Fear my *Drácula en la ducha* remark did not go down well. Now to sleep: big day tomorrow.

January 9
Disappointing presentation and audience reaction due, in the first instance, to catastrophic PowerPoint failure and, in the second, to idiot questions posited by academic rivals.

That insufferable Melissa Rhodes-James, now slumming at Oxford apparently, inquires: *Does Ophelia necessarily need to have eight arms? Or is this mere consequence of the robot being initially designed on cephalopod principles?*

Thus, reduced to explaining in detail to a bio-engineer the principles of bioengineering. How Ophelia is a simple embodiment designed only to demonstrate our integrated design and additive fabrication strategy for embedding autonomous functionality. Emphasized how robotic end effectors with bioinspired and rapid actuation can be multiply deployable crawlers *and* swimmers with plethora of useful applications.

Response was moronic blank stare and follow-up query: *But why an octopus per se?*

Noted that the name was Ophelia and not Percy. Scattered giggles. Emphasized again how such a machine can handle delicate procedures and maneuver into tight spaces in search and rescue - or be useful for internal medicine. Reiterated that a soft body like an earthworm crawls more effectually than a rigid structure, such as a crab.

Still the same mutant stare. *Bear with me* (MRJ actually said that). *If one requires a chemical reaction inside the robot to turn the liquid fuel (hydrogen peroxide) into a volume of gas flowing into the arms and inflating them, why not simplify design? Why not a one-arm principle? Why not an earthworm robot? Why the need for an octopus?* Widespread amusement in conference room ensuing. *My dear boy, what's your obsession with the octopus?*

My pithy retort. *Can a worm grow to 100 pounds and 8 feet long and squeeze his boneless body through a hole not much larger than the diameter of its eyeball? Does a worm have arms covered with thousands of suckers that taste as well as feel? Is there a worm with a beak like a parrot and venom like a snake and a tongue covered with teeth that also shape-shifts, changes color, and squirts ink? Is there? Is there?*

Can your robot do any of that though? MRJ inquires, sporting gargoyle grin. *Isn't your Ophelia more prone just to run into walls at great velocity?* This uttered *sotto voce* and eliciting stifled guffaws from the Harvey Mudd contingent.

Clearly, we have a leak. Will investigate upon return.

Departed the presentation irate, but anger mitigated by chance meeting with delightful young woman sporting a pageboy and absolutely perfect cheekbones next to the lunch buffet.

"So, you'd be the octopus robot man," was her swaggering first introduction.

"No," I informed her affably. "I'm the bioengineer who built the octopus robot."

She did not smile.

Her name is Gillian Frankenthaler, resident research biologist at the city Aquarium here. Primary field of inquiry: the octopus. Had long conversation about octopuses (not octopi). Dr. F. is intrigued by possible replication of the three hearts of the animal and its use of a copper rather than iron-based carrier for oxygen. What would engineering equivalent be? Multiple power sources and a different conductivity? How might a robotic octopus replicate the original's extensive nervous system and cognitive complexity? If the majority of neurons are in arms that taste and touch and control basic motions without input from the brain, what kind of electronic circuitry is comparable? Stimulating tête-à-tête. Invited to visit aquarium to study the original in habitat. Invited her to the lab to meet the design team. This has the makings of a productive collaboration.

March 14
Research visit to aquarium approved by committee. Erica deeply skeptical. Inquired if my 'Doctor Frankenstein' is attractive. Recall suddenly that, as a graduate student, she studied in Rhodes-James's Ph.D. program and worked in her lab, a notorious viperous nest of seething Sapphic desires. Might the pair of them have once boarded the love craft, as it were? No definitive proof, as of yet. Investigation on hiatus while the lab is shut down for repairs after the recent incident (raccoon, power line).

May 12
A most educational albeit disquieting experience. The aquarium was moist and dim and upon the sand were shrub-like clumps of sponge. To my eye, the geometry of the tank was confusing and wrong. One could not always be altogether sure that water and glass were horizontal. Down amid the coiled seaweed I spied, lurking, an animal the size of a cat. The only parts in any way focusable upon

were its small head and eyes. Its color perfectly matched the seaweed, except segments of skin folded into tiny peaks with tips matching the bright orange of the sponge. Ligeia (its name) is a fifty-pound, six-foot-long, two-and-a-half-year-old giant Pacific octopus.

As Dr. F eased off the lid, it oozed from a far corner to the top of the tank to investigate me. Its arms boiling up, twisting and slippery, outstretched upside down. A melon-sized head bobbed, left eye swiveling in its socket to meet my gaze.

"She has eyelids just like we do," Dr. F observed, sliding a hand near one of the creature's eyes, causing it to wink coyly at me. "She's looking right at you."

I reciprocated the thing's gaze, staring deep and long into the horizontal pupil of a large prominent eye. It seemed to stare right back at me. But what was it thinking?

"What a look she's giving you!" Dr. F noted. While she stroked the creature's soft head with her fingertips, it changed color, ruby-flecked skin turning white and smooth, as it set about the curious task of tasting and feeling her at the same time.

"You have a way with octopuses," I noted. "Might I venture a touch?"

No idea at all why I made this request. Immediately realized I had never wanted to do anything less in the entirety of my earthly existence.

"Well, I wouldn't want her pulling you into the tank," Dr. F said, smiling eerily. "She seems to have gotten herself worked up into a right funk today."

It was at this juncture that, strategically deploying its funnel, viz. the siphon by the side of its head used to jet it through the water, it squirted a substantial drenching stream directly into my face. The deluge soaked me head to foot.

"Bad Ligeia," Dr. F said, shaking her head. "Who's a naughty girl then?"

Dr. F was at the time attired in extraordinarily form-fitting short shorts and a pink tee-shirt (beneath which she was most certainly *sans soutien-gorge*) and which bore the illustration of a smiling cartoon cephalopod, the phrase 'Handsy as Hell' etched in Baskerville font beneath its sprawling tentacles. Given her aquatic work environment and the consequent propensity of spillage, this would be an understandable sartorial choice if, perhaps, needlessly provocative. Observed also that Dr. F's pale bare arms were tracked by red hickeys. A strange and violent kind of sororal affection, this.

At dinner, Dr. F informed me the creature is often temperamental, sometimes turning off overhead lights, scooting jets of water at the bulbs above its tank to cause a short circuit.

"Catching her for the maze experiments took forever," she added. "You see, once Ligeia's got a grip of something she won't let it go. One time she got stuck in a filter and we couldn't get her out for love or money. She'll plug the outflow valves by poking her arms all the way in there. She gets a kick out of flooding everything. Eight kicks, I suppose it'd be. She's quite the delinquent."

"The thing sounds mildly psychotic," I observed.

"God!" Dr. F smiled at me fetchingly.

"What wonder that across the earth a great architect went mad?" she intoned cryptically, then giggled slightly.

"What?" I asked.

She shrugged and I supposed the above to be a quotation of unknown derivation. Dr. F is somewhat of a reader I surmise.

"Well, Ligeia is totally super-smart," she continued. "She can open the childproof caps on Extra Strength Tylenol. Put a crab inside a Mr. Potato Head and she'll have it dismantled in no time."

"I have colleagues can't do that," I observed.

"Open a Potato Head?" Dr. F asked, ridiculously.

"No," I clarified. "The Tylenol business."

May 13

The thing is uncanny. When I turn away, I can feel its eyes follow me through the glass. The papillae above the eyes look like horns and I see why one name for these is 'devil fish.' Earlier, Dr. F regaled me with tales of neurotoxic flesh-dissolving saliva venom, suckers that tear flesh, how a Pacific octopus can overpower a weak person. What I dislike most about it, though, is its continually changing color, shape and texture. One moment bright red and bumpy, the next smooth and veined with dark brown or white. It is so mutable - one second, a silk scarf, the next a beating heart, a gliding snail, a rock covered with algae. The thing mutates endlessly. It can be everything, and therefore is nothing. At least until it melts into octopus again, the webbing of its arms flecked with lichen green, gazing at me hungrily through that hair-thin slit, the second before it soaks me. Five times today it was.

"Good God," Dr. F said, smiling nervously. "Ligeia really doesn't like you."

I am glad to be leaving this place tomorrow. I need to be back in the lab where I belong. There is much to be said for a controlled environment.

May 30

For the narrative I am about to write, I neither expect nor solicit belief. I merely put these words onto the page in some semblance of sequence in these, the still small hours of the morning. To record for myself the events that transpired this evening - and hope these words are sufficient, at the least, to traduce my own belief hereafter.

I would that all was different and I could now celebrate the inability of the human mind to correlate all its contents. Such bliss it would be again not to understand! But, in truth, I suspect now that we live on a placid island of ignorance in the midst of these lack seas of infinity, and it was not meant that we should ever voyage far. I know I wish *I* hadn't.

There was some unpleasantness in the lab today, not unrelated to Erica's situation, albeit her dismissal was for sufficient cause. In any case, a minor fit was thrown.

"You," she snarled, like an enraged animal, pointing at me accusingly, admonishing. "Are a pathetic excuse for a human being."

"Be that as it may," I ventured.

"You have no feelings," she screeched. "You're a monster, but you're not even an interesting one. You're a boring one. You're some kind of infinitely boring monster."

I regret to say campus security was summoned and my erstwhile assistant dragged, protesting, away - arms flailing wildly in her wake. Then Soo-Jin took it upon herself to storm out also, accompanied by her teeth, firing a number of creatively choice epithets in my direction ('misogynist creepster,' 'incel wankerboy,' 'new fogey fuck-up' etc. etc.). I didn't even know she spoke English. It was, to say the very least, an unfortunate and disconcerting turn of events.

Erica's departure complicated the project's timetable going forward and, for that reason, I stayed late in the lab - in order to review her progress towards fashioning a synthetic form of cephalopod skin that can transform from a flat 2D surface to a three-dimensional one - with requisite bumps and pits.

While perusing her often unintelligible and cryptic notebooks, apparently written in one of the lost languages, I became conscious of a nasty slopping sound and, soon after, a pungent and pervasive odor. Given the lab's recent infestation issues, I assumed that some animal had died in our ventilation system. I made a note to have the janitorial staff investigate and continued with my analysis of Erica's cryptology, only again to feel my concentration challenged as the smell thickened into a wet stench percolating inside my nostrils. This became, in time, positively distracting.

I caught a glimpse of movement out of the corner of my eye. Disconcerted, I realized it was Ophelia. She rocked back and forth gently, an almost imperceptible swaying. The realization caused no small perturbation on my part. Ophelia was disconnected for repairs and not charged. The only possible explanation was that there was something *behind* her, causing the movement. My initial assumption was another mouse had made its way into the lab.

I approached, wielding a Bunsen burner as makeshift club, fearing a rat - with a creeping horror I find almost impossible to explain in rational terms. For, as I came nearer, it was as if the very geometry of Ophelia's motion back and forth was abnormal. That, as it rocked, seemingly autonomously, in a *diagonal* fashion, that this directionality upset our normal rules of matter and perspective. I found myself blinking repeatedly, as if to right the dimensions, or as though to get awake. I wondered if, as a malevolent parting gift, my disgruntled ex-employee had booby-trapped the thing.

I acknowledge that the day had been long and fraught and upsetting. No doubt the incident of a bat flying into my study, the evening previous, had left me overtired and susceptible to fancy and perhaps even - such cases are known - prone to hallucination. But as I commenced my tentative exploration of the robot, I noticed that a thick viscous fluid was seeping through its vent orifices, as a sort of slime-green ooze, making a syrupy pool over the table upon which it rested.

Then, drawing still nearer this green slick, aghast, clutching the Bunsen tightly between my fingers, a jet of that same oily fluid spewed up into my face, gelatinous liquid blinding me in its spatter.

I frantically daubed at my eyes, which were now thoroughly coagulated, went careening across the lab in the fashion of the Cyclops. I forced my lashes open against the resistance of the mucus-like stickiness in which they were caked, just in time to witness a second spurt of the sickly fluid splat against the fluorescent lighting above. A rain of bright orange sparks lazily descended and the lab was plunged into deep darkness.

I groped in the impenetrable murk for minutes that might have extended into centuries, trembling uncontrollably. I felt the liquid goo slide down my cheekbones. A buttery-yellow fingerbone of moonlight suddenly illuminated a larger blubbery secretion on the floor, a thing sperm-white and squat in the darkness. This hugeous gluey gob slid towards me inexorably, squelching as it came, avalanching forward.

I was chilled to stone, a mad disorder in my thoughts. I heard a clicking sound, as of a parrot's beak, and watched in terror as the crawling shape coalesced into the form of a tumescent blob. I glimpsed the hair-thin slit of its eye, swiveling at me, cruel and malevolent.

I knew then. I turned, groped madly for and, somehow, located the door handle. Pulled it almost off its hinges and ran out into the night where something, maybe me, was screaming.

I have lain awake in the dark for hours thinking on these events, as uncounted millions of years rolled by outside. My thoughts go drifting through me as the wind does a jackal's skull in the desert. I record them here but not for posterity. I cannot stay in my room tonight. I know not what rough beast I have unleashed - only that it is hideous and awful and lays outside the door of my apartment now, as a boa of snow. It wants in. I can hear its arms scraping at the knob like a satchel of eels. My God, I can hear it dripping.

This may be my last testament. Should it prove so, my final thoughts are these. If I do not survive the eldritch terrors of this night, I pray my executors put caution before audacity and see that these words meet no human eye.

The Killing Pen

Pauline Yates

Faster, faster. Knit, don't knot. The fishing line needs to unravel. Otherwise...

Otherwise, I'll waste weeks of practice on deer carcasses and Joe 'Skinner' Johnson, the pathetic human who lies drugged in the killing pen, will escape the punishment he deserves.

My father's punishment, too, for appointing Joe as the company's CEO.

Packer Leather's success is attributed to expert knowledge and a commitment to ethical practices...

Bullshit. Our company's testimonials are lies designed by Joe to hide the truth about the tannery's production process. Lies Joe groomed me to believe. So well groomed, I also hid the other things Joe did.

"Breathe, Grace," I mutter.

It's my chance for retribution on both counts. Focus. Loop, secure. Loop, secure. Joe can't feel a thing; he's...

Shit. He's awake.

Joe fixes his eyes on me - two black beads staring from puffy, stitched skin. There's no time to admire my handiwork. Gathering the fishing lines that hang from his body, I slide the boning knife into the sheath on my belt and scramble to the killing pen gate. A buck stands at my left, its liquid brown eyes brimming with the same hatred that infects me. I avert my gaze - never eyeball a buck, Gracie. He'll view that as a challenge and charge.

How ironic that I'm using Joe's warning to exact my vengeance. I want the buck to charge, just not yet. Pulling a phone from my back pocket, I set it to video and press record.

Joe sits up.

"What'cha doing, Gracie?"

He's groggy, unaware of his delicate position. That will change.

"Something I should have done years ago." I keep one eye on him, the other on the buck. The deer lowers his head and threatens with a shake of his antlers. I say a silent prayer - *please don't charge, not yet.*

Joe clambers to his feet. He looks at the lines of knitted stitches running up his arms, across his chest, and down his midriff, then touches his face. Awareness rushes in, pushing the drug haze out.

"What the fuck did you do?"

"What you do," I say, for my father's benefit. This video is for him. "I know how you keep the deer hides soft. Your skinning method is barbaric."

"You think you know better, Gracie?" Joe smirks. "Do you understand how to get a premium price for deer hide? Buyers don't want a pale, tough hide. They want it soft, dark. You don't get that from skinning dead deer."

"No, you get that by flaying them while they're still alive, as the blood flows through their hide. Before calcium ions leak into the cells and rigor mortis sets. I've done my research, you piece of shit."

The buck shifts his attention to Joe. It would be sweet justice if it pierced his belly with its antlers and splattered his guts onto the ground. But that won't stop Packer Leather from continuing Joe's live-skinning method. My father needs to be shown why his method is wrong.

Joe grabs the fishing lines dangling from his body.

"Gracie, you listen now. You're forgetting who looked out for you down here on the killing floor. Worse bucks than that standing there who wanted to chase you, remember?"

Out of all the men who worked the killing floor, there was only one I feared. Joe, with his hard hands and whispered threats. He corrupted my mind, violated my body, turned me into a plaything for his sick desires. Kicking the gate open, I raise my hand so the fishing lines pull tight. The buck snorts, shifting his attention back to me.

Joe tugs on the lines, reeling me in. I lean back, pull against the wires, but he's so strong. Blood trickles through my fingers where the lines cut into my hands but I don't let go. I can't. If Joe doesn't die, I will.

"Don't kid yourself, Gracie." Joe leers at me. "You were a tease, tagging after daddy wearing short skirts and pink knickers. You liked the attention then and you like it now."

I want to slap him, hit him, rake my fingernails down his face. But I step back, keeping the fishing lines taut.

"My memories differ from yours, Joe. I remember how you picked me up so I could pet the deer over the fence. How your hand slipped under my skirt when father wasn't watching. But I should thank you. You made it easy who I chose to help with Packer Leather's ethical re-education."

I eyeball the buck. He lowers his head and charges. I jump aside as he bolts through the open gate, dropping my hand so the fishing lines catch across his chest. The buck swerves, but I run behind so the lines tangle around his body. Letting go, I jump the fence into an adjacent laneway, then aim the camera at Joe. The buck darts every which way, pulling hard against the fishing lines.

Joe utters a guttural gasp as my knitted loops pull undone and the stitches unravel. Body jerking, his gasps change to a high-pitched shriek that scream of unimaginable agony. Panicked by the noise, the buck bolts along the fence. I zoom in to capture a close up of Joe's skin, peeling from where I sliced it with the boning knife. Entire sections, from wrists to shoulders, the front of his chest, his neck up to his forehead, leaving only his eyes and mouth. Torn from his body, his skin drops to the ground, rendering Joe a raw, bleeding mess of stinging nerves and severed sinew. Pain receptors overwhelmed, his body shakes uncontrollably, like a live-skinned deer.

I stop recording after Joe collapses and his carcass ceases twitching. Then send the video to my father, so he's forced to witness what he refused to see. The buck stands nearby, nostrils flared.

Pulling out my boning knife, I reach through the fence and cut away the lines.

Then I open the gate and set him free, like me.

The Swallow

Mark Wheaton

"Can't lie," the radiology nurse says, returning with a plastic bottle. "This stuff tastes terrible. Chalky. Remember Maalox? It tastes like Maalox."

Mrs. Beeke nods absently, her mind already calculating the bottle's volume. If the shifting liquid inside is about twelve ounces in mass after subtracting 9.25 grams for the weight of the bottle, she guesses the density of the barium swallow she's meant to drink is around 2.5 grams per cubic centimeter. This is on the high side. She'd read that some radiologists prefer 1.4 g/cm3.

Then she notices a powder around the bottle's rim.

"What's that?" Mrs. Beeke asks.

"Oh, I add a little strawberry flavoring," the nurse says. "Doesn't do much."

Mrs. Beeke blinks.

"How much do you add?" she asks.

"Not much," the nurse replies. "It doesn't dilute the solution."

"A pinch? A dash?" Mrs. Beeke asks. "Quarter teaspoon?"

The nurse arches an eyebrow. As if dealing with crazy isn't on her to-do list.

"Sorry," Mrs. Beeke says, feigning contrition. "Nerves."

"S'alright." The nurse softens her tone. "I use one of those plastic coffee stirrers. Maybe a quarter-quarter teaspoon."

Mrs. Beeke recalculates. The density is closer to 2.4 grams per cubic centimeter.

"Everyone ready?" the radiologist, Dr. Upadhyay, asks, breezing into the imaging room.

Mrs. Beeke nods demurely as the nurse leads her to the X-Ray, a gargantuan machine that looks like a photocopier turned on its side. The nurse indicates where she is to sit, places a lead apron over Mrs. Beeke's shoulders, and swings the X-Ray's metal arm around until it is aimed at her chest.

"We'll watch through there." Dr. Upadhyay indicates a window on the opposite wall. "You'll hear a beep as I turn on the digital fluoro-scope. When I say, take three swallows of the solution. Rather than a still X-Ray, it takes video of your gastrointestinal tract as the barium solution travels through your esophagus to your stomach. The esophagus can't be seen in an X-Ray, but the barium can, which allows us to check for irregularities."

"How long does it take?" Mrs. Beeke asks.

"About half an hour," Dr. Upadhyay replies. "But you won't be exposed to radiation the entire time. Most is taken up adjusting the angle between captures."

If she was younger, Mrs. Beeke might've been worried. But she lives in nearby Terranova, a sprawling Florida retirement community where doctors pay off their yachts with insurance company kickbacks. She can't remember the last time an annual physical didn't result in appointments for further testing. For several residents, the appointments are welcome diversions to their routines.

"Are you okay, Mrs. Beeke?"

The voice belongs to Psamathe, one of the ghost-mice (brain volume upon dissection: 435 cubic millimeters) that lives in her head.

All is well, Mrs. Beeke silently whispers back.

The first beep sounds. Mrs. Beeke raises the bottle to her lips.

Mrs. Beeke's bones, muscles, and organs appear gray and ghost-like on the screen. The barium solution - dark, as promised - enters her mouth. Her epiglottis closes to block her windpipe. The solution slides into her esophagus.

What happens next is… *transformative*.

The spectral tube subtly bows and arcs like a dancer, decelerating and separating the swallow into three parts. So divided, these sluice through the lower esophageal sphincter into the stomach. Mrs. Beeke stares at her esophagus's fading outline in amazement.

"Looks good." Dr. Upadhyay taps the screen with a pen. "No tears, no constrictions that might indicate tumors. No polyps."

He's about to turn off the video when Mrs. Beeke snatches his hand away.

"Can we watch it again?" she asks.

"Um, of course," he says. "Did you spot something irregular?"

"No, I just…I've never seen anything like it."

The radiologist restarts the clip. Mrs. Beeke stares as her esophagus's shadowy presence returns to the screen. It expands, contracts, tightens and swells before vanishing again.

Mrs. Beeke is dumbstruck. In a body full of symmetry - paired eyes, arms, legs, ears, breasts, feet - it's like a strange truth hidden away. Something ugly and utilitarian yet graceful, even elegant, in its function. She feels silly for being so taken by a part of her anatomy she's barely considered before but can't pretend otherwise.

"Again," Mrs. Beeke demands.

"I can e-mail you a copy, Mrs. Beeke," Dr. Upadhyay suggests cautiously. "If it's so interesting to you."

"Oh, yes," she agrees. "Yes, please."

Mrs. Beeke boards the shuttle back to Terranova, phone in hand. It's been ten minutes. If she calls to ask when the e-mail will arrive, she worries she'll look crazy.

"It's okay, Mrs. Beeke," one of the youngest of the ghost-mice, Thalassa (volume of brain upon dissection: 182.2 cubic millimeters), whispers. "It'll be here in time."

"I know," Mrs. Beeke says under her breath. "I only fear they'll forget."

Her mind wanders to her esophagus's volume. She estimates it around eighteen centimeters long. Two centimeters in diameter when inactive. That isn't the interesting part. The inconstancy is. It roils, expands, and turns, forever changing its shape like a nebula.

"Or a pufferfish!" Psamathe's sister, Laomedia (volume of brain upon dissection: 395.1 cubic millimeters), suggests.

"Yes, but one that never stops expanding and contracting," Mrs. Beeke agrees. "A pufferfish exhausts itself and dies after three inflations or so. This goes and goes."

The shuttle drops Mrs. Beeke off at the edge of Terranova, as the retirement community's roads are golf-cart and pedestrian-only. She thanks the driver and walks home.

Terranova, she's long decided, is a strange place. Part outdoor mall, part golf course resort, part abattoir - given the number of near-weekly deaths. Its shops, restaurants, and exercise pavilions are designed with old-fashioned Americana facades meant to suggest they'd been built centuries ago, despite Terranova being only twelve years old. The illusion is confined to the exterior as a store decorated like a nineteenth-century ice cream parlor will only sell tepid, taste-free probiotics. A cobbler's shop with leather goods in its window case will specialize in Crocs. Why her late husband decided they should retire here, Mrs. Beeke would never understand.

"Hi, Mrs. Beeke!" someone calls from an outdoor café.

She waves back but doesn't slow. She thinks only of her esophagus.

Her phone vibrates, announcing the arrival of the swallow videos the moment she gets home. Elated, she makes tea, hunts down a notepad and pencil, and plays the video on a tablet. As she watches, she calculates the changes in her esophagus's volume with every swallow. It becomes both more beautiful and more alien with every attempt to quantify it.

The limitations of the 2-D X-Ray are quickly evident. Video or not, her calculations are based on estimates. After several hours of work, she snaps her pencil in frustration.

"Mrs. Beeke? You all right?"

Mrs. Beeke opens her eyes. She's fallen asleep at her breakfast room table. Sally Sorondo, one of Terranova's most popular, most tanned, and most toxically positive residents, peers at her through a window.

"Morning, Sally," Mrs. Beeke says, hastily wiping her face with a tea towel before opening her front door. "How are you?"

"Excellent." Sally sweeps into the apartment in an ensemble of red, white, and blue Spandex. "More importantly, how are you? How was your swallow? Nothing out of the ordinary, I hope?"

"Nothing at all," Mrs. Beeke replies, pouring cold water on her neighbor's lust for gossip. "I'm in the pink."

"Gratitude to Gaia," Sally says, elevating her palms as if in imitation of some YouTube wellness guru. "Althea had her GI scoped at Dr. Woodall's last month and they found enlarged veins. Now she needs a liver transplant."

"Dr. Woodall has a fluoroscope?" Mrs. Beeke asks.

"He does!" Sally says. "Bought it when he expanded his practice last year."

"Doesn't she work there?" Sao (brain volume upon dissection: 287.3 cubic millimeters) asks.

"Don't you work in Dr. Woodall's office?" Mrs. Beeke echoes.

"I wouldn't call what I do *work*." Sally dusts her response with innuendo. "I merely help with community outreach. Why?"

"Does he keep video records of swallow tests?" Mrs. Beeke asks. "I'm not interested in names. Just samples I might compare to my own."

"Thought you were in the pink?"

"I know what the doctor says." Mrs. Beeke feigns worry. "But I also listen to what my body tells me."

"Of course," Sally says reassuringly. "Dr. Woodall's off today volunteering at Memorial Hospital, but I have office keys. Shall we go now?"

Dr. Woodall's office is in a building made to look like a frontier general store. Sally unlocks the front door and leads Mrs. Beeke in. In contrast, the inside is like any other bland professional building in Florida.

"The videos are on the control room computer," Sally explains, leading her to a small alcove adjacent to the imagining room. "You want a Bloody Mary?"

"What? No."

"Mind if I make one? Dr. Woodall keeps good vodka in the lab freezer."

"Be my guest," Mrs. Beeke says.

After Sally heads away, Mrs. Beeke dives into the video files. There are hundreds of swallow tests. Each begins with a ghostly image of a patient's upper torso including faint ribs and shoulder bones. The barium arrives next. Then the reveal of the esophagus.

It's never not spellbinding and otherworldly.

Mrs. Beeke rough-calculates the area of each one, restarting several of the videos to get it right every time. After deriving the same number for a handful, she realizes she's looking at the same esophagi.

"Holy cow, you're right!" Sally exclaims after Mrs. Beeke shows her two videos she believes belong to the same person. "According to the log key, those are both Mrs. Kershaw's."

Mrs. Beeke smiles. The thickness of the epiglottis gave it away.

"That's some crazy talent," Sally says, swigging a second Bloody Mary. "I wonder how many doctors could tell the difference."

Mrs. Beeke has two doctorates but doesn't think that is any of Sally's business. Besides, she has problems of her own. The 2-D X-Rays, while inspiring, remain deficient. They are flat. A one-sided glimpse.

"Dr. Upadhyay didn't say how much exposure was too much," whispers Despina (brain volume upon dissection: 222.7 cubic millimeters) one of the more introspective of the ghost-mice.

Meaning what? Mrs. Beeke asks.

"He switched angles to focus on certain points. What if *you* switched angles to approximate a 3-D image?"

Mrs. Beeke glances to the fluoroscope on the other side of the control room window.

It'd be hard to coordinate from in there.

"Not you, silly," Thalassa says, jumping in. "Aren't you trying to create a baseline formula that can be applied to any esophagus?"

Mrs. Beeke realizes she means Sally. Her neighbor's Bloody Mary is so laden with vodka it's practically clear.

"Might you help me with this?" Mrs. Beeke asks.

"What do you need?"

"The videos are excellent but insufficient," Mrs. Beeke explains cautiously. "I'd like to capture one myself so that I may choose the angle."

Sally comments on her swallowing ability. Mrs. Beeke understands her remark is sexual in nature but ignores it all the same. What matters is that Sally knows how to turn on the equipment. She retrieves a barium solution bottle from a cabinet and settles onto the stool in front of the fluoroscope, Bloody Mary in her other hand.

"Let me know when to drink!" she says.

Mrs. Beeke alters the angle of the fluoroscope with a joystick. When it's directly over Sally's esophagus, she turns on the X-Ray. It responds with a beep.

"Swallow," she says into the microphone.

"Bottom's up," Sally replies.

On screen, the barium solution slides through Sally's mouth and into her esophagus. Her esophagus's outline soon appears. Mrs. Beeke quickly calculates the circumference at several points before it vanishes. She then alters the fluoroscope's angle by a few degrees.

"Another swallow, please?" Mrs. Beeke asks.

Sally sips her cocktail first, then the barium. What amazes Mrs. Beeke is how the esophagus differentiates between the density of the drinks. Though barely visible, the vodka-heavy Bloody Mary slides to the stomach without obstruction. The barium swallow makes the esophagus expand slightly, slowing its progress.

"Another swallow?" Mrs. Beeke says after switching the angle.

"Out of barium," Sally calls.

"The Bloody Mary works."

"Music to my ears!" Sally exclaims.

Mrs. Beeke grins and jostles the joystick. She captures several contrasting angles in a row, the differences of shape and volume making her calculations ever more precise. Each time she thinks it's good enough, the next X-Ray reveals room for improvement.

"Couple more," she says into the microphone.

"All good," Sally calls back, slurring her words.

Mrs. Beeke captures a lateral angle next. It reveals bends and kinks that throw off her calculations yet again.

"Few more," she urges.

Sally's hand appears on screen giving a skeletal thumbs-up. Mrs. Beeke laughs. So do the ghost-mice.

Soon, she doesn't even need Sally to swallow. She can make out the esophagus's outline, not by the barium, but by what's missing from the hazy skeleton behind it. She maps each indentation as it affects the esophagus's circumference from top to bottom, finally stopping when the computer tells her she's run out of memory.

"Oop," she says. "We're done, Sally."

Sally doesn't respond. Mrs. Beeke peers through the window. Her neighbor is passed out, likely from the booze. Except, much of Sally's skin is inflamed. Her sweat glands ooze yellow pus. Mrs. Beeke checks the clock. It's been seven hours.

She races into the imaging room but knows Sally is dead before she checks her pulse.

Mrs. Beeke gasps in anguish. What has she done?

"You didn't mean any harm, Mrs. Beeke," Halimede, a speckled ghost-mouse (brain volume upon dissection: 302.9 cubic millimeters) says.

"No," Mrs. Beeke replies, voice a pained rasp. "But to not even notice…"

"People die here all the time," Thalassa adds. "What's one more?"

"Sally was in perfect health," she replies, scoffing. "She wasn't going to die any time soon."

"You sure of that, Mrs. Beeke?" Sao asks. "Maybe check Video 177."

Mrs. Beeke shuffles back to the alcove. She calls up the 177th video (of 392) and watches the barium slide down her throat. There's a slight twist at the midpoint she hadn't noticed before. A cluster of tumors nestles within her esophagus's lining.

Sally wasn't long for this world after all.

Terranova's first mention on national news was when video of a seventeen-foot alligator climbing out of one of its golf course water hazards hit the internet. It was so large people weren't sure it was even real. Mrs. Beeke, transporting Sally's corpse to the golf course that night, prays it is.

She'd waited until dark to leave, shutting everything off, deleting the videos she'd made after copying them onto a key drive, and cleaning the place from top to bottom. She can't do anything about the security cameras in the front of the building that saw her and Sally enter that morning - but exits through the camera-free backdoor regardless.

Once she's rolled the body into the water hazard, Mrs. Beeke races home, consumed by guilt and shame.

She awakes the next morning, not to the expected knock from Sumter County sheriffs, but silence. She slips out into the village only to find the quiet is omnipresent. Residents gather at the same diners as the day before, but the mood is somber. All watch TV news reports that cut between photos of Sally, footage of police unspooling crime scene tape at the golf course, and stock images of alligators.

Mrs. Beeke picks up fragments of hushed conversation.

"…heard she was drunk…"

"…body torn to pieces…"

"…such a lovely person…"

Mrs. Beeke's fear of capture diminishes. Her shame does not.

To assuage her guilt, Mrs. Beeke spends the day rewatching the footage of Sally's esophagus and calculating its transitory area. It's soothing, as if Sally herself might be gone but this engine inside her lives on, too strong to die. Yet something else gnaws at her after a while.

"What is it?" Laomedia asks.

"I should have taken it with me," Mrs. Beeke replies.

"Taken what?"

"Her esophagus," she says. "It would've been messy, but I could've studied it here. Made my formula even more complete."

Triton, the oldest ghost-mouse (brain volume upon dissection: 501 cubic millimeters), scoffs.

"You have a comment?" Mrs. Beeke says.

"It would've disintegrated like mealy tripe," Triton replies. "A wet bag."

Mrs. Beeke knows Triton is right. She sighs and is about to acknowledge this when she realizes he has more to say.

"Something else to add?" she asks.

"You told us never to say the word."

Mrs. Beeke is taken aback. She can't imagine what Triton is referring to.

"Say it anyway," she demands.

"Resin," Triton says.

Mrs. Beeke's mouth drops open.

Decades earlier, she'd been a biochemistry professor at the same Southern California university where her husband taught economics. Known as much for her no-nonsense approach to lab work as for generating topflight chemical engineers, she'd had but one quirk her colleagues found objectionable. A tinkerer by nature, she used the lab to develop glues, epoxies, hardeners, and resins that could be put toward a variety of uses. What she used it for was to create posthumous figurines from the bodies of mice she'd dissected. She then displayed them in whimsical poses around her office.

When other faculty members protested her hobby was too gruesome, Mrs. Beeke brought the figurines home. Her husband viewed them as a harmless eccentricity. Unencumbered by scrutiny, she expanded her work to include the occasional possum, raccoon, squirrel, or even neighborhood cat. This might've continued ad infinitum, too, except her husband brought the chancellor and her wife over for coffee one afternoon. The terrifying screech the latter emitted upon spying her own cat, Brownie, frozen in resin and posed on the mantle, told Mrs. Beeke her time in California, if not academia altogether, was over.

She'd had to leave her figurines behind when they'd moved to Florida. Her husband found a position at another university. Mrs. Beeke settled on a job as a pharmacist. She missed her mice terribly, so when their ghosts began speaking to her, she was delighted.

"Resin," she says. "How perfect."

It takes a few tries to make a resin capable of hardening muscle tissue without breaking it apart, but Mrs. Beeke finally comes up with one. To her surprise, it's even easier to find suitable test subjects. Her criteria are simple. Subjects should be aged, have no next of kin, and selected cremation on their advance directive (alligators only really feed once a month, she knows). To access a state database and search for candidates, she tries her old pharmacist's login. It still works.

Florida, she thinks.

Whittling the search to a local hypochondriac named Jay Healey, she rings him up to say a recent physical suggests he needs a barium swallow test.

"Is this Mrs. Beeke?" Healey asks.

"It is!" she replies cheerfully. "I've been helping Dr. Woodall with community outreach. Are you busy today? We could squeeze you in."

Mr. Healey, sounding delighted to have something to do, agrees. Mrs. Beeke uses Sally's keys to access Dr. Woodall's office, makes sure he's still volunteering that day, and preps for Healey's arrival. When the old man arrives, Mrs. Beeke injects him with a large dose of Valium she says is an anti-inflammatory and settles him in front of the fluoroscope. She proceeds to take over 400 digital X-Ray videos of his esophagus before readying the resin.

"You ready for this?" she asks the old man, already fading in and out of consciousness.

"Sure," he says, as if his mind is miles away.

She pours the resin down his throat. His esophagus tries to reject it, so she injects him with enough Valium to knock him out. Once all the resin is past his pharynx, she waits for it to harden, injects Healey with potassium chloride to stop his heart, then unrolls two shower curtains and places them at his feet.

With an oscillating saw used to remove casts, Mrs. Beeke begins the dissection. Unfortunately, the touch of the saw's blade against Healey's breastbone shoots adrenaline into his heart.

"Whaaa...!" the old man screams, returning to life.

Startled, Mrs. Beeke quickly tugs a corner of the shower curtain over Healey's head and drags the spinning blade across his carotid artery. He stills.

Rattled, Mrs. Beeke hurriedly cuts through the breastbone, pries open the rib cage, removes the lungs, and pushes aside the trachea. The esophagus lies beneath. Unfortunately, the resin only hardened the upper half while leaving the lower section limp.

Still, it's a start.

Mrs. Beeke severs the esophagus between the pharynx and stomach then readies the rest of the body for disposal. Instead of going to great lengths to obscure what happened, she realizes she simply needs the documentation to give a funeral home so they can file for a death certificate with the state. This proves readily available in Dr. Woodall's office. She provides it all to the bored funeral home workers who arrive for Healey's corpse, saying it's their third Terranova body that day. All she must do is provide an address for them to send the urn following cremation.

She spends the next several days alternately calculating the area of Healey's esophagus and working to improve the resin. Once this is done, she rings up her next potential subject, a former high school choir teacher named Sabrica Zabala. After coaxing Zabala to Dr. Woodall's office, she pours the new resin down the old woman's throat, cracks open her chest, and discovers that her esophagus was three-quarters hardened before tapering off.

Though incomplete, the 500-plus X-Ray videos she made of Zabala's swallow before killing her, in concert with her data from Sally and Mr. Healey, get her even closer to her formula.

"Hooray!" the ghost-mice cheer.

"Don't celebrate yet," Mrs. Beeke retorts.

After improving her resin one more time, she recruits Elliott Porteus, a carpenter and recent widower. He smiles as Mrs. Beeke brings him the barium solution.

"What?" she asks.

"I prayed this would happen," he says.

"Prayed what would happen?" she asks, preparing a syringe of Valium.

"Oh, everyone knows what you're doing," Porteus continues. "I want to be with my wife. Each new treatment keeps me from her. You'll give me what I want."

Mrs. Beeke freezes, terrified by the man's dying words.

Everyone knows it's you?

Porteus's esophagus turns out to be perfectly preserved in the resin. But, as Mrs. Beeke cleans up the office, she can hardly revel in the success. If people are beginning to put two and two together, she may be running out of time.

She locks herself away and sets to work. Now with three recovered esophagi in various conditions and over a thousand videos, she creates a complex equation that allows her to plug in new measurements that reveal an esophagus's relative area depending on the density of what it's swallowing. It's like trying to quantify the movement of individual water droplets in cresting waves, but she gets closer and closer.

She fills notebooks, the backs of envelopes, and old stationery with her calculations. Long after the ghost-mice are bored and fall asleep, she remains at her desk, pencil in hand, lost in her ecstatic reverie. It isn't until the fourth day that she realizes something is amiss. By the fifth, her suspicions are confirmed.

It's a simple flaw but fatal, nevertheless. She has considered the esophagus in isolation, but it is never that. It's packed in. Surrounded by the rest of the body's organs. Moreover, the body is constantly in motion. Her calculations are for a state an esophagus is never in.

Her reverie breaks. People have died. And for what? Her poor mathematics? Her inability to write a simple equation?

"My beautiful formula is a calamity," she admits to the ghost-mice. "I thought it would be easy, but there are too many factors and likely many more I've overlooked."

There is a long silence from the ghost-mice. Finally, Psamathe speaks,

"I thought the esophagus is the beautiful thing," the little ghost-mouse says.

The words echo across Mrs. Beeke's mind. She smiles for the first time in days. All thoughts of numbers drain away.

"Of course," she says. "You couldn't be more correct."

That night, the streets are silent as she heads to Dr. Woodall's office. Terranova residents are typically home by sundown, businesses closing soon, thereafter. But the stillness of the evening without a single golf cart on the paths is unsettling.

Mrs. Beeke ducks down an alley to approach the doctor's office via a different route. When she emerges behind the general store building, she finds several security company vehicles lying in wait.

"What'll we do, Mrs. Beeke?" the ghost-mice ask in a panic.

Fret not, she whispers back. *I've got a backup plan.*

The Terranova Flea Market is the largest indoor mall in the area. Dealers from all over the region fill stalls with everything from rare books to antique jewelry to vintage furniture, in hopes of enticing locals to spend money on things they don't need. Mrs. Beeke slips in through a broken side door, stopping off first at a stall filled with decorative farm implements, then to a corner where numerous light fixtures hang from the ceiling. She switches several of these on, drags over a dining room table, and positions several mirrors around it.

Within twenty minutes, her improvised surgical suite is ready.

"Are you sure of this, Mrs. Beeke?" Thalassa asks quietly.

Mrs. Beeke closes her eyes to still her mind and takes off her clothes. She places a hand sickle, pliers, and a handkerchief on the table next to a cooler bag of sample liquids, then injects herself at various points on her torso with large doses of lidocaine. As the numbing agent takes effect, she adjusts the mirrors once more, lies down, and raises the sickle. She uses it to make two incisions, a wide one at the bottom of her throat and a second, deeper one on her left side, beneath her ribs.

Lidocaine or not, the pain arrives with such violence it blurs her vision. Though she was careful to avoid veins and arteries, blood seeps from the wounds. She's about to get to work when a pounding on the flea market's locked front entrance breaks her concentration.

"Mrs. Beeke!" yells a security guard. "Put those tools down and open this door!"

The guard is flanked by several sheriff's deputies. Someone bangs on the side door as well, but she blocks it with a freezer.

"Are you out of your mind?" A voice she recognizes as Dr. Woodall shouts. "You're going to kill yourself!"

Ignoring him, Mrs. Beeke slides her left hand inside the wound at her side. She worms her fingers under her ribcage and lungs until the shivering flutter of her panicked heart is at her fingertips. She wishes she could calm it. She closes her eyes and presses on.

She touches what she thinks is her esophagus, only to realize it's her trachea. She finds the real object of her adoration pulsing beneath. She smiles as she gently guides her fingers along it.

In an esophagectomy, once the esophagus is removed, the stomach is pulled up (a procedure called a 'gastric pull') and attached to the pharynx. Mrs. Beeke executes a variation on this by easing her esophagus up through the incision in her throat. A three-inch section arches to the surface like an earthworm being plucked from the ground by a crow. Still in agonizing pain, Mrs. Beeke slips the handkerchief under it, grips the cloth with the pliers, and pulls her esophagus a few more inches out of her body.

She's never seen anything so beautiful. She removes her left hand from inside her torso, reaches into her cooler bag for the first sample - a sippy cup of milk - and raises it to her lips to glimpse the action. The cup almost slips from her blood-slicked hand but she gets it to her mouth on the second try.

At first, it won't go down. She painfully props herself up on her elbows and gravity helps out. Her esophagus expands, ever so slightly, to send the milk into her stomach. It's gentle as a stalk of wheat blown by the breeze.

As the deputies kick down the door, Mrs. Beeke goes through all the liquids of varying densities she brought. Coffee, gravy, pureed potatoes, yogurt, consommé, and grits. After so many days spent imagining this action, simply watching her esophagus throb, shift, and work as it's meant to overwhelms Mrs. Beeke.

She delights in a feeling of inundation. Of gazing on the incalculable. The beauty of the infinite. Who dares apply a formula to the hand of God?

Glass shatters. The pliers slip from her hand. She grabs the final sippy cup and pours its contents of ant killer mixed with melted butter into her mouth.

"Drop it!" a deputy yells, but it's too late.

Her body recognizes the danger of the poison right away and tries to reject it, to send it back up her esophagus, but Mrs. Beeke sits up straight. Forces it down. Her esophagus is accepting of even this. It relents and fills her stomach with boric acid.

She searches her mind for the ghost-mice but can't find them. She's never craved their company more. Hadn't they seen what she'd seen? Didn't they recognize their shared moment of glory?

She spies them in the mirrors. There aren't simply the couple dozen she regularly interacts with - but hundreds of tiny, dissected mice. They smile and applaud and cheer as the deputies attempt to handcuff her, causing blood and poison to rush up her esophagus, through her epiglottis, and into her lungs.

She smiles as her esophagus fights to the death to save her life, awestruck by the unknowable.

Dragon Rufus Interrupts Class

Justin Hunter

Steve Polowski owned the Basho-Yo-Stains Laundromat and Grandmaster Steve's Viper Death Tornado Martial Arts studio. He'd just completed a workout and was gazing at himself in one of the many mirrors which covered the western wall, like a Spartan phalanx.

He had skin whiter than the driven snow. Thick brown curls swooshed at the top of his head. Sweat dripped from his 90s windowpane sized glasses. Oh yeah, he knew he was badass. A man alone, no student had shown up for class tonight. Just like the past several. Sure the carpets were filthy with the sweat and blood of a thousand hours of kicking ass. Sure the ceiling tiles were sodden and falling in several places. Sure half the lights were out - but he felt the lighting casting him in partial shadows made him look extra sexy.

Grandmaster Steve didn't mind there were no students tonight, or any night, for that matter. They would come. Even the ones that came and decided his place was shit and quit would come back again. Polowski was a name rich in martial arts history. He tracked it back to General Cao Cao of the Han dynasty at the local library just last week. He flexed his chest muscles, making his gi bounce furiously from diminutive pec pulses. He was the man.

The door opened and in walked a figure, wearing a black gi with a golden dragon cross-stitched down one arm.

"Dragon Rufus! How dare you break in and interrupt my class," Steve said.

"The door was open," Rufus replied. "I don't see anyone here. Why are you still bouncing your pecs?"

"Stop looking at me like I'm a piece of meat! That's sexual harassment!"

"I'm not," Rufus said, "But that's what I'm here to talk to you about. My student, Dragon Linda or, as she wants me to call her, Linda, said you've been stalking her. It stops now."

"I've never stalked her!"

"Stop bouncing your pecs! She wants you to leave her alone."

"I can't help that I break boards with my fist and hearts with my karaoke." Steve finally stopped flexing and turned toward Rufus. "Why do you cross-stitch those dragons? Get a patch."

"My grandma likes to do them. It's awkward."

"They look bad."

"I know...stop it!" Rufus stepped forward, waving an arm in the air. Ten men and women ran into the room. All wore matching black dragon uniforms.

"I've had enough. You're impossible to talk to. We are going to kick your ass."

"You see what I mean about the cross-stitch?" Steve said. "Some of those don't even look like dragons."

"They are dogs," Rufus replied. "She has dementia."

"I'm sorry."

"That's okay. It's been hard on everyone. My sister hasn't really stepped up to help as much as she should."

"Have you tried home nursing?"

"Yes. But finding someone qualified that I can count on is really... Stop it! Goddamn, I hate you so much! Get him dragons!"

Dragon Rufus held his hands forward and the ten students rushed Grandmaster Steve. Steve reached into his gi and spun around in a pirouette. The front two students fell backwards with shuriken in their heads. Steve reached behind his back and drew a katana. He stabbed the closest dragon and, pulling the blade upward, severed him in half.

He slashed sideways and took a woman's head from her shoulders. The remaining student cowered back behind Rufus.

"Holy shit," Rufus gasped. "Where were you hiding that sword?"

"None of your business. But you should know my sphincter has the elasticity of a circ du solei troupe. Now back off before someone really gets hurt."

"You killed four people. What do you mean *hurt*?"

"I'm standing my ground against marauders," Steve protested. "You're thieves."

Rufus began waving around at the dilapidated studio.

"This place is a dump. There's nothing here to steal."

"It's true. My laundromat pays the bills while here we learn the skills. The greatest thing within these walls is my martial arts secrets. You're not here to save sexy Linda from unwanted advances. You're here to kidnap me and take me back to your studio and pump me for information. You'll pump me. Your students will pump me. Linda will pump me. Everyone will pump me all night long and, maybe, tomorrow during my lunch break."

"That's it. Kill him."

The six remaining students surrounded Grandmaster Steve in a loose circle. Dragon Rufus advanced. Steve slashed the air with his butt katana. A student behind him lashed out with a roundhouse kick and lost his leg at the knee. Two more jumped forward. Steve disemboweled one, grabbed the other by the hair and plunged his face into the first's entrails. Steve held the struggling man's head as he gurgled and kicked.

"There's no way you can beat me without weapons," Steve said. "Give up before someone *really* gets hurt."

"Stop this now!"

Steve looked up to see Dragon Li himself enter through the studio door. He was resplendent in a gi made of silk. Cross-stitched golden dragons ran down both his arms, which were laden with sais, nunchaku, swords, claws and a net - something he seemed to be having a bit of trouble with.

"Father," Rufus said, bowing low. The surviving students bowed as well. Steve pulled the man's face out of the entrails and found he had drowned. He dropped him and wiped bloody hands on his gi.

"Well, Dragon Li, you are finally here," Steve said. "Now we can settle this once and for all."

"Grandmaster Steve," Dragon Li replied. "Long have I waited for this moment. You can defeat my students but can you defeat the dragon?"

"Be careful, father," Rufus warned.

"I've always wanted to know how you're his dad," Steve said. "He's a huge black guy and you're a five-foot-something Asian."

"He's adopted."

"What?" Rufus said.

"You honestly didn't know?" Li sighed. "Really? Your mom's Irish. It never occurred to you that you might be adopted?"

"You didn't say anything."

"I just thought you would naturally come to that conclusion."

"Well, you never said anything."

"I didn't think I had to," Li grunted, turning to Steve. "Do you see what I'm working with here?"

"Yeah," Steve agreed. "He's not that bright."

"I have a degree in industrial engineering from the University of Milwaukee!" Rufus stamped his foot. "I make more money than both of you combined."

"Oh, a state school," Steve said.

"Yeah, He couldn't get into ivy league," Li sighed again. "Bad SAT scores. Not enough extracurriculars."

"He should have gone out for show choir."

"That's what I told him," Li said. "He doesn't listen."

"Dad, he killed six of our students. We have to destroy him," Rufus urged. "Stop talking about me."

"You're big," Steve said. "Why didn't you try out for football?"

"I don't like contact sports."

"Enough!" Dragon Li demanded. "What's done is done. The past is the past and, even though it's terribly disappointing, we can't change it."

"Dad!"

"Stop! We have other fish to fry here, Rufus. Go industrial engineer something or whatever."

Rufus began to cry and ran out of the studio.

"Sorry about that," Li said.

"It's okay," Steve shrugged.

"Do you have kids?"

"No, but I want to start a family someday. It's just not the right time for me."

"You with anyone?"

"Not right now. It's hard to meet people."

"Did you try one of those online dating things? It worked out great for my cousin. She's been married three years now."

"Woah, that's great. You'll have to give me her number so I can get some information."

"Sure. Sure. But first we must fight to the death." Dragon Li dropped the weapons he was holding onto the floor. He reached back and took his own katana out of his sphincter. Steve nodded approvingly.

"This isn't about Linda, is it?"

"Not at all."

"I knew it." Steve sliced off the face of a student that got too close to him. "This is because of your dabbling in the dark arts of biological engineering."

The other students gasped. One took a tanto knife out of the pile of weapons on the floor and immediately committed seppuku.

"Yes," Li said. "You pried the information from me last week while we were bingeing on Old Crow and uppers.

"You gave it willingly," Steve protested. "I posted it on social media to stop you in your nefarious ways."

"You did. But you forget that nobody uses MySpace anymore. I kept my account just to keep an eye on you."

"I should have blocked you."

"Yes, you should have. And I use my bio engineering way with satanic and pagan stuff."

"Pagans are basically humanists. That doesn't make sense."

"I know. I ditched the pagan bit and now just do Satan stuff with it."

"You monster."

"You have no idea," Li said. "With my new bio martial arts creation, I will rule over all the small martial arts studios in all of the upper Midwest. They will sign expensive unbreakable contracts to learn from me, Dragon Li. Enter Juanito!"

A student dressed in black appeared through the studio door. Grandmaster Steve thought that he really should start locking it. Juanito was tall, dusky-skinned and had six arms which bristled with sinewy muscle. His upper body attached to his lower body like a Minotaur. He walked on eight legs, moving like a spider. Steve blushed.

"You've created…"

"The greatest martial artist in the world," Li said. "Attack Juanito!"

Juanito leaped into the air and came down on Steve's head with each of six legs performing different Tae-Kwon-Do kicks. Steve took a tremendous hit and fell to the floor. Juanito chopped with all four arms. Steve gracefully blocked two of the shots, but the other two fell home with solid thunks. Steve slashed out and his blade was knocked effortlessly to the side. He got to his feet and scrambled backwards. Stood up against the wall of mirrors. Blood dripped from the corners of both eyes.

"Kill him," Dragon Li said.

Juanito lunged. Grandmaster Steve jumped and flipped through the air, landing on the back (thorax?) of Juanito. He gripped the spider man's body with his legs. Juanito ripped at him but couldn't get a good grip. Steve pulled his penis out of his pants.

"Consent?" Steve asked. Juanito renewed his fury. Dragon Li laughed at Steve and his dick bouncing up and down on his greatest student.

"Consent?" Steve asked again.

"Why would I do that?"

"Because, together, we can create the greatest martial arts student that ever lived. Do you have a womb?"

"I don't know."

"Stop trying to kill me and please consent!"

"Fine." Juanito raised his backside into the air. "Do it!"

Grandmaster Steve used a little bit of saliva, gave a quick pump, then started jackhammering.

"What are you doing?" Dragon Li cried. He raised his sword and ran in to attack. Juanito shot a thick string of webbing which hit Li in the chest, sending him high against the wall, where he stuck fast. He began swearing and tearing at the webbing.

"I knew you had webs!" Steve said, increasing the fervency of his thrusts.

"We are going to make the next Bruce Lee," Juanito replied, hammering his hips back into Steve.

"Hell, yes we are!" Steve came. Hard. Juanito screamed in ecstasy, pushing Steve off with his back legs.

Steve fell back and cracked his favorite mirror.

The Tit-Haunted Man

A d a m   B r e c k e n r i d g e

I want to tell you about how an apple saved my life and all the horrible things that happened afterwards.

I encountered this apple at a grocery store, which should surprise no one. It was not the apple I was interested in. I never particularly liked apples. But I would feign interest in them all day when they gave me a chance to admire the rather generous cleavage of a young woman on the other side of the display - eyeing, I believe, papayas.

I couldn't take my gaze off her breasts. They were Everest and K2: huge, beautiful and arousing a sense of adventure in men's souls. I was certain I would be thinking of them later. Even if I was having sex with my girlfriend, they would be on my mind for a while.

I caught a flash of an angry glare from the corner of my eye and ducked lower, pretending to admire a particularly round specimen of an apple - yet never taking my eyes off the woman's cleavage.

Then her head exploded.

I heard the shot. Heard the screams - then the laws of physics saw fit to send a spray of her viscera in my direction - blood, brains, bone and skin splattering my face. When I watched her corpse drop to the ground, the only thing I could think was that her cleavage was considerably less sexy when there was no face to complement it.

I turned in the direction of the shot, which had come from behind me. Who did I see but Max Fischer, my girlfriend's psychotic ex-boyfriend. He had sworn to kill any man who screwed the woman he still believed was his. He had told me so himself, both before and after I had told him how often I was fucking her.

Hoo, lawdy had I fucked her! We'd fucked in her car and mine. In every room of her apartment and mine - and about half the parks and public restrooms in the city. Every time I spoke to Max, usually while chasing him out of Emily's bushes, wielding whatever implement from her apartment I could use as a makeshift weapon (one time a hair curler, another a bread knife), I would scream at him about all the places I had fucked her. Which, I should state, Emily found very funny and Max did not.

Now it occurred to me I should have taken his threats more seriously. Because, there was Max Fischer, with a gun pointed at my head. He had already fired one shot, clearly intended for me and, instead, dispatched a poor innocent.

Our eyes met and I saw a remarkable thing. Remorse. He had not wanted to kill the woman, I'll give him that. But, now, there was nothing between me and the barrel of his gun. For a second, I was sure this was my last moment - covered in a girl's blood and brains and bone and skin in a grocery store - while holding a single apple. It was not how I wanted to die.

Then his head exploded too - and the bloody corpse that used to be Max fell. I was grateful I was too far away to not have any of *his* parts spray on me.

From a nearby aisle emerged an old man, hobbling on a cane, carrying a revolver of some kind (I'm not very good at telling one make of a gun from another but it had a spinny bit). He was cackling and hobbling towards Max's corpse. He kept shouting something near-incoherent to someone behind him that sounded like *I got him*.

When he reached the corpse he kicked it a couple of times, still laughing, then looked up at me and with a big, toothless grin.

"Ah gawd um!"

I don't remember, but I must have said thank you, because I'd like to think I had the wherewithal to acknowledge the man who killed the man who killed an innocent woman because he was trying to kill me. I do have some wells of decency.

Now, obviously, the old man deserves a lot of credit for saving my life. I would be loathe for anyone to think I was ungrateful about his aim. One expects an elderly gent to have some capability for saving lives - but an apple? Nobody expects anything from an apple except to keep them distant from doctors.

I couldn't take an old man home with me and put him on a mantle. But an apple? Somehow that apple stayed in my hand through the arrival of the police and the interrogation and getting checked over by the ER and being given a ride home by a nice police officer who agreed that getting blood in my car would only make this worse.

"I can just wash it off at home," I said, "I mean, that's okay?"

"Well there's no need for you to go to a hospital so, yeah, clean up at your place. You're gonna have to toss the clothes, though, sorry to say. Hope you weren't attached to them."

"You don't need any of this as evidence?" I pointed at the viscera on my face.

"Not with a case open and shut as this one. Oh, and make sure you scrub yourself down good. Who knows what's in that poor girl's blood."

It made sense but seemed so unceremonious. She had been a human being and soon I would be washing bits of her down the drain. All those little pieces of brain, what had their function been? Was this bit on my cheek, under my eye, responsible for retraction of the Achilles Tendon? Was this spot on my shirt the memory of the first time she ate a tomato? Her tomato memory was going to enter the sewer system and mingle with the shit of the city. It was all so tragic.

When I got through my door and realized the apple was still in my hand, it occurred to me that I had basically stolen it. I didn't care, though. I had survived a murder attempt. I was entitled to a few hours of committing petty crimes. The apple, like me, was covered in the woman's viscera but I couldn't just throw it out. Not the apple that had saved my life. So I put it in a plastic bag and set it on the counter. It would have to wait until after I took the longest shower of my life.

I decided I was sufficiently clean when I had been in the shower long enough that I had scrubbed away half a bar of soap and the water had long turned cold. After I got out, I saw I had several missed calls from Emily.

"Are you okay?" she asked when I rang back. "The police talked to me. They said Max killed some girl who was standing nearby. He didn't get you did he?"

"I'm not dead," I said, "I mean, even if the police hadn't mentioned it, I'd think calling you would have sorted that out."

"Sorry, I'm a little high-strung right now," she said. "He probably would have come for me next - but you stopped him."

"Actually, it was some old guy with no teeth who stopped him."

"Well, I know you would have if you could. How are you managing?"

"I just finished washing the woman's blood off me."

"Great! I'm coming over."

She made good on her promise and was at my door a few minutes later. I opened it to the sight of her sad eyes staring up at me.

"We need to have sex," she said.

"What? Now?"

"Yes. There's a life that's gone because of things we did and we have to compensate."

"Um, sweetie, there's two lives gone."

"Max doesn't count. He got what he deserved. But the girl who was killed, we need to make a new life to compensate for hers."

"I've had a vasectomy because we decided we never wanted kids."

This clearly hadn't occurred to her.

"Okay. Well, we need to do it with the intention of having a kid. Even if we can't, we still have to have sex like we mean to."

"That doesn't make any sense."

"Just shut up and fuck me."

"Um, I don't know if I'm really in the mood right now. I mean, I literally just finished washing the woman's brains off my face a few minutes ago."

She threw her arms around my neck and kissed me on the cheek.

"A piece of her brain was right there, you know. Right on that spot you just smooched."

"Oh really?" she said. "Where else were there brains?"

I pointed to a spot beneath my eye.

"Here."

She kissed there.

"This isn't sexy."

She kissed me on the lips.

"Any brains there?"

"Just blood. And maybe a bone fragment."

"Take me now."

I really wasn't in the mood. But there are very few times in a man's life when a woman, even one he is dating, will throw herself at him, begging for sex. And, when those circumstances arise, it's best to just go with it. So went with it I did, dragging her into the bedroom as we kissed and stripped. Such unbridled passion is never sexy - it was a lot of slobbering on each other and tripping over our clothes, yet we made it to the bed with only a few bruises. I did my best to work up an erection but it was a precarious one, inclined to melt if my mind strayed even a little - and I had a lot on my mind that day.

Then the dead woman's breasts appeared before my eyes, disembodied and blood-smeared, and all hope for arousal was gone.

I rolled off Emily.

"I can't do this," I said. "Not right now and probably not for a while."

"We have a debt to pay off, baby. We owe what's-her-name a life."

"We're gonna have to do it some other way, honey. Maybe we can not squish the next cockroach we see, or something."

"Her life was worth more than a cockroach."

"Okay, fine. We can become vegetarians. But can we please not have sex for a while?"

I didn't sleep well that night. The woman's boobs were in my dreams too, floating after me as I ran away screaming, always managing to appear in front of me when I rounded a corner. Finally, her top flew away to reveal eyes where the nipples would have been and the boobs shouted 'boo!'

That was not a fun dream to wake up screaming from.

Next morning Emily took me back to the grocery store to get my car. We parted ways there, her reminding me of the promise to replace the life our actions had taken. I struggled with that rare and difficult task of trying to get back to a normal routine, after having something completely insane happen. The police had warned me I might suffer from PTSD. That I would find myself reliving the events of the moment, over and over, in my head.

But I didn't. I actually found it surprisingly easy not to think about the actual event, vivid as it was. Yet, everywhere I looked, I saw those disembodied tits - the eyes-for-nipples now a permanent fixture of their appearance. The specter of their presence was so convincing I could almost believe they were an actual ghost. All day they stared at me, spattered in blood, eyes judgmental, daring me to get aroused. I don't know if there's a word to describe the opposite of horny - but I was about as not-horny as anyone could be.

That evening Emily called me.

"I adopted a cat."

"Does that mean we're square on the whole 'taking a life' thing?"

"Yup. I went to a kill shelter and adopted one that was soon up on the execution block. Apparently, nobody wanted him. He's a little aggressive but I'm sure he'll calm down. Now, what was the name of the woman who died?"

"Huh? Somehow I don't know that. Hang on..."

I pulled up Google to do a search and found a news article about what had happened.

"Uh oh," I said.

"What's the uh oh?"

"Well, her first name is Maxine."

"Oof. Sounds a lot like Max, doesn't it?"

"An awful lot like Max."

"Does it give her middle name?"

"It does."

"And?"

"It's Emily."

"I'm not okay with that," she said. "What's her last name?"

"Smith."

"Then the cat's name will be Smith. Ouch."

I heard moggie-like commotions over the phone.

"Still aggressive?"

"He attacked me unprovoked. Perhaps Maxine Emily Smith is still angry with us."

"You do realize that, even if reincarnation is real, her spirit couldn't have been reincarnated in that cat, right?"

"Have you got a better explanation?"

"Yeah, he's an angry cat."

"Well, I saved his life so I'm sure he'll learn to love me."

I didn't want to argue. I mumbled agreement and hung up.

A couple of days later, I went into the kitchen to see if there was anything edible there (a rather rare occurrence for my kitchen) and spotted the apple, still covered in viscera and wrapped in plastic. I had to do something with it, but what?

I remembered an art project from middle school - our teacher had us peel apples and carve faces into them. She used vinegar to preserve the fruit, which caused them to shrivel up over the semester, until they resembled ghastly shrunken heads. We had been so excited at the beginning of the semester. Then we slowly grew horrified as we watched our creations age a lifetime over the next few months - from beautiful, youthful carvings to shrunken, wrinkled monstrosities.

Perhaps I could carve Maxine's face into the apple and preserve it with vinegar? It would allow her face to age as it never could have in life. The apple could be for me what the cat was for Emily.

There was only one problem: I couldn't recall Maxine's face. In fact, I didn't even know if I'd actually seen it - I had only been staring at her cleavage. I Googled her name again. News articles about the shooting, all of them accompanied by pictures of the exterior of the grocery store. One of them even had my Facebook profile pic - me and Emily at Halloween, when we went as serial killer and victim.

There was Emily play-screaming with her fake neck gash while I was dressed in my underwear and clown mask, pretending to slit her throat. I was now deeply regretting that picture.

I tried doing a Facebook search for Maxine Emily Smith but got back a couple people who definitely weren't her. I tried a Google image search and turned up a bunch of pictures of different women, none of which looked quite right. I tried seeing if I could recognize her by the cleavage - but couldn't definitively say that any of them were the cleavage I was looking for.

Well, I thought, *Since I can't find her face, maybe I should carve the apple into the shape of her breasts.*

At least I knew what those looked like.

I washed the blood and viscera off the fruit, peeled it, and set out some knives on the kitchen table. It had been a long time since I had carved an apple but boobs aren't terribly difficult to render and the image of Maxine's were burned deeply into my mind.

As I was working, the specter of her breasts materialized over my shoulder.

"You really think those look like me?" they said.

"You *talk* now?"

"If that's what you want to call it. You've got the curves all wrong and they're too small."

"How can they be too small? I'm not carving the whole body. There's nothing to compare them to."

"Look at me," the breasts said.

Reluctantly, I turned my head. Maxine's disembodied bosom was floating in the space over my shoulder, nipple-eyes glaring.

"Does that carving look like me?"

"Well, it's the idea of them, really. I mean, you're the inspiration."

"Not really flattering to be the inspiration for that middle-school piece of crap."

"Look, I'm sorry. I'm doing the best I can, okay? You know, I really feel bad about the whole thing."

The breasts' eyes narrowed.

"If you could go back and take the bullet for me, would you?"

"Um…"

"You die like you were supposed to, so I could live. Would you do it?"

"Well, you know, maybe I could have worked it so that neither one of us had to die. I kind of like being alive, you know."

"So did I," the breasts said.

"Emily rescued a cat for you."

"I was allergic to cats."

I tried to tune out Maxine's breasts as I completed the carving but I did give them eyeballs for nipples. After I finished, I realized I would have to go to the grocery store to get ingredients to preserve the apple. I'd hoped Maxine's breasts would stay behind in the apartment. No. They followed me to the car and floated in the passenger seat.

"I hope you're not a backseat driver," I said to them.

"That's not what I'm here for." They continued to glare at me.

In my distraction, I drove by instinct to the grocery store where the shooting had happened. It was the first time I had been there since…

The employees clearly recognized me because they were all staring. At least they couldn't see the ghost-boobs floating over my
shoulder. The area where the shooting had happened was still cor-
doned off.

"You know how much it sucks to have shopping for papayas be the
last thing you were doing before you died?"

"Hey, it would have been apples for me."

I realized only my half of the conversation was audible to everyone
else in the store, so ignored the badgering of Maxine's breasts as I
finished my shopping. When I was leaving, Emily called.

"What's up babe?" I said.

"I'm not feeling very good. I think I need to get to a hospital."

"Do you want me to drive you?"

"Please?"

"Be right over." I hung up.

"You know, I blame her more than you," Maxine's breasts said.

"And what about Max? He's the one who pulled the trigger."

"He was sick in the head and you two pressed him too far. If you'd
laid off, I'd still be alive."

"He was stalking Emily. We couldn't get him to stop."

"You still pushed him over the edge with your taunting and insults
and all the times you humiliated him."

"Goddammit, you are a figment of my imagination. There's no
way the real Maxine could have known this stuff."

"Maybe I am - but good luck ignoring me."

I got to Emily's apartment and knocked on the door. When she
opened it I saw she was covered in scratches, many openly bleeding.
She looked pale and tired.

"Good god," I said. "What happened to you?"

"Smith. I've been trying to get him to love me but he's not being
very cooperative."

From somewhere in the apartment I heard the low growl of an angry cat. Suddenly a massive ball of fur pounced on me, hissing and

clawing at my face. I grabbed it and threw it off, then watched the cat vanish under Emily's couch. I barely even saw what color he was. My face was burning from the cuts.

"I'm sorry," Emily apologized. "I think he may have been abused as a kitten."

I wanted to clean myself off before we left but was afraid to step back into the flat with that… thing still there.

"Let's go," I said.

"Don't you want to wash up?"

"I'll be fine."

On the way to the hospital, Maxine's breasts were chewing me out.

"That's *her* tribute to me? A ball of psycho fur? I don't know whose homage I'm more insulted by…"

I couldn't tell her to shut up because I had not yet told Emily I was being haunted by the breasts of the woman who died - and I didn't think she'd take the news very well.

She was looking progressively worse as we drove. Whatever she was sick with, it was working on her fast. By the time we got to the hospital she could no longer stand and I had to carry her in. The nurse took one look at Emily and called for ER. I don't know what she saw that I didn't, yet before I knew it, Emily was being whisked away on a bed. I was pointed to a waiting room and told I'd be updated shortly.

"You should wash these cuts," the nurse said. "You don't want them getting infected."

I scrubbed my face in a bathroom and started calling any of Emily's family members I had contact with, which was not many. Her family didn't like me. For some reason they thought Max was the better catch and had never forgiven her for leaving him. Then again, her mother believed Ted Bundy had been framed. There was no way such a nice-looking man could be a serial killer, she insisted. The conversations with her brother and dad were bad enough but I knew her mom would be the worst.

"Why are you calling me?" she said.

"Emily's in the hospital…"

"What did you do to her?"

"Nothing. She's sick."

"What did you infect her with?"

"Nothing. I don't know. It's nothing I did."

"You don't even know what she's sick with? Humph. Max would have cared for her himself."

"I drove her to hospital."

"Max would have carried her on his back."

"Max was stalking her for the last year."

"He was loyal."

"He tried to kill me."

"Too bad he screwed it up."

I hung up after that. If I had to be the one to deliver bad news to the rest of her family, I'd be wishing Max *had* killed me.

Maxine's boobs were still staring.

"Why am I not surprised no one likes you?"

"I have friends and family. And Emily cares about me."

"I had friends too, you know. And a boyfriend."

"Just think about how sad Emily and all my friends would have been if I'd died."

"Mine would have been sadder," Maxine's boobs protested. "I was younger and prettier and had my whole future ahead."

"I'm 28."

"I was 23."

"How was I supposed to know that?"

"Hmm, something about Maxine you didn't know? Maybe I'm not just a figment of your imagination."

"I could have made that up."

"Maxine Emily Smith. 23 years old. Studying physical therapy. Boyfriend's name is Carl. He has a parakeet named Sweetybird."

"Then I *am* just making all this up and projecting it through the vision I have of your breasts."

"Of course," the boobs said. "That's all I am to you. A pair of tits."

"Even if you hadn't died, all I'd have done was look at you in a grocery store for fifteen seconds and maybe jerk off later. How could you have possibly been anything *more* than a pair of tits to me?"

"You sure are one with the ladies. Is that all *Emily* is to you?"

"No, I actually care about Emily, for fuck's sake."

That's when I noticed the doctor to my left glaring at me. I scrunched my right shoulder to my ear.

"I'll call you later." I pretended to put away a cell phone.

"Are you Emily's husband?"

"Boyfriend."

"She said you were her husband."

"She was kinda delirious when I brought her in."

"Well, I'm sorry to say she's in very bad shape."

"Is she going to live?"

"She'll live but she developed a severe case of sepsis. Are you familiar with this condition?"

"That's a blood disease, right?"

"Blood poisoning. It can sometimes happen from an infected cut, of which she had quite a few. I take it you two got a new cat?"

"She did. I met him for the first time earlier today."

"I can tell. We're going to need to get you checked out. The cat's claws were probably very dirty, especially if it was a stray. That could lead to this kind of infection."

"What happened to Emily?"

"Sepsis really takes hold in the extremities and, in cases like Emily's, the only way to keep it from spreading is to amputate."

The bottom of my stomach dropped out.

"Um, which limbs did you have to amputate?"

"All of them, I'm afraid. The infection was in both arms and legs. You have to understand, we had to do it to save her life."

How had Emily gone from healthy to a quadruple amputee in just a few hours? I heard Maxine's boobs snickering behind me but ignored them.

"Can I see her?"

"She's asleep now and I want to get you tested, so tomorrow would be better. I'd also strongly recommend you get rid of the cat."

"I don't think that's going to happen."

I was free of any infection myself. When Emily woke and found out what had happened, she had two requests. The first was that I be the one to take care of her. The second was that nothing happen to Smith.

"It just makes it much more important that we rehabilitate him and make him feel loved," she said.

Of course, I agreed to all of these things. What the hell else was I going to do? At least Maxine's boobs had nothing to say.

But, holy hell, did her family make up for that. Over Emily's protests they kept insisting I couldn't take care of her and they wanted Max to do it. The conversation informing them Max was dead (which they somehow didn't know) did not go well. But with Max no longer an alternative, they agreed I could have the job. That only came about after I offered to let them do it - each of them suddenly having an excuse for why they couldn't.

Since I lived on the ground floor, we decided she would move into my apartment.

Getting Emily settled in was actually pretty easy. Getting Smith in, on the other hand, was not. I had already gathered that Smith was not a pleasant cat - but did not truly grasp just what a bundle of evil he was. Until I had to catch him.

He destroyed half her apartment as I was chasing him around, sometimes deliberately knocking over furniture to trip me up. I learned quickly not to reach under a piece of furniture unless I wanted my hand to come back out a bloody mess. But, if I flipped over the furniture, that's when he attacked. Maxine's boobs, whose haunting presence I had come to accept as a permanent fixture of my life, enjoyed the show - taunting me and cheering on the cat, as I failed to snag him.

Finally, after an hour of blood and destruction, I managed to force him into a crate. Once he realized he couldn't escape, he began pissing and shitting until a mixture of bodily fluids was sloshing through the door onto the back seat of my car. I thought about arranging an 'accidental' escape for the monster - but all I could think of was Emily, sitting in her wheelchair, with her stumps still swaddled in bandages, waiting patiently for me to bring her Smith back.

Releasing him into my apartment was something I did not want to do. I begged Emily to let me keep him in the crate for a while.

"He needs to be free," she said. "He's happy when he's free."

I opened the door and Smith darted out, making straight for my TV. He jumped on top and, squatting over the vents at the back, pissed into it. Given the biblical outpouring of urine he had unleashed in the crate, I couldn't see how it was even possible. Yet, somehow, he unleashed his longest stream yet.

"Oh no," Emily said, "I hope he didn't ruin it."

But ruined the TV was. As was my desktop computer, which he targeted next, as I was trying to power the TV on. I had to open all the windows to keep the smell of cat piss from overpowering us.

"Just give him time." Emily stretched out the stumps of her arms. "Carry me to bed."

I picked her up and carried her to the bedroom, Smith attacking my ankles as we went, then rushing ahead to piss on the bed before I could lay her down.

One new set of sheets and an open bedroom window later, Emily was as sprawled out on the duvet as much she was capable of.

"I want you to do something for me and it's really, really important."

"Of course," I said. "Anything."

"I need you to have sex with me. I need to feel like I'm sexy and, if we fuck, I'll know you still find me attractive."

Maxine's boobs started laughing. With some horror, I realized it was really difficult for me to still be turned on by Emily. Since Maxine's boobs had started haunting me I'd also found it impossible to get an erection.

"What's the matter?" the breasts sniggered. "She still has *her* tits."

I had learned not to respond to Maxine in the presence of others. Instead, I started undressing Emily, running my hands along her body, trying to feel some stimulation.

"Just think about me," Maxine's boobs said. "I sure turned you on, didn't I?"

Not even a tingle.

"Are you hard yet?" Emily asked.

"Getting there," I lied. Even focusing on Emily's body, which still looked great, I could not get aroused. I took my shirt off and that was when Smith, apparently finding the sight of so much unmutilated flesh too much to bear, attacked me.

He moved faster than I could fathom, clawing at my back then moving to my stomach. Finally, I threw him off and he bolted out of the window.

"Oh no," Emily screamed. "You have to get him."

I looked at her.

"I have had it with that cat."

"Please, please. You have to find him. We have to heal him. It's so important."

She was near tears. I put my shirt back on, which quickly started soaking with blood, and ran outside.

I searched the parking lot for Smith but couldn't find him. Then he leaped at me from a bush, sinking his claws into my face. I grabbed him and threw the bastard off. He landed in the parking lot and hissed, backing away as I approached, until he was in the middle of the road. I started to lunge at him - and that's when he was run over by a speeding BMW.

Smith was stretched across ten feet of asphalt, his tire-smashed guts sprayed over the road, severed head staring at me in a death snarl.

"Goddamn fucking cats." The owner of the vehicle climbed out. "You fucking assholes can't keep your sodding furballs on a leash and then this happens."

He looked me in the face.

"Goddammit, you probably referred to him as your fucking fur baby. You look like the type." He opened his wallet and shoved two one-hundred-dollar bills in my hand. "What's the going rate for a cat right now. Aw, fuck it."

He shoved another hundred in my hand.

"Just don't fucking sue me, okay?"

He got back in his car and screeched off, leaving me to stare speechless at the gore that was formerly Smith the cat.

"So, what was it she said?" Maxine's boobs were laughing uncontrollably. "*Replace one life with another*? You two sure know how to honor the dead. But, hey. At least you've still got the apple tits you carved for me, right?"

My carving. I had completely forgotten about it after I'd had to rush Emily to the hospital. I ran back into the apartment. Where had I left it? I'd hardly been home since Emily had fallen sick.

Through the stench of cat piss, I could make out the smell of rotting fruit. There, on the counter, at the other side of the toaster.

The apple had rotted into a pile of maggot-infested mush, brown goo staining the countertop, the form I had carved into it now indistinguishable. The apple that had saved my life.

Maxine's boobs were still laughing and I heard Emily's voice from the kitchen.

"Sweetie?" she said. "Is Smith okay?"

How to Read a Woman

SJ Townend

To him, freckles were dot-to-dot maps, heralding secrets of the future. Each woman with mottled skin was an unread book. A mug of tea leaves ready to be interpreted. A human tasseological chart waiting for his fingers and blades to explore. Raised or flat, regular or scruffy-edged, plain nubs or cancerous, he loved every one. He loved the splatter of all of God's kisses.

Patterns on a lady's skin would always unearth a story and it was his own form of astrology. He'd taught himself to read in this way. It was what he believed in and knew to be true. Only by connecting the beauty spots and pockmarks on a woman's shell with lines, with the rich red stretches a blade would proffer, could he clearly see the prescient constellations dictating his own future.

He'd killed earlier that week and the skin he'd laid and dried and etched with a thousand small, razor lines showed him a representation of the street on which he now lurked. So, he followed his stars and sat in wait. He hoped he would strike lucky again.

In his bag, he carried a variety of tools to help him bisect his next piece. A razorblade. A scalpel. A steak knife. A hacksaw. An axe.

Cheek-by-limestone-jowl, he crouched amongst the darkness, between the pressing faces of towering walls belonging to the empty university buildings. He waited under the watchfulness of a strong moon, certain he would find someone suitable - young, marked - to give him what he needed. No idea yet who she would be but he knew the darkness of the night would deliver. It always did. It had always done.

He sat tight. With only the deserted cityscape, a rucksack of bundled blades and a blanket of light pollution for company, he waited - hidden - near the nightclub. Bassline music thrummed from under its steel-portcullised entrance. It would open soon.

Cars passed, oblivious. The little hand on his watch crept closer to eleven. Taxis spilt out groups of Friday night revelers, loosely drunk, high on their own youth and everything else the city had to offer. The night smelt for them of pheromones and hope. For him, it would soon smell of cheap perfume, sweat, fear and coppery vermillion. Nothing was quite as fragrant as the pages of a freshly skinned book.

From his crevice, he watched for the right one. Many passed in groups but none arrived alone and none were covered in markings. He'd dealt in stretch-marked flesh more than once but found it disappointing. Here, he would find youthful skin, tight skin, decorated only by a natural reaction to sunlight. It was the sweet, freckled ones he had a taste for. Those were the women he wished to peel back layers from.

This dive of a student club was a gamble but he had no better place to be. At least it was secluded at night-time, being in the central business district of the city. The area was heavily built up, providing plentiful spots for him to lurk.

A people-carrier pulled up to the taxi rank near the entrance, a stone's throw from his watchful glare. And, solo, out she stepped.

His green eyes sparkled with the light of Lucifer at the sight. This would be his takings, for sure. He could not wait to cut and slice, from this girl, the narrative of her very spirit. What stories would the map of her markings reveal?

She was wearing a black dress with a zipper running from neckline to hemline. Auburn curls tumbled from a high ponytail. Her exposed arms and legs were translucent as rice paper, thin and marked as pages from an old bible. He stretched his neck to watch her strut into the club, careful not to reveal himself too soon. He needed her drunk first, intoxicated, so he could have his wicked way. His heart revved and pumped blood, laced with expectation, to his keen fingers and toes. Her skin was laced with prophecy. She'd keep him busy. What a read this one would be.

Three hours passed. She stumbled out through the safety net of bouncers, into the mouth of the night. Would she call and wait for a taxi? Would she walk the half-mile to the kebab shop, the only remaining source of food in the city at this ungodly hour? He waited with bated breath.

Bag swung over his shoulder, he scuttled between the shadows behind her. She walked past the empty taxi rank and, staccato-heeled, tip-tapped around the corner. This was his chance to approach. Not a soul present other than the pair of them.

"Excuse me, madam."

This slip of a girl, early twenties, skin of treasure, turned to face him.

"Hello," she replied.

"Saw you in the club," he lied. "Was going to buy you a drink, but you left before I'd got the chance."

He'd never set foot inside of that boom-box building of noise and promiscuity. He was not the partying type, more the studious type, always reading. He preferred to while away his daylight hours alone, at home, amongst his library of hung-flesh fiction.

"Hope you don't mind me approaching you like this?"

"No," she interrupted. "Not at all,"

That took him aback. He could not smell fear permeating from this one's beautiful body. He relished a challenge, though. He would make her feel terror. He would enjoy watching the colour drop from her cheeks.

"I'm Lamia." She moved closer. "And you are...?"

He clutched his bag. Even in the moonlight he could see threads of purple veins running below her skin. He could trace the ribbons of blood vessels snaking around underneath crops of freckles.

"I'm...." She did not need to know his name. He changed the subject. "Would you like me to escort you home?"

"How very gentlemanly. That would be divine."

Lamia pushed her thin arm through the loop of his. A stream of pleasure shot through his very core. His eyes darted around the translucent, bespeckled skin of her shoulder, as she recounted the non-events of her evening.

He didn't hear a word she said. In his mind, he was already slicing through her cold body, connecting the largest, protruding moles he might find first with his fingertips, like Braille. Then, with a simple razor blade, he'd provide a sketch of his future, an outline. After, he would hack through this framework with his axe to split the parts of the story her body would reveal. Once separated into chapters, he could wipe away her red ink and join the smaller brown and orange marks which decorated every visible part of her, with the steak knife or scalpel. This would reveal the beauty in the sentences of each page of her flesh.

"So this is me." She delved into her purse for a key. "It's been lovely chatting. Divine."

Her eyes mocked coyness and she bit her lip playfully.

"Would you care to come in for a..."

His eyes flitted left, right and behind to check they were alone on the steps of her apartment. This was all too easy. Adrenaline flushed his cells at the thought of the joys to come.

"Yes. Yes I would. That'd be... divine." He was too distracted to select new words of his own.

He followed her up the steps, eyes tracing the star-charts of heavens that scattered in freckle form over the backs of her legs.

"Tea or wine?" Lamia called from the kitchen.

He sat perched on the edge of the sofa. Where would he place the pages of derma once he'd ripped apart the story of this redhead?

She came back in with an opened bottle of Malbec and two glasses.

This one would whiten with fear, he thought. All colour from her would vanish. Her face, round like the moon, would pallor. The dusting of freckles on her cheeks would pop against an ashen canvas. He felt himself harden with excitement as he took the glass.

Whilst she'd been out in the kitchen, he'd sequestered his tools. The axe lay hidden beneath the sofa cushion, the steak knife was tucked in the cuff of his boot.

"You've beautiful eyes." She perched next to him. Her bare leg brushed against his knee. He felt ecstasy.

"Thank you," he replied. "And you have beautiful skin."

"You've seen nothing yet." Between her fingertips, she took the zip which lay above her delicate décolletage. "Would you like to see more?"

"Very much so."

His night was about to peak, his future revealed. Between the cushions, his fingers felt for a weapon. He placed his other hand on her knee and traced a small crucifix patterning of freckles. Further up her leg, his index finger slid over a stretch of pigmentation, premature age spots curving round like a scythe. Old Father Time. He pressed on the curve of her hip. The girl was an hourglass. He couldn't wait to carve and connect the grains of sand.

She drew down her zipper. He drew up his weapon.

She continued to peel open her skin-tight dress and a scream ripped from his throat. His face, stamped with the mark of terror, could not believe what she had revealed.

Before his own eyes were tens of hers, a hundred. Blues, greens, browns and all shades of hell in between.

From breast to pelvis, myriad eyes burst from her skin. Clusters and patches of eyeballs, small and large, lashed or not. Some ogled side-by-side, matching partners. Some bulged alone. Others blinked.

Where her nipples should have been, poked out the largest two - irises of red, pupils black holes. The eyes blinked and twitched like faulty Christmas lights. They dilated and flitted around the room, before all settling forwards on him.

"Your eyes," she said. "I need *your* eyes."

She draped slim arms around his thick neck, pressed crimson lips against his and stared directly at him. Her hands gripped and forced open his eyelids, so he could not close away from the terror. Her eyes held the suction power of an oceanic drain.

They yanked his own eyes out from their sockets, lashes and lenses first - white sclera splitting apart like a cracked egg. Her full lips slurped his eye juice and it trickled down inside her. Fluids from within his orbital sockets sprayed onto her face, each drop absorbed through translucent skin, each freckle sucking in the liquid. Like water down a plug hole, his face was lapped up. His body was guzzled in through her portals to the underworld, circular doors which led to the outskirts of the universe.

In a blink, he was gone. She sat alone on her sofa.

Lamia felt a familiar tickle, this time on her inner thigh. Where before, two dark moles of the warty variety had been, new green eyes rolled underneath. The opals throbbed against the top sheet of her paper-thin skin until, miniature volcanoes, they erupted from her flesh. Crowning out from the surface near her groin, his eyes opened, full of emerald fear.

They started to weep. Tears of regret and confusion and insanity trickled down her thigh and fell between her legs onto the sofa. She patted and dabbed at his sadness with her fingertips.

"Cheer up, love," she said. "It might never happen."

Lamia zipped up her dress and rubbed each of her sore eyes through the fabric. They had seen enough for now.

Satisfied with her accomplishments of the night, she finished off her wine and fell asleep.

Moonlighting

Mark Watson

Hoolahan knew he needed to kill Galloway. It was the one thing he remained certain of, in the wake of the confusion. He loathed the prospect but he was the only one left. It fell on him to see it done. He placed his back against the towering stone pine behind him and, ignoring the conks that crumbled against his hunting jacket, slid down its moss-shrouded trunk. He furrowed grimy fingers through sweat-drenched hair and listened to Galloway's wretched hitching breaths plead with him more profoundly than words ever could.

Farther off, over the rise to his right, he could hear the sickening crunch of fresh wet bones and the grotesque slurping of marrow.

"C'mon, Darren," he urged himself. "You're running out of time."

The thing that had attacked them was nearly finished with Peterson. When it had begun feeding, Peterson had still been alive and conscious. His gargled, steadily weakening screams, which had diminished to croaked gibbering near the end, stood testimony to that.

Peterson's death had been unspeakable. The creature had dined leisurely, beginning with the soft parts. It would be inhuman to allow Galloway to share this fate but Hoolahan couldn't bring himself to put a merciful end to the young hunter's life. Lowering his head between raised knees, he knotted his fists in slick tangles of nape hair and grieved the lament most common for those who fall victim to harsh consequence.

Why had he ever gotten himself into this? As a hunting guide, Darren Hoolahan had a humble client base with deep and generous pockets. He didn't need the money that Peterson and Galloway had offered. They had contacted him, seeking a hunting adventure in the unexplored wilds of the great Canadian Shield and Hoolahan had initially resisted. He had culled his regulars down to twelve groups which ranged from two to four individuals, all experienced woodsmen who adhered to his rules. He had little interest in moonlighting a thirteenth outing, especially in the company of two hunters with whom he shared no history.

Frank Peterson and Chip Galloway were affable and unpretentious, despite their wealth. Peterson hailed from Minnesota and Galloway was a good ole boy from Texas. Hoolahan didn't generally take to Americans who ventured to the Great White North, finding them largely condescending toward their Canadian hosts. Yet these two exhibited no trace of superiority at all. They were both ex-soldiers. They had met each other and become close friends during basic training. Then they had ended up in the same unit overseas during their one and only tour of duty in Iraq. They hadn't fifty summers between them but shadows behind their eyes told Hoolahan they'd seen enough for a lifetime.

When he met with them, he liked both instantly. Liked their easy way with each other, their quiet respectful humility and their undemonstrative confidence. He decided to go against his better judgment and guide their wilderness outing. Hoolahan was scarcely older than - but they had immediately looked to him as their leader, even before entering the wilderness. He accepted the role, doing so for the greater good, in deference to his wilderness experience. Yet he felt like an imposter.

He had never been in the military, never experienced combat and never taken a human life. These two young men, who were prepared to place their fate in his hands were, in many ways, more capable than he. They wanted a hunting adventure and a hunting adventure they would get.

On this excursion, however, the role of hunter would not long be theirs. Soon enough, they would become the hunted and his leadership would fail them.

Galloway shifted beside him, pulling Hoolahan from his somber reverie. He glanced down at his companion, not without some measure of difficulty. Galloway was lying on his back, directly to his right. The young soldier's lower left leg was cragged within the confines of his forest print cargo pants and the left sleeve of his hunting jacket and the chambray shirt beneath it were torn off at the shoulder stitching.

The arm was gone as well.

Hoolahan's eyes fixated on the shiny white lump of bone that jutted from the swollen fleshy mass where Galloway's arm had been. It was still glistening, despite being encrusted with pine needles and forest floor debris. It looked grizzly. Hoolahan wished he had his canteen so he could, at least, rinse off the offensive filth. Oddly, the pine needles, twigs and leaves that were clinging to the raw flesh revolted him more than the wound itself.

Galloway was breathing in short, ragged gasps. His eyes were now open and aware, staring straight in front of him, as he focused on his breathing. He was in shock but wasn't close enough to death to suit Hoolahan. He'd last long enough for the beast to get at him, if he wasn't spared that horrible fate.

There was another loud, popping snap a hundred yards or so away, beyond a fern-covered rise to their left, followed by more grotesque slurping sounds. It served as a grim reminder that time was running short. Hoolahan thumbed off the snap on the sheath of his hunting knife. His mind drifted back to the attack. The thing had come at them with such bladder loosening suddenness, none of the trio even comprehended what was happening.

They had made their way up the Churchill River, full of exuberance and awe, in Hoolahan's twelve-and-a-half-foot inflatable raft, powering through the opposing rapids with a small four-stroke out-board motor. The progress was slow and tedious but none of them had minded. The journey was a large part of the experience and they luxu-riated in it. A swimming moose elicited a stir of conversation. A bald eagle soaring above inspired quiet awe. Even the commonplace white-tailed deer, glancing up from drinking along the shore as they passed, added flavor to the trip. The sky above was clear, blue and as elevated as their spirits.

Hoolahan navigated a route familiar to him, directing the raft along some tributaries and across a couple of small lakes until they came to his predetermined location. The area he selected had the dual benefit of offering virtually untouched wilderness to his adventure-seeking clients and remaining within two hours of civilization and medical assistance, should the need arise. After setting up camp near a lake that had no name, they idled in campfire camaraderie, too exhilarated to bed down for the evening.

Hoolahan knew there were some nights, even in July, when the temperature could dip below zero this far north in the Manitoba wil-derness. Tonight, however, the air was fine. It was chilly enough for jackets, yet not cold enough to induce any real discomfort. The moon etched a crisp circle in the clear night sky and the stars accentuated eternity. Regarding ambiance, Hoolahan couldn't have asked for a better opening night to their wilderness adventure. Peterson and Gal-loway were pleased with him and he was pleased with himself - until they were set upon by a living nightmare.

There was no clear antecedent to the attack. No low growling. No disturbed underbrush. Not even so much as a snapped twig. The three adventurers, completely oblivious to the impending threat lurking in the darkness beyond their small dome of light, were perched on fold-ing tripod stools on the lee side of their modest campfire, away from the smoke. The mood was light, as was the conversation. They talked about their homes, families and aspirations. More than anything, they complimented the beauty and serenity of their surroundings. They could hear a gentle lapping of wavelets caressing the shore of the small unnamed lake. As they sat amidst a forest of tall, pillar-like stone pine, with naked trunks and bushy tops, they could hear the soothing rustle of leaves far above. It did not occur to them, not even Hoolahan, that they could hear nothing more.

No owl queried the night. No bird chirped nor did any chipmunk chatter. The forest was warning them that a predator was close at hand but they were so engaged by its opulence that nature's counsel went unnoticed. The heavy carpet of moss and accompanying fungal growth bestowed the area with a serene primordial countenance. There were no signs of previous human presence at all.

Hoolahan had taken pains to erase all traces of his earlier excursions here after each outing. Remnants of old campsites tended to spoil the effect.

"I could go the rest of my life without ever hearing another car horn."

Peterson unscrewed the ceramic cap of his canteen and raised it to his lips. He couldn't remember the last time he'd felt so at peace. They had freshly refilled their canteens from a glacial stream a few hours earlier, relishing the pristine clarity of the water as they had done so. Hoolahan had deliberately detoured to the babbling brook for this very reason. It was part of his tour and it never failed to pay off.

His clients ate it up every time - a welcome diversion from bottled water lifestyles. Hoolahan forbade the consumption of alcohol on his excursions. The wilds of the Canadian Shield were no place to dull your senses. He bore the teasing inferences that he was turning his back to his Irish ancestry with good-natured guile, whenever such hints had been made.

Neither Peterson nor Galloway had offered any. When it came to maintaining a sober mind in a potentially hostile environment, they shared Hoolahan's views completely.

"You can say that again, brother. It's God's country up here." Galloway tipped his own canteen in agreement with his partner's proclamation.

Then it was upon them.

Galloway was still holding his canteen out in salute when Peterson was suddenly writhing, eviscerated, on the forest floor - wailing and trying to gather his innards. His shrieks were short bursts that sounded like wordless questions.

Ignoring the victim it had just disemboweled, the creature grabbed Galloway's extended wrist and simultaneously arced a swing at Hoolahan. Even while swiping backhanded, its clawed hand faced forward. This thing was a slasher, not a bludgeoner.

Hoolahan flinched away and reflexively threw up his left arm in defense. One of the creature's claws nicked the outer heel of his hand in passing - but just barely. Hoolahan didn't even feel it. His stool tipped, toppling him back from the beast. He rolled with the fall, clambered to his feet and ran blindly into heavy fern growth - up a gentle rise toward the deeper forest. His feet tangled in the undergrowth and he fell to the ground, cowering in numb horror.

Galloway had only served one tour of duty in Iraq but he was a combat veteran, nonetheless. He had seen a soldier's head suddenly disappear above the eyebrows, vaporized by a sniper's high caliber bullet, before he'd even heard the shot. He had watched dispassionately as fleeing insurgents, floundering in heavy dunes, were crushed beneath the tracks of unyielding tanks. He had heard their screams and the crunching of their bodies without so much as twitching an eyebrow. There was steel in him beyond the measure of his years, forged in battle. He had also given a hungry Iraqi child the last of his field rations without knowing when he would receive more. There was heart in him as well. He was a United States Marine and he comported himself accordingly.

Hoisting Galloway up like a slaughtered hog, the creature drew back its powerfully muscled, fur-draped arm. Its claws were splayed, and it prepared to disembowel him with a single stroke. Dangling in the air, Galloway lacked the leverage to deliver as powerful a blow as he would have liked - yet he managed to send a smart chopping right fist into the beast's left eye.

"Semper Fi, motherfucker!"

The monster roared in pain and brought its free hand to its eye without relinquishing its hold on the defiant marine. In a tantrum of rage, it hammered the two-hundred-pound combat veteran into the ground repeatedly, wielding him like a sack of potatoes. The small campfire was dashed to scattered embers and the gear and supplies were knocked pell-mell. The beast hemorrhaged fury as it dashed Galloway's limp body this way and that, again and again, into the hard forest floor. In the frenzied maelstrom of its rage, the beast failed to notice when Galloway's body tore free from the captured arm and was catapulted several yards into the ferns.

Galloway flew through the air, passing between a pair of stout tree trunks with inches to spare on either side. He was still alive but his body exhibited no signs of that, as it limply described a slow spinning somersault through the night air and skidded into the heavy growth a few yards from where Hoolahan was cowering. The creature, seemingly oblivious to Galloway's separation from his arm, continued to batter the disembodied limb against the forest floor with the unchecked enthusiasm of a berserker.

As Hoolahan lay cringing in the forest shrubbery, he didn't smell the sour, bitter stench of the mulch bedding. Nor was he aware of the sharp broken branch that jabbed at his side or the bead of sweat that trickled behind his ear like a crawling spider. His senses were heightened but not tuned to notice such mundane harmlessness.

He did hear Galloway's valiant cry, the beast's enraged bellow and the horrible thumping sounds that followed. He even felt the impact tremors at this distance, or imagined he had. He dared not move, remaining still and quiet in the greenery that bowed over him protectively. He was a small rabbit hiding in the tall grass while an owl circled above.

When Galloway's body whisked through the ferns and slid toward Hoolahan, he felt certain the beast was upon him. A startled squeal escaped his lungs and he tensed for savage desolation, clenching his fists in the mulch and squeezing his eyes tightly shut. After an eternal moment, he realized the creature was still at the campsite, several yards away, thrashing about. Tentatively, with tension permeable enough to taste in the back of his throat, he eased himself forward to investigate.

It was Galloway and he was alive! He was in real bad shape, though. Battered, bloody and missing an arm. The fucking thing tore his arm off! Hoolahan winced at Galloway's quick, short, gasping breaths.

In his youth Hoolahan had worked as a log piler for a chainsaw operator, cutting pulpwood. One day, his associate, Kirk McKay, was sawing through a spruce whose top was bowed under the pressure of a deadfall. Kirk had sawed halfway through the tree when it split up the middle of the trunk, snapped off and kicked back - striking him in the chest. They called it barber-chairing, when a tree split up the middle like that. Kirk had suffered four broken ribs and his breathing had been very similar to how Galloway's was now.

Not sure what he hoped to accomplish, Hoolahan slithered up to Galloway, grabbed hold of his hunting jacket on either side of the collar, and began laboriously dragging him through the thick fern growth. Their only remote chance to escape was the inflatable raft and they were heading away from that, deeper into the forest. But he had only two prevailing thoughts. The foremost was to put as much distance between them and the rampaging creature as he could manage. The other was that he wouldn't abandon Galloway again. They would see this through together.

They had made it down the opposite slope of the fern-covered hill and into a hollow, populated with slender stone pine, by the time the creature had exhausted its furor. Hoolahan pulled Galloway's unconscious form up to a particularly stout trunk, then he leaned against the rough moss-covered bark, panting.

"NO! PLEASE! DON'T!"

This was followed by a warbling scream that tested the boundaries of human vocalization. Hoolahan's wheezing gasps for air halted instantly and he cocked an ear. The creature had begun to feed on Peterson.

Nearly an hour had passed since then and Peterson's screams and pitiable whimpering had gone on for a good quarter of that. The rifles were still in their cases, back at the campsite, and Hoolahan didn't carry a sidearm. Galloway didn't have one either. The only person who had sensibly brought a handgun into the wilderness of the Canadian Shield was Peterson - and his Colt 1911 service issue would do them little good now. For all Hoolahan knew, the damned thing had eaten it.

Another bone snapped and he could hear marrow being slurped ravenously from it. The thing was thorough, it sure liked to clear its plate. It occurred to Hoolahan that his mother would approve and a small snorting titter escaped him. He didn't like the sound of it. He was becoming unhinged. He liked the noise of the beast's voracious feeding even less. It didn't sound like its hunger had been satiated in the least. There was no doubt in his mind the creature would sniff them out quickly, once it finished with Peterson's remains.

"It's a werewolf, ain't it?"

Galloway's query was spaced with quick, short gasps for air but his voice seemed calm and matter of fact. Hoolahan met his eyes. They were also calm.

"I don't know. I didn't get a good look at it."

He *did* know, though. There was no way not to.

"I did… Black as shit… Blazing yella eyes… Head like a wolf. Even had a tail."

"Maybe it was a timber wolf. They get pretty big up here."

Galloway looked up at him flatly and Hoolahan shifted his eyes away.

"It lifted me in the air with a hand, Darren, not a paw. Felt its fingers around my wrist."

Silence fell between them, as they struggled to add the existence of such a thing to their knowledge of the world. For Galloway it was like adding water to a glass that was already filled to the rim. The added water simply forced existing contents out over the top. For this thing to be, other things, previously thought to be true, could not.

Hoolahan's absorption of the new information was considerably less simplistic. For him, it was like trying to add water to a sealed bottle without removing the cap. His brain began to buzz and he felt his mind slipping away.

"Fucking thing made me drop my canteen," Galloway's abrupt lament helped Hoolahan bring his mind back to focus. "Wish I'd held on to it. Thirsty as hell."

It occurred to Hoolahan that Galloway had lost the arm which had been holding the canteen, so it scarcely mattered one way or another if he'd held on to it. He saw no profit in voicing this - but the logical nature of the thought brought his mind back from the brink - and he was grateful for that. Ultimately, he decided that the creature would soon put an end to him, anyhow, so losing his mind was not that great a concern - all things considered.

"I wish I could help you out." It sounded lame but Hoolahan could think of nothing else to say.

"I guess, maybe... you can,"

Galloway fixed his gaze on the sheafed knife strapped to Hoolahan's thigh. The grotesque slurping sounds continued to assault their ears from over the rise.

"I was in and out of it there, for a bit, but I heard Frank screaming. I'd just as soon have my spirit flown before that thing gets at me."

Hoolahan said nothing. Buzzing began to rise in his brain, like an agitated bee swarm. He squeezed his eyes shut and clenched his fists. Galloway could see his consternation.

"After you free my spirit," he ventured. "Maybe... you could slip away while it's... while it's busy with me."

Freeing your spirit would have no impact on my chances one way or another.

The coldly ungenerous thought came unbidden, a foreign intruder in Hoolahan's mind. The buzzing intensified. He felt on the edge of blacking out. A cold rush ran across his shoulders and the tiny nick he'd received earlier from the beast flared like a hot needle.

He had to see this done before he lost consciousness. Galloway drew in a quick sigh of relief when Hoolahan reached for the blade. The guide had looked strange for a moment, like he was harboring thoughts of abandoning him to his plight.

Hoolahan grasped the hilt of his knife with a shaky right hand and positioned its tip to the left of Galloway's sternum. He closed his eyes and drew in deep, stabilizing breaths in an attempt to dispel or, at least, reduce the intense level of throbbing in his head. He carefully placed his left palm over the compass bulb that was screwed into the hilt of his knife and prepared to force the blade through the young soldier's chest, into his heart.

Galloway watched until he was satisfied with the positioning, then laid his head back and closed his eyes. His lips moved in silent and earnest prayer. Hoolahan began to feel a rustling, crawling sensation in his hands. It ran up his arms and spread across his back. He looked down and gasped out loud.

The freckled backs of his hands were now covered with coarse hairs, sprouting and writhing like long thin worms. Suddenly, his body was wracked with spasmodic cramping pains, so powerful an anguished cry escaped him. He let the knife slip from stretching fingers and hugged himself around his convulsing abdomen, overwhelmed by sudden, fervent agony.

Galloway felt the discarded knife fall on his chest and opened his eyes. His face shuddered in horror and disbelief.

Hoolahan was changing before his eyes. His formerly clean-shaven, face was contorting under a fresh growth of surging dark hair. His irises, a pleasing shade of blue moments before, had become a baleful rusty yellow. His cheeks were drawing back, as his nose and mouth stretched forward into a snarling muzzle, exposing teeth growing into sharp canine points. His slight build expanded in length and breadth until it strained, then burst through the seams of his clothing. Thick bristles of fur jutted out through the torn and rendered seams.

Galloway had braved the fury of the creature at the campsite, but this macabre transformation was too much for him. Blithering nonsensically, he fumbled for the knife that was lying on his chest.

He was too late.

Galloway began to scream and continued screaming for a long time.

The thing that had once been Hoolahan pinned his body to the ground with powerful talons and began to dine leisurely, starting with the soft parts

Something to Do on a Rainy Day When You're Dead

David Wesley Hill

It was a rainy morning and Courtney and I had nothing better going on so we went to the basement and watched our brother, Sam, tumble in the dryer. His head, as corrugated as a pumpkin and the same orange color, was split by a toothy grin.

The area around the machines was finished with linoleum tile and particle board, but the recesses of the room were natural rock and dirt. In one dark corner Sam had burrowed a tunnel. I had no idea where the left branch led. The other divided like a human artery into a thousand capillaries, providing clandestine access to every building in the neighborhood, which really came in handy during a pandemic.

Courtney, sprawled on the ancient faux leather recliner beside the laundry hamper, blew a bubble, popped it, and began masticating the gum again.

"You know, Frank," she said, "Covid really sucks."

"Tell me about it."

"I mean, pestilence is my thing. I'm all on that. Give me Ebola. Give me anthrax. For gosh sakes, I'll take the plague any day. *Bring out your dead*. Remember?"

"I do."

"COVID, though… "

Courtney popped a bubble in disgust. She was as bored as I was. Sometimes it seems I've been bored for eternity. My entire life.

191

The dryer finished cycling. Sam popped his round head through the circular door. Steam threading from his cranium, he said:

"It's time, guys. Let's have some fun!"

We followed Sam through the labyrinth of tunnels to the basement of 28 Oak Street. The house belonged to Randolph "Randy" Pearlmutter. Randy had been a truck driver for thirty-two years. A month after he retired, his wife divorced him. Since then, Randy had entertained himself by shit posting on social media.

Some weeks back, Sam had seeded the house with medical waste from the community hospital. Soon Randy contracted Covid. On Monday he drove to the ER - but no beds were available and he was sent home with an oxygen bottle.

Randy wasn't vaccinated. Now he was too weak to stand. His O_2 saturation was at 84 percent. He was lying in a wet mess of bedding, his breath coming in gasps, while he pecked at his phone and argued with strangers, since he didn't have any friends.

"Well, hello!" Sam snatched the phone from Randy's hands.

You'd think such a grotesque visitor would appall the dying man, but Randy wasn't surprised by the apparition at his bedside. Instead, he smiled happily at Sam. All his cherished paranoid fantasies were being validated.

"Christ, you're one ugly son of a bitch," Randy wheezed, his lungs shredded by the virus. "What are you? Some kind of mutant? Deep State assassin? Yeah, that's it - a kiddie raping alien hybrid pervert. I've done my research."

"Wrong, wrong, wrong!" Sam said.

"No, Mr. Pearlmutter," I pulled up a chair while Courtney pressed near his unshaven cheek, wrinkled her nose like the cute witch in that old sitcom, and inhaled a deep sniff of his sickness. As she sighed contentedly, I went on:

"We are not members of the Deep State. We have no political agenda. We just want to watch you die, that's all. Up close and personal, if you know what I mean."

"What the fuck for?"

"Because we're *bored*," Courtney explained with a moue, as if it were the most obvious thing in the world.

We timed our visit just right. Randy had only hours to live. No one else called or came by. We were his only company and we weren't good guests.

Just for kicks, Sam caught a rat and demonstrated how he would abuse Randy's body once the trucker expired. Courtney popped bubble after bubble, while staring into his eyes, occasionally leaning forward to lap up his tears. I bent close to his ear and, in a whisper, detailed all the ways he had been wrong about every little thing he had ever done.

Eventually, Randy lapsed into delirium and let the last dregs of himself drool away.

That's when I kissed him. The foulness on his tongue reminded me of what it was like to be alive. Soon, though, the moment passed.

Sam kept his promise. He immediately began violating Randy's corpse while Courtney and I returned home and joined Mom and Dad in the living room.

Wearing a wife beater and boxers, Dad was in his La-Z-Boy, drinking vodka and streaming a porn video. His right leg was half the width of the other. Dad tells people he had polio as a kid but that isn't true. He was born with the deformity.

Mom was on the couch, doom scrolling through Facebook. Every so often, she paused, frowned, and used one of her thousand sock puppets to post a lie of her own.

"Where's your brother?" she asked.

"Paying his respects to Randy Pearlmutter," Courtney answered, plopping herself on Dad's lap to watch the video with him.

"Who?"

"An idiot who died with neither grace nor illumination," I said.

"You were expecting different?" Dad asked.

"Not really. Sometimes, though, I wonder what the point is."

"The point of what?"

"I don't know. Everything."

"There is no point," Dad said. "That's the point."

He was right. Meaning was mortal bullshit. Yet, for a fleeting instant, in the pain of others, I'd almost felt like a real human being.

I suspected that proved something. I just didn't know what.

"Hey, Frank! Courtney!"

Sam had returned. His grin exposed teeth like black pegs.

"Randy's no fun anymore," he said. "Come on, guys. Let's find someone else to play with."

I glanced out the window. The afternoon was overcast and dark.

"Why not?" I said.

It was something to do on a rainy day.

Never Give Up

Geoff Hart

A disembodied circulatory system, heart pumping madly, floated before my eyes. Not just any circulatory system, mind you. Mine.

My last memory before this unfortunate situation arose was crossing the heliopause. When the *Voyager* probes made that transition, there were no repercussions. No trumpets and drums, no alarm sirens blaring. Just a scientifically interesting change in the ambient electromagnetic environment. A change that reassured us we truly understood the universe through the power of science and that the universe, though inhospitable, was at least safely navigable and ours to command. But when *Bright Hope* made that transition, it was like rupturing the amniotic sac that holds a fetus safely suspended in a warm, comforting environment. Safe from the hostile universe that lies outside, its hostility unsuspected by anyone other than occasional whack jobs like Lovecraft. Before we could so much as high-five each other on the bridge, something detected our presence and sprang upon us with what can only be described as predatory delight.

Hello, by the way. I have no idea who you are or how I'm communicating with you. I hope you're not me. This is weird enough already without getting into the whole echo-chamber thing.

In an instant, I went from looking at a display of magnetic field density on the science station's screen to hovering suspended in darkness so absolute it was unrelieved even by the occasional flashes of light that bored retinal cells invent at night behind one's eyelids. (I

195

used to think they were caused by cosmic rays intersecting neurons. Live and learn.)

Where was I? Oh, right: Darker than the void at the heart of a corporate lawyer, which is several steps darker than the dark at the center of a black hole, which is only a poseur by comparison. A Platonic ideal of blackness, unrelieved by any sensation.

It was like floating in a sensory deprivation pod, but not in a good way. More like being suffocated by claustrophobia while clawing at the coffin lid, trying to escape before they put you in the ground.

The darkness didn't last, which was a good thing. I could feel it sucking at my brain like a kid slurping on a frozen fruit juice stick during an August heatwave. Something like a sea anemone - if sea anemones were the size of the Burj Khalifa - emerged from the darkness, its writhing and moistly glistening tentacles glowing with that disturbing shade of violet that lies right at the edge of the human visual perception and looks like it's persona non grata in our universe and wants to take you with it when it leaves. The creature undulated towards me in complete silence, moving without motion, if you'll accept for a moment that that's a thing. Like using the zoom lens on a camera when you're looking over the edge of a cliff, with the same void in your gut, but with the world compressing and foreshortening as the zoom increases. I could have been the one moving. It could have been moving. The universe could have been contracting around us. I had no point of reference by which to judge. In any event, it felt fricking big.

It would have been nice to say a hearty welcome, or at least to shriek and flail my tongue in the air like one of those old Don Martin drawings in *Mad Magazine*. But I had no mouth and could not scream.

As the creature drew closer, it set my nerves vibrating like a plucked guitar string - which I could tell, because my nervous system had joined the circulatory system, hovering in the void. This, as you can imagine, was acutely uncomfortable. Sticky tentacles wrapped around what remained of me. Its crushing grip wasn't precisely comforting but was a nice change from the previous lack of sensation.

Imagine, if you will, one of those weighted blankets that periodically come into and go out of popularity. Only this one was a Chinese knockoff in which the pirate manufacturer hadn't really grasped that the purpose was to comfort rather than crush the customer. A distinctly mixed pleasure.

The pressure abruptly changed to tension, like being torn apart on the rack but without the pain. That's what losing your nervous system will do for you: feeling no pain! Of course, there was still the 'ick' factor, which was considerable. On any given day, I preferred my insides to be inside. I watched, with an incipient sense of panic, as the creature's myriad tentacles dug under my skin, insinuated themselves between my muscles, and began peeling them from me like a tight-fitting coat. With a moist sucking, skin and muscles detached and floated free, joining the other bodily parts. The creature's excited hunger flooded my mind, the craving of a sociopath who wants nothing more than to pull things apart to see how they work and doesn't much care whether they can be reassembled.

Oh, by the way? I think I've solved the mind-body problem thing, since the me who's telling you this wasn't co-located with the nervous system anymore. Make of that what you will.

The sense of violation was bad enough, but worse was being forced to watch the creature as it detached my wrinkly, slack skin from the muscles so it could pick them apart to explore their connections. The skin's surface tension pulled it into a rough ball, flaccidly oscillating in an invisible breeze. Which would have raised the hairs on the back of my neck, except...

Yeah, that. No nervous system, at least not one sharing space with me. The circulatory and nervous systems formed an elegant and surprisingly lovely filigree, glowing in that bruised purple light against the blackness. Next, these miscellaneous viscera were joined by a complete digestive tract that leaked various unpleasant solids and liquids into the void. That left me, now presumably a disembodied soul, naked as a pizza deliveryman in a bad porno.

I think I would have panicked by then. But without a circulatory system to carry chemical signals throughout whatever remained of me, it was an oddly impotent form of panic. Sort of a meta-panic. A pseudo-panic. A start repeating yourself to avoid making blubbering noises with your non-existent lips panic.

Like that, only worse.

I felt a psychic sense of tentacles rubbing together in glee, then the creature set about disassembling my body into ever smaller component parts, like a kid taking apart a Lego kit and sorting the different bricks into categories. Except the bricks were my fricking body parts, being given all the respect of a bowl of yesterday's chili at an all-you-can-eat buffet.

About then, I'd had enough. It was time to fight back and score one for humanity, before being claimed forever by that creepy purple-lit infinite night. As I awaited my chance, I listened to my own internal playlist and did my best to avoid ear worms - because worms by the bowlful aren't a bundle of joy at the best of times - and in the present context? Ewww. Talk about carrying a metaphor too far, right? But, on the other hand, it gave me an idea.

At last, the creature turned to the me who's telling you this and began fondling whatever I now was in the most disturbing 'bad touch' manner imaginable. I'd seen enough hentai to know where this was going, so I was ready. (Okay, I lied. I've never seen any hentai. It seems creepy. Even by present standards. Just me, whistling past the graveyard, mutatis mutandis.)

With direct contact between the creature and me, we could now communicate, at least non-neuronal versions of communication. The creature flipped through my memories like a teenager flipping through an 'adult' magazine. (That's kind of like an iPad, but with static images on paper and bound together with staples. Adults used them before porn was invented. You can still see some in the better class of museum. But no hentai.)

The more shameful the memory, the happier the creature was. If I tried to hide something, it was like playing with a laser pointer before a cat. The creature dove right on it and savored my shame.

So it was that I laid a tasty, humiliating path of hidden indignity that led to a small, sequestered area, where I hinted that my utmost humiliation lay in wait. And when it ripped open the door to that area? Then, patient listener, my trap was sprung.

Playing in an endless loop was the ultimate weapon invented by humanity: Rick Astley's *Never Gonna Give You Up*.

Take that, you bastard. The earworm from Hell!

With a psychic scream that probably caused children to wake, breathless with horror, in the middle of the night back on Earth, the creature recoiled and fled into the dark from whence it had come, the notes of the chorus trailing behind it until they faded in the distance. (No, I have no idea how I was hearing them. If you figure it out, let me know.) If I'd had a mouth, and if it had finally stopped screaming, I would have smiled. As it was, I had to content myself with the notion that humans still ruled the space between the stars, and that alien horrors from beyond space and time trifled with mankind at their peril.

Which was all very satisfying until I realized I was now a disembodied something, orbiting a cloud of miscellaneous disassembled body parts, floating more than 100 astronomical units from Earth. The radio astronomers were going to hate that, particularly if the rest of the crew had suffered a similar fate.

So if you're still listening, and happen to be in the neighborhood, please stop by and give me a hand pulling my shit back together. I promise not to Rickroll you.

That would seem ungrateful.

Author's Notes

The phrase 'I had no mouth and could not scream' is a tip of the hat to Harlan Ellison's classic, *I Have No Mouth, and I Must Scream*. Best not read before bedtime, or indeed any time if you're not a big fan of insomnia. If Don Martin is before your time, Google his name plus Mona Lisa. In the unlikely event you haven't encountered it before, Rickrolling is an Internet 'bait and switch' meme, in which a Web site lures you to some promised payoff (e.g., cute kitten pictures) but instead delivers something else entirely - usually the Rick Astley song. (Which, to be honest, I kinda like. No shame here!) The ne plus ultra of Rickrolls was when BoingBoing linked to an article that explains why Rickrolling exhibited highly problematic 'dependence upon the semiotics of cisgendered discourse'.

Yeah, it was a meta-Rickroll:

https://boingboing.net/2015/05/28/rickrolling-is-sexist-racist.html

Consider yourself warned!

Pity the Penguins

M.S. Gardner

The time between dusk and dawn is the worst time for the penguins. The zoo keeper puts them in silk pajamas, purple with yellow polka dots and the penguins scuffle around, ashamed. For the penguins know this was not how their lives were supposed to be and they'd curse their parents if they could. Only they don't much remember their parents or, perhaps, their parents are gone or maybe suffered a similar fate at a similar zoo. Either way, it seems as if there has always been the zoo keeper and this enclosure with the piss warm water. And, as they slump about in their silk pajamas, red with gray stripes, they wonder if they really remember the cold, or if they had never actually felt icy Artic air, the bite of snow and sleet saturated winds. Instead it is just some ancestral residual memory and, when the zoo keeper brings them milk and cookies, they wonder if they had ever actually tasted a fish before - or if this, too, is a leftover memory - an instinct they have but can never really possess for themselves.

These are the dreams that haunt them as they lie awake in their little bunk beds under the itchy drab olive green woolen blankets, from dusk to dawn.

But, this time, the zoo keeper had gone too far. Those poor penguins. The wooly socks and silk pajamas had been extreme, yes ridiculous, and the boxer shorts had been humiliating and just a tad bit more than uncomfortable. But today it began to dawn on the penguins that the zoo keeper was not right in the head. Cookies and milk, canned sardines and ale and itchy woolen blankets on tiny bunk beds were all a bit much.

But today it was lederhosen. The zoo keeper dashed in with his hat askew and his plain brown tie knot pulled up all the way. In his arms were a dozen or more green and tan lederhosen, neatly hung on tiny hangers and the penguins did not resist. They did not know how to resist, as the zoo keeper scrunched their webbed feet into moss green wool socks and stiff brown boots and dark green velvet shorts pulled over their nonexistent bottoms. The leather suspenders kept slipping down because the penguins had no shoulders to rest suspenders on, but the zoo keeper was oblivious to this and the penguins did not know anything about lederhosen and suspenders so it mattered little to them that the suspenders hung limply at their sides like the skins of dead snakes. Except the penguins knew about as much of snakes as they did of suspenders, which was nothing at all. They shuffled along in their hard boots, making black scuff marks on the white and blue painted floor of their enclosure. Some of them tripped over the suspenders so often that they all finally decided to stand still and stare up into the stark robin egg blue sky and pray for the polar bears to come and eat them.

The penguins hoped beyond hope that it would work. They did not devise the plan themselves, indeed they had nothing to do with a plan at all. It was either serendipity, dumb luck, chance, coincidence, or perhaps Divine Providence. The hope they felt was not tangible, nor well-formed. They did not have the brain capacity for such thoughts. Rather, it may have been they picked up an awareness, or noticed the tedious tedium routine, the routine that ruled their lives, formed their meaning and existence, from the time they hatched in a hot house incubator without father or mother, was askew. Or, perhaps, it was the wooly socks they were forced to wear for the past fortnight. Itchy, prickly, poor quality woolen socks, knitted haphazardly by the zoo keeper in violent shades of puce, fuchsia, and bilious green. Knit one, purl two, with absolutely no thought of gauge, their webbed feet folded and rolled upon themselves and unnaturally forced into the itchy, hot, nasty wooly socks in magenta and chartreuse and violet. The zoo keeper's crazed knit two, purl one, increase one, knit two together.

The penguins would wonder, if they could ponder such things - but they couldn't - their minds numbed, erased, desensitized by the pale ice blue walls. Could they wonder, they would have speculated if the zoo keeper loved them too much, too violent a love which pressed too hard, too long. Or if the zoo keeper loathed, detested them and, as such, they were forced to endure the cruelty of nasty, hot, itchy wooly socks in colors of rust and orange and dead leaf green.

So when the plan, which wasn't really a plan but rather a poetic twist of irony or, perhaps, an act of Divine Providence executing righteous judgment against such unnatural acts inflicted upon them, happened, the penguins were initially hesitant, unprepared to seize the miracle that fell before them, like manna from the heavens in a rain of blessings. The zoo keeper entered their enclosure dancing a flamenco, dressed in drag, wearing an extravagant dress in red and black and layers upon layers of tulle, clenching a red rose by the stem in between his teeth - his lips painted a crimson red, his eyebrows plucked in thin arches, fake eyelashes fluttering in time to the samba music only he could hear inside his head. He carried brown paper shopping bags filled with miniature sombreros, tiny maracas, little woolen ponchos woven in red and white and green and a piñata filled with chocolate kisses and small dried anchovies. He minced across the enclosure, shiny patent leather dancing shoes clicking along, as his high heels tapped across the floor.

It was then that he tripped, his braceleted arms and fishnet hosed legs splayed out beneath him. His Spanish veil headpiece bounced off when his head hit the pale ice blue painted concrete and cracked open like an egg. His addled brains oozed out like broken egg yolk, his blood spilling, pooling, seeping and running down into the piss warm water tingeing it pink. Lipstick smeared across his face, one of his false eyelashes fell off.

The penguins weren't sure which one of them started first. Perhaps it was the one who pecked at the fallen eyelash, mistaking it for a millipede. Or maybe it was the one who snatched at the golden hoop earrings the zoo keeper wore in his lobes. Or maybe it was the one who gobbled the broken tooth that had flown out of the zoo keeper's mouth when his head hit the concrete, because it thought it was a fish egg, though none of the penguins had even eaten a fish egg before. But one of them was the first to taste the hot metallic twang of blood and soon all of the penguins scuffled over, their Birkenstocks sliding across the floor and their poorly knitted woolen socks sagging around their ankles, if they had any ankles, and supped on the zoo keeper.

The brains were soft, spongy, moist, and salty, his eyes gelatinous, the tender bits of face flesh so easy to peck and tear off in slender strips. When he had fallen, the piñata had broken, scattering silver foiled chocolate kisses and dried anchovies across the floor of the enclosure. The anchovies landed in the pools of blood, soaked up the viscous fluids and re-hydrated, until they became squishy and the penguins ate these as well. If the penguins could think such thoughts and speak to each other, or use sign language, or possess the ability to communicate telepathically, or could scrawl out messages in sticky blood ink, they would have all agreed they had just eaten the finest, best, most marvelous meal they had ever eaten in their entire lives, though they did not possess the conception of time, of seconds, minutes, hours, days, months, or years.

Once the penguins had eaten as much as their stomachs could hold and there wasn't much left of the zoo keeper that they could easily consume, as they did not have fangs and claws like the polar bears had, they all sat down and waited for the next thing to happen.

But nothing happened. No one came. And the penguins died.

Sugar Mice

Ishbelle Bee

It was the summer of 1863 and I was going to spend the school holidays with my Grandfather, Vezzibean Quick, a bad-tempered warlock. He resided in his ancestral home on the edges of the tiny rural village of Dot. The Quick family had lived in the dilapidated mansion for eight hundred years, acquiring a reputation as misanthropic eccentrics and avid practitioners of dark magiks. I was Vezzibean's only grandson and considered, due to my distinct lack of sorcery skills, a ghastly disappointment.

Grandad, adoring his solitude, rarely left the confines of his crumbling mansion with its sagging turrets and sunken observatory. His household staff were limited to two automatons, mail-ordered and constructed in New York, which he conjured into life upon their unboxing. One was given the role of housekeeper, tending to meals, laundry and cleaning. The other sufficed as a gardener, adept at pruning rose bushes and walloping poachers over the head with a garden shovel.

After a dreary seven-hour journey, bouncing about inside a carriage over English country roads, the surly coachman dropped me off at the village green of Dot - flinging my luggage roughly by my feet. The summer fete, with cake stalls, cricket match and sprightly Morris dancers, was in full swing. A pig's bladder was playfully bounced off my bottom as I passed.

I meandered towards my grandfather's home, relieved to be far away from my insane Geography Master, who lurked the school corridors at night wielding a leather bullwhip, which he cracked into the air with a shriek of delight at imaginary burglars.

As I stepped through the iron gates to Quick Manor, I spotted the automaton gardener digging up parsnips and flinging them into a wheelbarrow.

Grandpa was peering out of the wonky turret window.

"INSOLENT WHELP!" he shouted, "You have returned!"

I waved.

"Come inside." He curled a finger. "I have to speak to you,"

I located him in the dining room, sitting at the head of an oak table surrounded by flickering beeswax candles. He sported a heavy velvet robe of purple with a bronze tasseled belt - and I suspected he was wearing the curtains. Above the table a small iron cage dangled and, although it was empty, its occasional soft creak made me feel distinctly uneasy.

"While you were away, Percy," Grandad informed me. "There was an incident. I don't want to alarm you but it's rather serious,".

"Did you teleport the Vicar into the pond again?"

"No. I inadvertently blew up the housekeeper. It was a complete accident. I was recharging my black orb and it rolled off the dressing table and acted as a surprising electrical conductor for a random lightning bolt. The surge of power rebounded toward her whilst she was folding laundry and she exploded."

"I see. Have you ordered a replacement?"

"Yes, but there is something else dear boy."

"Go on."

He looked sheepish.

"The explosion also removed the back of the house, so your bedroom's gone. Sorry about that. The ping pong room and main staircase are reduced to rubble but you can ascend to the second floor by levitation or a garden ladder, which I have propped against the wall."

He tried to smile.

"I suppose I can sleep on the library sofa," I suggested.

"Yes, yes. The library remains quite intact. But alas, due to the now vast and unstable structural problems, the house may very well collapse at any moment. So be prepared to flee."

"Anything else?" I queried, a little suspicious.

"Yep," he stared blankly at me.

I waited.

"The powerful magical surge discharged from my black orb after bouncing off the housekeeper and various walls blasted its way through the floorboards into the basement."

I was worried now. Grandad twiddled his thumbs.

"As you know, buried under the house is the twelfth century sealed well of St Winifred of Woes, also known as a Backdoor to Hell."

"Is it open?" I panicked.

"You could say that."

A sudden high-pitched scream vibrated through the air, followed by manic laughter and a rubbery squeak. Grandad grasped my hand.

"My dear boy, we are in terrible danger. I should have trained you in the dark magiks but you never showed any interest or aptitude. Your skills have always been elsewhere. You're wonderful at ping pong and were always exceptional at making a walnut loaf."

"I'm assuming, in this particular situation, those skills are some-what useless." I cursed my proficiency at ping pong.

"I still need your help, Percy." Grandad looked desperate.

"Why don't we just run? Get as far away as possible?"

"If we leave now, we condemn the village of Dot to the horrors of Hell. They are good people, Percy. We cannot abandon them."

"Even the Morris Dancing team?"

"There's always an exception to the rule."

"Has something from the *hole* emerged? Have you seen anything?"

"I had a brief conversation with a ten-foot green devil on the re-mains of the landing."

"Was it constructive?"

"No. He informed me he wanted to eat my feet. He said he had a pet name for humans. Liked to call us his 'sugar mice.' I had to teleport myself into the outdoor privy to escape."

"Why does he call us 'sugar mice'?" I queried.

"I suppose devils regard us as sweeties," he gulped. "I think it's best, since you have no abilities as a dark conjurer, that you should use this."

He handed me a cricket bat from under the table.

"You want me to smack demonic entities over the head?"

"Precisely dear boy. Give them a good wallop while I attempt to shut the back door to Hell."

I gave the bat a test swing.

"Are you ready?" he asked.

"Yes Grandad. I'm ready."

Together, we headed out of the dining room towards the kitchen. The downstairs toilet had sunk into the floor and we had to wobble precariously over planks of wood.

A whoosh of bats materialized between the cracks, zipping out through a window.

Grandpa booted open the library door and I leapt inside, cricket bat held aloft. I was surprised to see the green devil relaxed in a leather armchair engrossed in a novel- *The Passion of Widow Twilley* by Baroness Gump.

Perched on the spinning globe sat a red raven who cawed mischievously.

The devil's yellow eyes peered over the book, staring at us with horrific intensity. His thick horns twisted like tree roots into spirals. Closing the tome and placing it on the reading table, he grinned, revealing a row of scissor fangs.

"I shall have to suspend the passions of Widow Twilley, little sugar mice. Do come and sit with me. We can have a *chat*."

The raven cackled, its blood-coloured wings ruffling.

I thought it was ill advised to try smacking him over the head straight away and wondered if I could sneak up behind him at a more opportune moment.

"Not advisable," the devil smiled. "I would be really rather upset if you walloped me. I'm rarely surprised or anxious, although I find tripe deeply upsetting."

How annoying that he could read my mind.

"Yes, it must be very irritating for you." His grin was fixed. Grandad moved in-front of me.

"Devil. Your presence is unwanted. I command you to leave. Also, for your information, my feet are completely inedible."

"Why are you wearing a curtain?" the creature arched an eyebrow, "Do you not own any trousers?"

"HOW DARE YOU!" shrieked Grandad, grabbing a tropical spiked pot plant. "Shove THIS up your arse!"

"I will take your suggestion under advisement," the devil stuck out the tip of his tongue and whistled. The raven flew over and perched on his shoulder, cackling,

"Isn't he gorgeous? I call him Sweetmeats."

Enraged, Grandad shouted an incantation, conjuring a purple mist which oozed from the cracks in the floorboards beneath his feet, swirling in hoops about his legs, weaving and enclosing sparks of energy.

The monster yawned and clicked his fingers. The floor beneath my grandad collapsed and he disappeared, screaming, into the hole.

I leapt over the sofa and smacked the devil with the cricket bat. Completely unaffected he glared at me with mild disdain.

I bounced the bat off his head again.

"Seriously?" he exclaimed.

I twatted him thrice with the bat!

He swatted me with the back of his claw, the power of which propelled me, at alarming speed, into the bookshelf. The books wobbled, landed on top of me and I fell into unconsciousness.

I awoke dangling in the cage over our dining room table. Grandpa lay underneath, bound by thick ropes, an apple stuffed into his mouth. About him was a selection of fruits, elaborate garnishes of crimson berries and a sculpted cucumber canoe. The green devil, with the pet perched on one of his horns, sat at the head of the table uncorking a bottle of claret.

"HELP! HELP! HELP! HEEEEEEEEEELP!!!" I screamed.

A banana hit me in the face.

"SILENCE STUPID HUMAN!" the devil commanded. "Or I shall be forced to throw a coconut."

A pair of gardening sheers zoomed past me and sunk deep into one of the devil's horns.

"WHAT THE HELL?"

Leaping through a window, the automaton gardener performed a series of dazzling high kicks and karate chops in front of the confused creature.

The devil picked him up by the scruff of his neck and flung him back outside.

Undeterred, the automaton gardener, with a warrior cry, threw himself back through window, karate chopping the air.

"STOP IT!" cried the devil, "You're making a prat of yourself."

The automaton, balancing on one leg, kick-flicked himself into a somersault, landing on the other leg.

"What was the fucking point of that exactly?" The agitated devil demanded. Grabbing the aggressor, he booted him violently up the backside. The automaton flew, with the speed of a rocket, through the wall and continued another half a mile into the garden, landing head first in the shrubbery.

There was a low rumbling sound as the walls of the house wobbled - its structure trembling on the verge of collapse.

Grandpa spat the apple out of his mouth and quickly muttered something.

I was teleported onto the lawn with Grandad grasping me by my ankles.

The house fell apart into a mass of rubble.

Grandpa zapped off his ropes using a magic incantation and smiled with relief.

"Phew. That was close."

"What do we do now?" I noticed the heels of the gardener sticking out from the shrubbery.

"Technically, the backdoor to Hell is still open," Grandad said. "But that devil, for the moment, is squashed flat."

Together we pulled the gardener from the bush, straightening him out with a few thwacks from the garden shovel and propping him against a tree.

"I must now prepare a complex ritual to close the well of St Winifred of the Woes," Grandad announced soberly, hitching up his robe, which was starting to fall off.

"Is there anything I can do?" I offered dutifully.

"No, no, no, Percy. This is something I can only achieve alone. It will require a lengthy meditation and several hours of monotonous chanting, before gathering rare fungi under moonlight in the woodlands, which must be harvested in the ancient appropriate way before being stewed. Afterwards, I will bathe in the juices to purify my aura and offer thanks to the woodlands and moon for their support in my quest. Finally, I have to perform a freestyle jig on a ley line."

He looked at me wearily

"Fuck it. Let's just get the hell out of here. I really cannot be arsed."

Cherry Bomb

Jan-Andrew Henderson

Austin, Texas 1996

The Cherry Bomb killed children. Cute, pint-size, little children. Then he hid them in people's cars. It created a nice double victim scenario.

Pepe Pineda was the owner of Janet's Eatery on 32nd and Guadalupe. A stocky, unassuming second-generation Mexican immigrant, he looked like a cross between Sitting Bull and Bob Hope.

On Sunday at 9.00 am, he walked, yawning, from the early morning bustle of his restaurant and slid into his car, easing gingerly over the scalding seat leather. Starting the engine, he maneuvered between the slumbering vehicles in the parking lot, squinting sleepily at the low-slung sun. He bumped over the balding grass verge and onto the slip road between his property and the neighbouring Posthouse Bar. As he shifted gears, his old Lincoln Mercury died.

Now there were two dead things in the alley.

Mr. Pineda climbed out of the car in the face-stinging heat and lifted the bonnet. An oily scrap of card, torn from a milk carton, hung lifeless on the radiator cap.

Oops! Look in the trunk....

Pepe Pineda spat. He circled the Mercury and read the note again. Shit. What the fuck was this?

213

He warily unlocked the trunk of the car. It was stiff. He felt a stab of fear followed by a pang of hunger. Hunger won.

Standing to one side, Pineda leaned over, pulled up the cover and skipped quickly back.

A tattered, fleshy snake shot, glistening, into the air. The shaken driver later likened it to a giant Chinese firecracker, splintering into a thousand silent sparks. The sparks showered Pepe Pineda, turning his sweat-soaked shirt red.

It was blood.

Bobbing in front of him was the body of Kimberly-Anne Thackery, a ten-year-old abducted from Northwest Hills the day before. She had lain all night inside the sweltering Mercury, attached to the lock mechanism by a hook and wire apparatus. When the hood flew up, it pulled Kimberly-Anne's intestines out through the razored slash in her stomach.

Pepe Pineda was hospitalised for shock.

One of the witnesses, eating breakfast in Pepe's restaurant, was a tall consumptive diner called Brett Parker. Parker was a part-time local DJ, playing smoky jazz on K-NAC from ten till midnight. That evening, in the murky studio, he told his story over the air. Ash fell like a glow-worm from his cigarette.

"When I seen that kid's insides fly up in the air... it looked like some kind o' terrible cherry bomb," he rasped laconically, languishing in his fifteen minutes of real limelight.

And, suddenly, the killer had a name.

That was the basic pattern of the slayings. A month later, another car broke down at Round Rock. The driver got out, lifted the hood and found a similar note. Knowing of the Pineda case, he faced a choice. He could open the trunk and pray the message was an adolescent hoax, or he could call the cops and risk losing time and looking stupid.

He went through the usual process of self-denial.

It can't happen to me, he thought. *I'm too busy to have a dead kid in my car.*

He opened the trunk and found the cheapness of human life displayed in a pool of congealing blood.

Three weeks later, the same thing happened to a motorist on Hayes Boulevard in west Austin.

The fourth and fifth casualties fell prey to a new strategy. Both suffered wheel problems and went straight to the back of the car to get a spare or tyre iron. Inside, each driver found his very own dead child.

The patrol car always arrived with siren clamouring and lights whirling but the white-lipped driver was no longer in any particular hurry. He would be standing at the roadside, perhaps smoking a cigarette, crying bitterly in the crisp morning air.

Commuters went through an agony of indecision each time they ran out of gas or saw their engine overheat. The Triple-A became so popular they could have built bigger offices. The Austin Police Department, on the other hand, grew jumpy and irritable. The victims were random strangers, neither deserving nor undeserving. The body count was relatively low compared to a highway pile-up or tornado, but the primal fears aroused were much deeper.

Frightened parents began keeping their kids home from school and spied on them at play from behind cracks in the curtain. Out there roamed the bogeyman. The stuff of legend. This guy was killing kids. Little fucking kids.

And he wasn't leaving any clues.

The absence of leads haunted Detective Ettrick Sinclair. He was new to the Austin Police Department and wanted to prove his worth. He had a dozen theories and not one was heading anywhere concrete. Still, he clung to the belief that his enthusiasm could make up for the tired cynicism of the dozen experienced detectives now working on the killings.

Besides, the Cherry Bomb had started off as *his* case. He had responded to Pepe Pineda's original call and that made him the primary on the Kim Thackery murder. But his Captain had panicked and replaced Ettrick when department big-wigs realized what they were dealing with. There was no way a rookie would be allowed to head up an investigation this size. Politicians and newspapers would soon be screaming for results and pointing fingers if they didn't get them quickly enough. Instead, the Cherry Bomb case was assigned to Grimm and Scharges, the department's most experienced detectives. Their *best* detectives.

Ettrick had fumed for hours at that. He had nothing against Grimm but, in his opinion, Scharges was a corrupt Neanderthal dick. Got where he was by kissing ass and beating convictions out of perps who were probably innocent.

Well... fuck him.

Each day and each hour he had to himself, Ettrick worked on the killings. He assembled every conceivable bite of information about Cherry Bomb he could beg, steal or con. When he took a rare coffee break, the doughnuts reminded him of car tires and the bites were wounded flesh.

No matter how irrelevant a detail seemed, Ettrick chased it up and wrote it down. He showed up on the doorsteps of traumatized drivers. He ranged for miles questioning the shattered relatives of the dead children. He talked to any onlooker who would talk back. He was everywhere, a wiry powerhouse in denim jeans and white t-shirt. Asking and asking and asking ...

In the locker room, Scharges joked snidely that 'Sinclair would crawl up a guy's butt crack just to see what he had for lunch'.

Ettrick ignored him. His superiors frowned on this one-man crusade, but what could they say? The legitimate investigation wasn't doing any better and the press and public were wired to fever pitch. But the other cops were pissed off by his zeal and his wife, Madison, was particularly disgruntled.

"I'm tired of my life being full of broken appointments and constant interruptions," she moaned. "I don't wanna be wakened at three in the morning so you can go chase a lead. We got no friends and don't have fun these days. I know more about these dead kids than you do about your own live one."

"You gotta give me time!" Ettrick retorted. "You're always saying how, if you'd worked harder at your old job, we'd be rich by now. Well, this is my chance to get somewhere. You should be glad I'm so Goddamned dedicated. It's gonna take dedication but it's our ticket to success."

"Your ticket."

"My ticket. Our ticket. Look, it's just this one case! After that, I'm established. Hell, I'll be around so much, you'll wish I was dead."

Madison accepted this. She knew she'd failed in her own vocation. Years ago, she'd fled from her boring but promising white-collar job and lost herself to the dream of becoming an artist. It was the same kind of nebulous hankering that plunged her into marriage with a poor but handsome, no-frills cop.

Success had eluded her and the pull of middle-class safety had grown stronger every year. Now she was back in the rat race, working in advertising, hauling herself grimly up the lower rungs of a corporate ladder she could have ascended years ago.

Her dream had faded. Lack of commercial reward in both her chosen and necessary endeavours fuelled her frustration until it tainted every plane of her life.

She couldn't honestly begrudge Ettrick his chance. Besides, she was mad about him.

And catching Cherry Bomb might get him promoted to a nice safe desk job.

Ettrick Sinclair's problem was not his wife, nor the rest of the police force. They'd all come around if he cracked the case. It was the fact that his self-assurance was taking a career-ending nosedive. He didn't dare show it, but felt he'd staked everything on a first reckless dash up a slope, slick with easily crushed ambition.

And he was absolutely stumped.

The detective was sure he had collected enough information. He just wasn't doing the right things with it. He needed help. An expert to go over the facts with him. Someone whose brain could spawn the leaps in logic his own mind couldn't muster. The Austin police, in their desperation, were dabbling in everything from outside profilers to psychics. It wasn't doing them any good either.

Ettrick needed his own medium.

What the hell. He'd go get himself one.

The detective dug out the telephone directory and wrote down a list of analysts in the private sector. He began sending them emails. Then he made telephone calls. Tried to get the masters interested in tinkering with the mechanism of a mind that killed children. And many *were* fascinated - but not for less than $200 an hour.

"We would do it for nothing," they pondered, nibbling their Ralph Lauren, wire-rimmed glasses. "But... You take one case like this for free, you'll always be expected to do it. It's the principle."

"Why should those bastards care?" Ettrick grumped to Madison whenever he managed to get home. "There's no way a psychopath's ever gonna bump any of them off. One of those head-shrinkers most likely has the fucking Cherry Bomb as a patient. Probably trying to get him a job as a shower attendant in some children's home. With a garage next door."

The next day he got a call from R.D. Slaither.

"I hear you need help catching the notorious Cherry Bomb killer." A happy Scottish voice sang down the telephone. "Overheard some of my acquaintances discussing it over lunch. My name's R.D. Slaither and I'd like to offer my services."

"You're a psychiatrist?"

"Analyst. Got a bunch of initials after my name the length of an alligator sausage, to use one of your fine colloquial phrases. Actually, that's not true, but I'm awful good. I used to work in partnership with Justin Moore."

The detective liked the sound of R.D. Slaither immediately. Ettrick's grandfather had come from the Scottish borders, hence his own exotic name. R.D.'s down-to-earth speech smacked pleasantly of an unexplored past.

"Justin Moore. I would know him?"

"Probably not." The disembodied voice sounded unperturbed. "But he was a true innovator in the treatment of clinical depression a few years back before he... eh... retired. Look us up in an old *Who's Who.*"

Ettrick was suitably impressed. He mentally crossed his fingers and gave R.D. the bad news.

"This is a private investigation," he volunteered sadly. "The police won't pay you and I sure as shit can't... S'cuse my language."

"Not at all. To be honest with you, I'm calling because I'm a wee bit bored. None of my patients are loopy enough. I need a challenge. An adventure, if you like."

His inflection dipped conspiratorially.

"Cherry Bomb fascinates me. As far as I can see, you're after a very, very clever man. Apart from one serious psychological flaw."

"A tendency to kill children?" Ettrick added dryly. "Uh... yeah, funny, that's what the police shrink said."

"If he was any good, he wouldn't be working for the police. You need me. Plus, Detective Sinclair, I happen to have a great aversion to children dying in cars. It's just a quirk I've got."

Ettrick stayed mum, holding his breath.

"I have some ideas I'd like to discuss," said the voice. "I thought we might meet for a drink tomorrow night."

Ettrick pictured them both sipping daiquiris in *Les Amis*, over on the Guadalupe Drag. He pictured a canny silver-haired Scot, a twinkle in his wrinkled old eye and a kilt barely covering his knees.

"Drink?" Ettrick interrupted. "Shit! You just got yourself a dinner invitation."

When the detective arrived home, he found Madison sitting on his study floor, weeping over an island of spiral notebooks. Her polished black fringe dripped mournfully onto the paper. His elation quickly deflating, Ettrick scurried overo.

"What's wrong, honey? What are you crying for?"

He knelt beside the huddled figure, pushing his fingers awkwardly through her hair, trying to shuffle her emotions back in order. Across the wall, blown-up photographs of Cherry Bomb's five victims leered in eternal frothy joy - a rogue's gallery of wispy hair and missing teeth.

"Oh, just the usual," she sniffed with tearful sarcasm. "Thinking. Thinking how I work in an ad agency and try to fool people into buying my shit. How in my spare time, I paint God-awful pictures and try to fool people into buying my shit. Then I think about how you work full time at catching child killers. How in your spare time you work at catching child killers."

Her mouth crumpled.

"At least you're doing something meaningful. Even if you're failing."

"We'll both succeed in the end," Ettrick protested, trying to project the correct amount of sympathy. He knew better than to try turning Madison's mountains into molehills, or to attempt cheering her up by pointing out the good things she had. Like a husband who loved her to pieces.

Instead, the detective suffered miserably by her side, an ineffectual scarecrow for her fears.

"I'm sorry. I'm really sorry." Madison gestured at the walls. "It sometimes seems the whole world is turning to crap out there, but only we've got a little fucking showroom displaying it in our house."

"What are you doing in here, anyhow?"

"I was cleaning."

"You were being morbid. You never clean this room."

The tears vanished.

"I do so!" she barked. "Maybe if you were around to notice."

Ettrick felt his temper rise. That wasn't what he meant. She *knew* that wasn't what he meant. How come she never took the time to map the good intentions behind his words? The temptation to snap at her hung like a sour green apple. He let it drop this time.

"Look," he took her in his arms. "I don't give a flying fuck how often you vacuum the damned study. I don't like to see you upset, is all."

Madison glowered at him from the depths of her dark, dark eyes. The balance swung. Ettrick fell deeply in love again, as he always did and always would.

"I'm sorry." He hugged her tight, forcing a gasp from her pouting lips. To his surprise, Madison laughed.

"At least you don't have a picture of your own son in here."

"That would be tasteless, honey," Ettrick smiled.

But he knew one more harsh phrase now echoed in the canyon. Another drop of water pushed against the dam. He'd better solve this fucking case soon.

"I'm sorry too," said Madison. "I'm just feeling low."

"In that case, I got pretty good news." Ettrick grinned wider. "We have an analyst coming to dinner. A real, live looney-link fixer."

"Really?"

"Says he's the best."

Madison wrinkled her nose doubtfully. Ettrick eyed the dozens of folders, files and notes jigsawed into every corner of the room.

"If he's right," he coaxed slyly. "All this will go."

"He's got a truck?"

"Make him something nice. Huh?"

Ettrick turned from the window and lit a Marlboro. The incoming light bled him of colour, a living bookend to a string of sun-faded photographs, dealing in death.

He didn't remember much about his own childhood. Nothing too terrible had ever happened to him, that he could recall. His parents had died when he was a teenager and weren't around to administer familial warnings. Not there to talk him out of doing anything stupid or dangerous, like becoming a cop in Texas.

Ettrick exhaled a worm of smoke. He could hear the soft sighs of his own infant son over the intercom system connecting their rooms.

"When's this guy coming?" In her mind, Madison was already opening cookbooks and culling after-dinner topics, enthused at the prospect of proper intellectual conversation. She'd quickly abandoned attempted cultural forays with Ettrick's colleagues when one referred to modern art as 'whut wimmin and fags were into'.

"What do analysts like to eat, anyhow?"

"Food for thought, hopefully."

Ettrick absently stubbed out his cigarette and pulled down the blind.

The detective was a thorough, methodical man. He tried to be spontaneous for Madison but common sense pretty much ruled his life. He figured he was just a normal guy doing a captivating job. Exciting things happening to him, not because of him.

He liked the sound of R.D. Slaither but that didn't mean he wasn't going to snoop a little.

Robert Duncan Slaither had a Ph.D. in Psychology from Edinburgh University in Scotland. That was promising. He advertised himself as a therapist but was not a member of the Texas Medical Association. That wasn't so hot. Maybe it was because he was Scottish. Perhaps it was because he wasn't very good, after all.

Ettrick went to scope out his potential ally's place of business. Slaither rented an office on 5th Street, up near the river. It wasn't the most up-market locale in town but was no slum either.

He remembered R.D.'s reference to an ex-partner, Justin Moore. A direction shaper on the field of clinical depression. That's what the analyst had called him.

He picked up the telephone and dialled. Madison answered.

"Hello, Possum-Pig," Ettrick smooched, glancing around the squalid, heavily populated squad room. Someday a detective like Grimm or Scharges would overhear how he talked to his wife, take him out back and shoot him.

"Hi, baby," Madison answered cheerfully.

"Listen, you got a big old bookstore next to your agency, don't you? Could you do me a favour? Could you drop in during your lunch hour and get me something?"

The next day was Sunday. Ettrick surprised Madison eating Frito pie and strudel in the early afternoon. He solidified in the sun-speckled kitchen door and rambled between the hanging plants. Their big black cat, Boo, swiped at him lazily from the top of the fridge. Ettrick left his baseball cap tangled in the hairy paws and continued on to the sink.

Madison sat at the back of the room, holding a coffee and admiring the copper wiriness of her husband's small body, insulated from her stare by his usual tight white t-shirt and faded 501 jeans. Ettrick made himself a fruit tea, unaware of the attention, watching the steam blebbing on wet Yucca leaves.

"What's on your mind, shorty?" Madison asked.

"This R.D. Slaither. Gave me a man called Justin Moore as a reference. Said he was once a big deal in the medical field."

"And."

"I called some of those psychiatrists back. Y'know?" Ettrick sauntered over to the table. "The ones I talked to earlier?"

"The shitheads?"

"Yeah," he grinned. "Anyhow, only three of them would speak to me without getting my fucking credit card number first. I asked them if they'd ever heard of a scientist called Justin Moore. Or a guy called R.D. Slaither."

"Had they?"

"Sort of, but…" Ettrick rubbed his hat-head. "They were so vague. Can I have a piece of that strudel?"

"Sure, porky." Madison slid the plate across. Ettrick took the pastry, but not the bait.

"Two of them said they remembered a scientist named Moore. He did neurological research, a few years back, for the Daler Corporation. They've no idea where he is now."

"Swell. And the third?"

"Said that Slaither and Moore left the company under a bit of a cloud. Their work was 'all smoke and no fire' according to this guy."

"Professional jealousy?"

"Could be. Apparently, their research was cancelled after there was some scandal surrounding their team - but I couldn't get any more details. You know how these types stick together."

Ettrick pushed a hunk of strudel into his mouth and wiped crumbs from the corners of a frown.

"I want a criminal psychologist, sure. But not a *criminal* psychologist. I can't even find mention of him or Justin Moore on the web."

Madison put down her piece of pie and gave a big brown grin.

"Guess I'll have to save your old sleuthy butt," she beamed

"Sleuthy butt?"

His wife dipped into the shoulder bag below the table and pulled out a thick, paper-backed volume.

"I asked the woman in the bookstore. She said this was what you were looking for." Madison handed it to him with a stern look. "It cost me $55. In paperback!"

"An *American Medical Compendium* from 2000. They *had* one of these?"

"Who was gonna buy it?"

Ettrick attacked the book, scattering morsels and bending pages.

"Matthews. Mellick. Mitusch..." His eyes thumbed down the page. "Here he is ... Justin Moore."

Madison scuffled around the table to get a better view. Ettrick could almost feel the softness of her face, even from feet away. He smiled, despite himself, simply because she was there.

He began to read.

"Moore. Justin Fenton. Got his M.D. at Johns Hopkins. Resident at Walter Reid. At the time this book was compiled, he was with the Daler Corporation doing neurological research. Working on a system to combat clinical depression and psychosis using an experimental system of retroviral drugs intended to stimulate dendritic growth in the brain." Ettrick shook his head. "Means nothing to me."

"Keep going," his wife urged.

"Moore's 'Cocktail' produced extremely positive results when tested on animals. How can you tell if an animal is depressed?"

Madison nudged him and he carried on.

"Moore was short-listed for the B.R. Clanton prize for advances in the field of Biology... Shit!" Ettrick slammed the book shut. "Don't sound like all smoke and no fire to me. I wonder what the hell happened to him?"

"I looked up Slaither and he's not in there." Madison smiled. "So I checked the web too. Took me a while but I finally found one entry by some freelance hack. This guy R.D.? He was Moore's second in command at Daler. When the project collapsed, he was in charge of PR and eh... financial allocations. Apparently, he was suspected of dipping into the funds, though it was never proved. The writer claimed the Daler Corporation hushed it up but didn't offer any real evidence."

"Well, that's just great."

Madison leant close to Ettrick's ear. He noted with pleasure how her milky lambency pitted against his olive hue.

"Just cause he's a tad dishonest don't mean he's stupid," she whispered. "Let's set a thief to catch a thief."

"We're not after a thief. We're after a child killer."

"Well, if he turns out to have killed any kids, he's not getting into the house." Madison began putting the rest of the dessert back in the fridge.

"I don't care how smart he is."

R.D. Slaither turned up next day, wearing a single-breasted jet black suit and matching sunglasses. Madison loitered by the window in her own simple black dress, lips glossy red and short hair shining. Hearing a vehicle draw up and a car door slam, she peeked round the sill and jumped back with a squeal.

"You didn't tell me he was one of the Blues Brothers." Her mouth shaped a glistening O.

Ettrick hung warily on the other side of the window, watching his guest walk uncertainly towards the house. R.D. Slaither was a stocky man, short, with an almost military crewcut. He removed the sunglasses and sad, sleepy pond-green eyes laughed in his oddly handsome face.

Ettrick looked down and gave a chuckle.

Two bulging Circle-K carrier bags hung like fat plastic tears from each of Slaither's arms, the seductive outline of beer bottles moulding each sack.

Madison jerked open the front door in time to catch R.D. pressing the buzzer with his nose. He jerked his head away and the bags clinked together, an alcoholic Newton's Cradle that threatened to swing him back down the porch steps.

"Eh... hello," he twitched awkwardly.

Madison opened the door wider, ushering the man inside.

"You look like you're here to get us drunk!" she laughed.

"Eh..." R.D. shrugged. "Aye... sort of." He plunked his burden down in the hall and shook Ettrick's hand.

"You must be detective Sinclair." Smiling breathlessly.

"Ettrick. Yeah, that's me." The detective had expected some aged academic, but R.D. looked to be in his late forties and his buoyant, boyish manner projected the image of an even younger man. He wiped perspiration from his forehead with a black sleeve.

"I kind of thought... Well... If I end up working with you - and hopefully I will - I might be here quite a lot of the time... If that's all right with you, Mrs. Sinclair?"

"Sure, it's fine. And call me Madison."

"The thing is, I'm quite a shy person till you get to know me, and this is a sort of traditional Caledonian way of breaking the ice. It's called getting pished."

He waved at the bags.

"Circle-K didn't have much in the way of fine wines, hope you don't mind. I assumed you both drank since you're a detective and you're a detective's wife. But I can polish them off myself. After all, I'm Scottish. It's expected."

Ettrick opened his mouth. Finding no more fault than reason in his guest's deliberations, he shut it again. Madison probed the plastic bags.

"Rolling Rock and Mickey's Big Mouth?"

"I only drink out of green or brown bottles. It's a phobia. Agricultophobia, I think it's called. Reminds me of the rolling hills of home or something like that." R.D. pursed his lips rationally. "Even though I grew up in Edinburgh."

His face morphed into self-mockery. He seemed satisfied that he'd managed to say something amusing and relaxed a little.

Ettrick, casting a professional eye, was impressed. Though R.D.'s charm was being laid on with a trowel, he was making a sincere effort to be an agreeable dinner guest and that was appreciated.

Madison patted his arm, sharing her husband's sentiment.

"I like him, Ettrick. Can we keep him?"

And she led R.D., bags clinking, into the dining room.

They got drunk with a vengeance. The evening started as a functional thing, then mutated into a miniature party. Talk about the killings slowly turned to a wide-ranging discussion, the conversation coasting easily away from Cherry Bomb and up other alleyways of existence.

R.D. Slaither turned out to be eloquent and likeably comic. He drank like a fish and seemed to be having a fine old time. Ettrick was also enjoying himself. For a whole ten minutes, he hadn't thought about the case. He glanced over at his wife as she happily poured more drinks, delighting in the gangly elegance which perfectly complimented his own slim build. Madison spotted Ettrick's appreciative look and brushed at her hair self-consciously, a primed, easy laugh buzzing between her teeth.

R.D. caught the noise, his eyes browsing from one sozzled host to the other.

"You look like wee human salt and pepper shakers," he slurred. "That's nice." He took a hefty swig of Rolling Rock. "I was married once, too. My wife left, though."

"It happens." Ettrick tried to coast over the subject. He found that his conciliatory reserves got used up at work.

"Any kids?" Madison asked.

"One." R.D. scratched his cheek. "He died a few years ago, when he was two. In a car crash."

He smiled wanly.

"I was driving."

There was an embarrassed silence. Out in the street, a vehicle's horn sobbed twice.

"Oh," Madison said quietly. "I'm truly sorry."

"Is that why you're helping us?" Ettrick was tactlessly curious, a Pavlovian response to any statement about sudden death. Besides, he had done more checking and already knew about the accident.

"You said 'us' instead of 'me'. That's nice too." For a stuttering second, a lost look slid down R.D.'s face. Then it was gone.

"I don't want to go into how I feel about my kid's death," he stated matter-of-factly. "But, if I can save someone else's child, it'll go a long way to putting my mind at ease... know what I mean?"

He stood up to get another beer, signalling the termination of that particular topic.

"I'm sure it will." Madison let R.D. vanish into the kitchen, then scooted Ettrick a look of mortification. The detective had on his poker face. Madison touched the rim of the glass with her teeth. When the analyst came back into the room, she turned in her chair.

"Would you like to see our boy? You won't wake him. He sleeps like a log."

R.D. halted in mid-slope. He looked surprised then absurdly pleased.

"Yes... Thanks, I would." He glanced at Ettrick to check if he was being too familiar.

"Y'all go ahead. I've seen him plenty."

Ettrick took a long drag on his Marlboro, watching Madison and R.D. drunkenly ascending the stairs to his son's bedroom. They got along well. That was good. Now he was ready. Now things were going to move along. He felt confident.

He decided not to mention to Madison the fact that R.D. had been speeding.

It looked like he was being punished enough.

In the days that followed, Ettrick and R.D. began digesting the smorgasbord of information the detective had put together. As partners in solving crime, they discovered then accepted each other foibles comfortably. The psychologist appreciated Ettrick's foul-mouthed dryness and marvelled at his identical white t-shirt collection. The detective enjoyed R.D.'s stories about his chequered past, partly because they didn't consist entirely of murder, rape and robbery, like everyone else he worked with.

The analyst, it seemed, had an amusing anecdote tailored for every occasion. Yet, if the conversation ever touched on his wife or child, he would slide the subject adroitly under the table.

Ettrick respected his partner's privacy. Their relationship wasn't the kind that prompted emotional sandblasting. Besides, the detective was too engrossed with the Cherry Bomb investigation to waste time prying into his ally's psyche.

A new enthusiasm pervaded the Sinclair household. Madison cheerfully provided Ettrick with moral support and R.D. was handed a continual supply of beer in dull-coloured bottles. In return, their new partner shared baby-minding duties to help out the exhausted parents. He would lie on the floor with seventeen-month-old Frankie Sinclair and make endless faces at the bemused child, allowing Ettrick and Madison to eat the occasional meal in peace. When all three were busy, Madison would give one of the local teenagers a few dollars to keep an eye on the diminutive whirlwind.

Finally, R.D. suggested he help pay for a permanent babysitter. Ettrick and Madison gaped at him.

"Every time I come here, there's a different gum-chewing nymphet sprawled on the couch watching soaps. Women that age make it hard for me to concentrate." He brushed away the Sinclair's half-protests. "I got the very person. Besides, the wee one's getting on my nerves."

Ettrick and Madison knew that wasn't true. R.D. and Frankie would sit for a solid hour playing Poke-Eye or reading *Peter Pan*.

"That's a bit advanced for a kid his age," Ettrick had remarked.

"All children should know the classics of Scots literature," the analyst retorted. "After this, we're moving on to *Dr. Jekyll and Mr. Hyde*."

The Sinclairs allowed themselves to be outmanoeuvred. They figured R.D. wanted their son to have the things his own child would never enjoy and they certainly couldn't afford a proper nanny. Touched, they accepted his help.

R.D. wasted no time. He turned up next day with Meike, a politely remote Scandinavian. She appeared supremely competent, though only the analyst possessed the ability to make her smile.

"She's not a patient of yours, is she?" Madison whispered.

"Certainly not!" R.D. retorted. "She's my... eh... niece."

Ettrick coughed loudly into his glass of Coke.

At first, Madison treated Meike with veiled suspicion but Frankie seemed completely at ease with his silent sentinel and Ettrick appeared indifferent to her presence.

"She's too boring for me and not nearly as pretty as you," he told his scowling wife, once the Garbo-esque Meike had withdrawn to the spare room out back. "R.D.'s right. This will give us some real time together."

"I don't know."

Ettrick had picked up a little psychology from his new friend.

"Look at all the extra opportunities you'll have to paint," he enthused.

From then on, Meike drifted round the house, distant as a ghost but far more efficient.

R.D. and Ettrick smoked furiously in the study.

"The first killing is the key." The detective said, at last.

"Why?"

"It always is. Plus, it's the one where I have absolute first-hand knowledge. I was there minutes after Kim Thackery's body was discovered. I called the back-ups. I interviewed everyone at Janet's restaurant. It was my case."

"You're pretty annoyed at getting ditched."

"You bet your ass I am. Didn't do those fuckers at the station a helluva lot of good dumping me, did it?"

He pulled a wad of notes from under a pile of Genesee Pale Ale bottles.

"I was all over that fucking crime scene. I searched every inch of Pineda's car. I damned near crawled round the parking lot with a magnifying glass."

"You had a hunch this was going to be something big?"

"Hell no. I don't get hunches. I'm just good at my job." Ettrick looked moodily across the study desk. "Then there was a second and a third killing and I knew that bastard was gonna be my big break. I was there. When someone kills over and over, the first killing is always the key."

"The next four breakdowns." R.D. picked up his pocket recorder. "Did you get to the scene as quickly on any other occasion?"

"The second murder, I was too far away. After that, they took me off the case and that made it even harder. Fourth and fifth, I was there within, say... an hour each time."

"An hour?" R.D. grimaced.

"I aint the fucking Flash, for Chrissake! I moved as quick as I could. I even bought a C.B. radio so I could pick up police broadcasts in my bedroom."

"That must do wonders for your sex life."

Ettrick gave R.D. a withering look.

"The third kid killed, though? I was on the scene within ten minutes. Fuck... I was there before Grimm and Scharges."

R.D. glanced sideways at the detective.

"Which one of your parents wouldn't let you swear when you were a kid?" He nonchalantly lit another cigarette.

"What are you talking about?" Ettrick's beer paused on the way to his lips. "I'm an orphan."

"Nothing," the analyst said sheepishly. "I saw it in a play once."

He rewound his recorder and stood up.

"Let's go back to the Pineda/Thackery case. You're right, the original murder might well be the most important. If it was the first time Cherry Bomb killed, there's a greater chance of him screwing it up. And let's not assume it's a *he*. Could be a she."

"I know that. I'm the fucking detective."

"Is there anything different about that killing? Something clumsy? Something Cherry Bomb might have refined once he got into the swing of things?"

"Hah! You called him 'he' again," Ettrick pointed out.

"Excuse me. Are we trying to catch a mass murderer, or is this the *Abbott and Costello Show*?"

"Sorry." Ettrick thumbed through a report sheet. "There are a couple of major differences between the first and subsequent killings. This guy obviously knows cars, right? The department's already investigating previous offenders working as mechanics. But shit, I figure it's more likely he's a talented amateur."

"I concur," R.D. nodded. "Mainly because I like the word."

"So... he abducts and murders a child in the evening hours. No sign of sexual assault or brutality. He just strangles the kid."

"That's not the usual pattern for killings of children."

"I know. But, anyhow, he puts the corpse in the trunk of some poor bastard's car around dawn, then screws with the vehicle. I mean, this guy's got nerve. We're already looking for a missing kid and he has the body laying there, while he takes a stranger's vehicle apart in a driveway in the middle of the night! That's a helluva stunt to pull."

"Like he's playing some kind of elaborate practical joke."

"Yeah... it is. That mean anything to you?"

"It means our murderer's probably one of those annoying wee shits who superglues coins to counter tops and puts Cling-Film over toilet seats. But that pales a bit beside his other bad qualities. I'll think about it... you carry on."

"O.K. Usual pattern. In the morning, our unsuspecting drivers take off to go to work. As soon as they hit rush hour traffic, they have to stop and start, stop and start. Pretty soon, the car breaks down."

"But… Pepe Pineda's car conked out instantly." R.D. stopped Ettrick in mid-flow. "Simpler to do. Yet the dead kid was wired to the lock mechanism. Which is more elaborate than just sticking it in the trunk, like the next victims."

"Exactly! And here's another interesting fact."

"Hit me with it, Frenchie," R.D. lisped, doing a passable Bogart imitation.

"Pepe Pineda left Janet's restaurant at the same time every Sunday morning to have breakfast at Moe's café, up in the Farmers Market on Burnett Road."

"Any reason why?"

"Said he liked a break from his own cooking. Now… Pineda's place is always packed on Sunday mornings cause they do a great breakfast taco special. You ever eaten there?"

"Packed on a Sunday morning." R.D. opened another beer. "So anyone who ate at Janet's a lot would know Pineda's exact schedule? Including the killer."

"Shoot, I know what you're getting at." Ettrick picked up a beer of his own. "Surprise, surprise, the rest of homicide thought of that too. But Janet's has hundreds of regulars. When you think on it, anyone who bought produce in the Farmers Market would also see Pineda every week. If they wanted to know what part of town he came from, they only had to follow him home. Or, it could've been a lucky guess. Maybe Cherry Bomb drove down Guadalupe every day and noticed the old Mercury that was always sitting outside the restaurant was missing on Sunday mornings."

Ettrick took a huge gulp of Miller Lite.

"It's all ifs and could-be's, R.D. There's a million permutations." He put the bottle down and wagged a detecting finger. "But Pineda's vehicle? Like you said, that's something different."

"All the other cars broke down on the journey but Cherry Bomb fixed Pineda's car so it wouldn't start at all," R.D. mused. "If that was his intention, then this murder would be..."

"...It would be the only time when the killer would know *exactly* where and when the dead child would be discovered."

"It was his firstborn," R.D. affirmed. "Too important to miss."

Ettrick punched the air triumphantly. He loved being right.

"I knew it! He was watching, wasn't he?"

R.D.'s face lit up.

"You were the officer on the scene, Ettrick. You might have seen him. Even spoken with him!"

"Yeah, I remember the guy, R.D. He was the one with the hockey mask and the *I Kill Children* button." The detective lit a cigarette and inhaled furiously, little storm clouds writhing round his bitter words. "But there are three restaurants and six shops in the vicinity, where customers had a perfect view of Pineda's car. And two alleyways besides."

"Yeah. Cherry Bomb was probably long gone by the time you turned up."

"More than likely. And you heard the interview tapes of the people I did talk to. There's nothing suspicious about any of them. Then again, I obviously couldn't spot a psycho if he stuck a goddamned axe pole up my butt. That's why I got you. You're the nut detector."

"It's a long shot, I admit." R.D. got more comfortable in his chair. "But, just in case, I want you to tell me everything you remember about every person you encountered that morning. Again."

"Holy shit!" breathed Ettrick. "You better pack a lunch!"

He began to recount all the information he could, and it was considerable. He talked for three solid hours. They came up with nothing.

The next day Cherry Bomb claimed his sixth victim.

Peachy O'Neil's rusty Oldsmobile overheated next to the Wal-Mart on 68th and Lamar, spinning it into the store parking lot. The vehicle ground to a halt, trailing clouds of steam like a doomed warplane. Vapour hung in tendrils over the motionless car. Peachy was assistant manager in the men's clothing department of Sears out on Bee-Cave Road. Forty-two and still only assistant manager. And he was late.

Peachy ran to the back of the Oldsmobile to get a water can, heart racing, ignoring the feeling of doom, daring to hope. He threw open the trunk. He began to scream.

He was forty-two and still only an assistant manager. He was late.

And he had a dead child in his car.

Ettrick was shopping less than a mile away when he caught the terse police bulletin. He was at the crime scene before the first patrolman.

The analyst lay on Ettrick's porch in a black t-shirt, black shorts and army boots, a glistening iced tea balanced on his forehead. The detective stared at his outlandish outfit.

"What?" R.D. protested. "Bedouins in Africa wear black to deflect the heat."

"It don't make them look like a soccer referee."

"Scotsmen aren't designed to look good in shorts." R.D. looked down at his legs. "See how pale my knees are? Christ, they look like a couple of Faberge eggs."

"Do you want me to tell you about the latest killing or not?"

R.D. waved his hand and listened intently while Ettrick faithfully recounted the incident.

"OK," he sighed, once the detective had finished. "Let's go over this one again." Did you check the car?"

"No. I let one of the grocery clerks do it."

R.D. was accustomed to Ettrick's sarcasm and ignored the comment. He removed the dewy glass from his brow and sat up to take a sip.

"O'Neil didn't even look under the hood. He just went and opened the trunk." Ettrick read from his notes. "Same as always, no prints, no nothing. I questioned him at the crime scene. Handsome guy. Gay. Real name was Peter. No alibi for the time that Gina Windsor, that's the dead kid, was kidnapped. It don't mean anything, though. Few of the drivers do."

"Yes. I noticed that."

"Not surprising, really. Most of these guys are quiet and single or divorced. Mostly middle-aged. They stay home nights, do paperwork, and watch TV." He glanced up from his notes. "I imagine it's a pretty dispiriting life, huh?"

"Don't look at me." R.D. swilled his drink scornfully. "I don't expect to live twice the age I am now. And I've got a girlfriend."

He paused.

"Those drivers, though. White. Middle-aged. Solitary. The similarities between them must be more than coincidence."

"Well, duh!" Ettrick looked scornful. "It's gonna be a lot harder for Cherry Bomb to hide a dead kid in a car belonging to some suburban mom with a couple of teenagers sneakin out at night and a husband who might come home from the bar at any minute."

"Point taken. The guys he picked are the type to be tucked up in bed by eleven, with no chance of unexpected visitors."

"Mind you, driver number four was a woman," the detective reminded him. "Driver number one was Mexican with four or five children."

"Aye, but you said yourself the first murder was different, like a try-out. The woman might have been a mistake." R.D. grabbed file number four and held it up. "See… She looks like a man. Or maybe Cherry Bomb's trying to throw us off the trail."

"What fucking trail?"

"The one he's successfully throwing us off." The analyst got up stiffly and leant on the porch rail, idly watching his narrow black suit shift like a rebellious chess piece on Madison's wash line. He made his next move.

"Let's hear the tapes you made of Peachy and any onlookers when his car broke down," he declared. "And I'll need a bag of Pork Scratchings to help me concentrate."

The duo listened to five eyewitness accounts in a row, all of them excitable and conflicting. Ettrick went inside and made more iced tea. The tapes were putting him to sleep. Finally, he settled back into his deck chair and surreptitiously closed his eyes. Petals of light danced like shaman under his lids and the detective began to sink pleasantly into mental fluff.

R.D. nudged his arm.

"I'm playing this one again."

"You spot something?" Ettrick was instantly awake.

"Maybe. I don't know. Who is it?"

The detective swiped tea droplets from the discarded file and muddled through the pages.

"Here he is. He was just a bum... Sean Matula. Yeah, a hobo sunning himself at the edge of the parking lot."

"Listen," said R.D..

He played the tape.

"Ah wuz sittin here and... jus sittin is all..." The voice had a broken, cigarette-stained timbre. "An... People comin out o them stores, n'all the time ah wait for them to drawp things. I can pick em up once they're gone an that aint stealing... see? I aint ne'er stole. Not ever. I wuz brung up right, me... Then a car comes past over there... Big brown car... Big... An dirty.

There's a bang or somethin an... it stops, right over there... kinda swerves, y'know? The father gets out, all annoyed, an walks to the back of the car... I seen this. Then ah start to watch other stuff... like this big fat, black lady shopping, sweatin, maybe gonna drawp something... then all this commotion... screamin and people runnin, an shit... I don know whut..."

"Father." R.D. switched the tape player off. "That guy didn't say the driver. He said the *father*."

"So what?" Ettrick was dismissive. "He was a tramp and he was rambling."

"Actually, he's perfectly lucid," R.D. corrected. "He's mumbling but what he's conveying is coherent enough. Except... he called the driver the father. It's just an odd thing to say. Everyone in this city, bum or not, knows about these killings. Even if they didn't, there's no reason for any witness to think the driver and the dead child are related."

"You're giving me the fucking creeps," Ettrick said. "What're you getting at?"

"It's a pure guess but I'm taking this tape to a voice expert. I'm fairly good with accents. You should hear my Jimmy Stewart. Listen."

He sat back and put on an aw-shucks expression.

"Well, I shays to Jim Bridger, I shays... to thish day, I never did get a good look at the Rocky Mountainsh!"

"That's Jimmy Stewart?" The impersonation was eerily accurate, but Ettrick wasn't going to give his companion the satisfaction of sounding impressed.

"Aye. From *How the West was Won*."

"I thought it was Sean Connery."

"I'm even better at him."

"Will you get on with it?"

"This onlooker made a connection he shouldn't have," R.D. continued huffily. "And the way he enunciates doesn't quite ring true."

He held up the recorder.

"I wonder if this might actually be your killer."

Two days later, R.D. arrived at Ettrick's house along with the paper boy. The detective opened the door, furry-mouthed, sporting a stained blue cotton robe.

"You look like shite," the analyst said, munching a tamale.

"Oh, I can't figure why!" Ettrick's pink eyes fastened malevolently on his peppy breakfast companion. "It aint like there's anything on my mind, disturbin my sleep."

"Like this, you mean." R.D. dangled the tape between his fingers.

"Tell me!"

"I got it analysed by Matt Wadell, head of linguistics at U.T."

"And?" Ettrick hopped around his friend like a curious rabbit.

"He doesn't believe the guy on this recording is a bum. He thinks your tramp is putting on the gutter accent. Told you."

"Holy, fucking fuck!"

"Don't get too excited," R.D. continued sombrely. "Wadell wasn't 100% certain. He certainly won't swear to it in court."

The detective digested this while he fetched two glasses of orange juice from the fridge. He pushed one into R.D.'s oily hand and sat down glumly.

"I didn't even get a proper look at the bastard!" he moaned. "He was all hair and rags and wearing a big floppy hat."

He pushed fingers through his hair.

"We got nothing!"

"We know he's pretty damned good at disguises and voices," R.D. contradicted. "Which is going to make him even harder to catch."

"Thanks for that morale boost."

"Don't mention it." The analyst lifted his glass hesitantly. His eyes narrowed and he lifted a preparatory finger. Ettrick could almost see butterflies of thought chasing each other around inside his companion's head.

"But I think we've just found Cherry Bomb's self-destruct button." R.D. sipped his drink slyly. "And we thought he didn't have one."

"That is?"

"He wants to be more involved with the discovery of the body. First murder? I bet he was there watching, like we suspected. Sixth murder, he's there again. He has to *see* his handiwork discovered."

"How can he possibly know when a doctored car will break down?"

"I imagine he'll have studied the route each driver takes to work. And, as you say, he's awful good with cars. I bet he can figure out approximately where his sabotage will best take effect. Rush hour traffic with lots of starts and stops. Bumps on the road. Whatever. So he waits. This guy's a vehicle expert. He guesses. Sometimes he gets it right, sometimes not. Twice, at least, he's been close enough."

"But that random element stops us paying attention to the onlookers!" Ettrick thumped the table. "Clever fucker! I don't have a clue what he looks like, R.D. Not with that big ole hat on. His face was covered in shit!"

"If you scrubbed the dirt off, you'd probably find a solitary, middle-aged, white male underneath." R.D. put down his juice.

"Spill the beans, buddy."

"This man isn't happy just to kill." R.D. picked his way slowly. "He tries to see the discovery of the body. But now we know being an observer isn't enough. This murder? He didn't leave when the police arrived. He *wanted* you to question him."

"Why? Why risk everything?"

"I don't know," R.D. conceded. "A subconscious desire to be punished? An inferiority complex? Maybe to prove how smart he is. Outwit the dumb cops."

"Thanks," muttered Ettrick. But the analyst wasn't listening. His mouth was working silently, birthing a thought too sinister to be wrong. He gripped Ettrick's robe. The detective clutched it back, glowering at him.

"Listen," R.D. hissed. "The first killing, he watches the results. But by the sixth, he has to say his piece. Be in the centre of the action."

He clenched tighter.

"He's not going to stop there! He's going to try and get as close as he can."

"How much closer can he get?" the detective fumed. "He'd have to jump in the fucking trunk with the body."

"He could get nearer than that, Ettrick." R.D. smoothed out the crumpled bathrobe triumphantly. "He could be the driver of one of the cars."

The detective's mouth fell open.

"He's not driver one or four. They're a Mexican baby machine and a woman," R.D. continued calmly. "He can't be two, three or five either."

"Why not?"

"His risk-taking is obviously escalating. He wouldn't go from being a driver back to observing again." R.D. sipped his orange juice thoughtfully. "Let's rule out Peachy O Neil, because Cherry Bomb is probably the bum you interviewed in the parking lot and let walk away."

"Will you stop harping on about that?"

"OK." R.D. put both hands casually behind his head and stretched. "But any drivers from now on? I would seriously check them out."

Ettrick gawped at him. "You're a goddamned genius."

"It all fits," R.D. said admiringly. "He gets to kill children. Triumphs over the police department. The media makes him famous and he gets sympathy as a victim. I'd say he was the goddamned genius."

"I'll be over the next killing like a rash," Ettrick grunted.

"Go cover your arse." R.D. winced. "I'll get us a beer. After all, we've got to clear some room in your fridge for champagne."

Driver number seven turned out to be Billy Wise, a site engineer for the La Renne Petroleum Company, over in Henderson. On Martin Luther King Boulevard, a sharp crack butted in on his morning radio. Wise's white hard hat tumbled like a brittle baby from the rear window and the greasy smell of burnt oil filled his stalled car. In the trunk of the hissing Ford, he found the body of six-year-old David Hunter.

Ettrick made some discreet inquiries. Mr. Wise's hobby was scuba diving. He went to Galveston on weekly trips, to lose himself in silent translucent water. He was allergic to cats and separated from a younger wife, who had taken their son and moved to Portland. He had one conviction for drunk driving. Didn't look like much of a suspect.

Three weeks later, driver eight was much the same story. Des Roberts drove a Lincoln convertible and taught history at Bennett High. On a sunny Monday morning, his car gave up the ghost outside the gates of the school. Roberts opened the trunk and discovered Sarah Gere, wrapped in tarpaulin and baking in her own blood. Passing pupils picked up the incoherent teacher and carried him to the school medical office.

This time it took Ettrick longer to gather information. The department were getting more and more disgruntled by the detective's private investigation. It was starting to interfere with his other cases.

Again, there seemed nothing unusual about the man. Credit, work history and college records were all unblemished. Roberts, like Billy Wise, was one of the grey, quiet men. His students neither liked nor disliked him. He had a few friends at a local bar. Played slide guitar with a band at weddings.

"Neither of these guys is exactly serial killer material," Ettrick told R.D. over the telephone. "You sure about this?"

"Email the new stuff to me," his partner said. "We'll talk about it tonight. Get me some Habaneras from the Farmers Market if you go past. I want to make my infamous Apollo Chili."

"You reckon that'll shake loose the cobwebs, huh?"

"Oh aye... it'll burn them right off."

"We sure as hell need some kind of shock treatment... Jeez." The detective perked up. "You never can tell. Ole Cherry Bomb might just strike again and give us another suspect."

"Always look on the bright side." R.D. hung up.

The analyst was rummaging through Ettrick's fridge when he heard the front door slam. He grabbed the turkey, Jack-cheese and taco sauce hoagie he was building and hid it behind the bread bin. Seconds later, the detective stole into the kitchen.

"You home already?" R.D. tried to look innocent.

"I'm going out again," Ettrick said quietly. "He's murdered another kid."

The detective returned at 2.00 AM. Madison was asleep and R.D. was sitting silently in the gloomy lounge, drinking Genesee Pale and watching *The Wild Bunch* on video. Ettrick looked exhausted, close to tears.

"That bastard Scharges put in an official complaint about us," he said. "I got a final warning from the department tonight. Stick to my own cases or get the fuck off the force."

He threw a brown canvas bag the length of the room. It missed the table and landed on the floor, lying on its side like a weighty rodent.

"Here," he spat. "Another stack of fucking tapes."

"Don't worry about it." R.D. didn't take his eyes from the television. "The Cherry Bomb is Des Roberts."

"What? What you talkin about?"

The analyst hit the pause button and switched on a little desk lamp by his head. His face soaked up light until it kindled his eyes.

"I was going over the notes you sent me. Roberts drives a convertible."

"So?" Ettrick was too beaten down to try and understand.

"When his car stalled, the top was down. One hundred ten degrees in the shade and the top was down. Rush hour traffic in the blazing heat and he's driving an air-conditioned car. But the top was down."

"So what? Roberts is a Texan, not some wimp-assed Scotsman that can't stand a bit of sun."

"Oh, really? Well, I phoned the principal of the school where the guy teaches and pretended to be you."

"You did what?"

"Like I say, that's one of my many fucking talents," R.D. drawled proudly, staging a fair parody of Ettrick's languid tones. "I can do all sorts of accents, imitate voices. When I was a student, I used to have an act with a university theatre company where I..."

"Would you get to the damned point?"

R.D. returned to earth.

"I asked the principal if Roberts ever put the top of his convertible up. He said no. Never. Not even when it rained."

"I may be up for moron of the year award," the detective seethed. "But I don't see exactly where all this is getting us."

"The man's claustrophobic." R.D. tilted his head like a hawk. "Not in his home or in his classroom. I checked. Just in his car."

"And?"

"Phobias are usually caused by childhood trauma, Ettrick. It might be a long shot, but I assume Mr. Roberts had an unhappy upbringing. I'll bet as punishment, someone used to lock him in the trunk of a vehicle. His father would be my guess."

"Jesus Christ!"

"Think about it." The analyst sat up excitedly. "Just suppose Des Roberts' dad was a really nasty nook... eh? Had a habit of locking his son in the boot every time the boy misbehaved. In the heat of Texas, remember. Can you imagine what that would do to a child?"

"He'd go crazy."

"Aye... of course, he would. Roberts probably grew up all warped inside. One day he snapped. Maybe his life got stuck in a rut. Maybe his car got stuck in a traffic jam. Could've been any number of things that set him off."

He sat back and tapped his nose.

"So, he starts to kill children. He hides them in the trunk of cars owned by white, middle-aged men. Men that remind him of his father... see? When the symbolic driver-cum-father opens the trunk, he doesn't find a repentant child. He finds a dead one. It's every punished kid's dream. I'll die and you'll be sorry!"

"Shit!" Ettrick slammed his hand on the table. "It's right! It's gotta be right!"

Sinking onto the arm of the chair, he gave his friend an admiring but lifeless pat on the arm.

"You're not pleased?" R.D. looked puzzled.

"It aint that." Ettrick's shoulders sank. "It's just we need hard evidence to back up your theory, even if we know who the killer is. And we haven't got any. But, if we sit on this, we'll be holding back the official investigation. From now on, Roberts is gonna have to be monitored round the clock."

"Aye. Why can't we do that?"

Ettrick sat down heavily in front of the television, its lustrous glimmer casting phantoms across his misery.

"I've been warned, R.D. Anyone catches us casing Roberts, I'll get thrown off the force and you'll likely get tossed in jail for stalking. We have to share this info with the rest of the department before anyone else dies. Then it won't be my collar. It'll belong to Grimm and Scharges. After all this fucking work."

R.D. switched off the TV altogether, always a sign he was deadly serious. Shadows leapt forward to conspire with him.

"What if we got a confession? Would that do?"

"That'd be swell," the detective sneered. "I'll just run on over to Robert's house and beat one out of him."

"Aw, you Texans. So quick to use blunt force." R.D. pointed the remote at his sullen partner then swung it slowly back to the TV.

"You find me all the information you can on Des Roberts' father."

He pressed a button and the TV winked on again.

"I'll get you that confession."

On a muggy Sunday evening, a few days later, Des Roberts arrived home to find Ettrick sweating on his doorstep. A thin, pale man with white hair and large, square glasses, Roberts politely asked if the detective wished to come in. Ettrick declined, equally courteous, insisting it would be better if the teacher accompanied him to the police station and answered a few routine questions.

Des Roberts obliged.

"I'm sorry about the lateness of the hour," Ettrick apologised as they sped downtown. Roberts didn't seem to notice that the detective was driving a squad car rather than an unmarked vehicle. "We crime fighters are just snowed under these days. What with a serial killer on the loose an all."

He glanced sideways. Roberts had rolled down the window.

"I can switch on the air conditioning if you like."

His passenger held up a pasty hand.

"S'all right... I like the breeze."

The south-side station was quiet on a Sunday night, only a skeleton crew staunching the flow of sin. Ettrick hurried Roberts, unchallenged, past the front desk and up the stairs. There they talked for an hour in a windowless interview room.

The detective fished, always civil, pulling his verbal punches. As expected, Roberts gave nothing away. Eventually, Ettrick drained the last of his coffee and looked at his watch.

"Thank you for your help," he said politely. "I'll drive you home."

The detective, still careful not to attract attention, nodded to a few beat cops - who couldn't care less what he was up to - and ushered Roberts out the back door. The men stepped into a moonless walkway, leaves hanging like dried bats on the deserted, tree-lined avenue. Buttery pats of streetlight blobbed on the ruffled surfaces.

"I'm afraid I'm off duty now, so we've gotta take my own car. It's in an underground lot a couple of blocks from here."

"Sure. No problem."

The men strolled silently down the star-speckled sidewalk, then turned onto a deserted concrete parking grid. Ettrick stole a glimpse at Roberts as they descended the stairs to the lower level. The man gave him a nervous smile.

They headed for the farthest corner, sidling past a subterranean landscape of discarded cartons and crushed beer cans. It was hard to tell what ground underfoot, for most of the light fixtures seemed to have been shattered and the floor had turned to ink. Ettrick tisked as he walked.

"I don't know how in hell these things get smashed," he said. "It's all reserved parking down here - with the police station round the corner, no less."

They rounded the last pillar and the detective heard a gasp from the man beside him.

In front of them, a leviathan slumbered in the gloom, a '76 Packard, blunt and shark-like. It was too dark to make out the colour or the license number of the car but the shape appeared unmistakable to Des Roberts.

Small wonder. A '76 Packard was the vehicle his father used to drive.

"I know, I know!" Ettrick sighed wearily. "It looks like a pile of shit but I got the thing for next to nothing. Last owner couldn't wait to get rid of it, for some reason. I'll let you in the back."

He opened the front door with a vicious pull. Roberts stiffened.

"Would it be all right if I sat in the passenger seat?" His nervousness was apparent.

"Shoot... Can't let you, I'm afraid," the detective replied cheerfully. "Some dumb police rule. Oh, the back doors don't work."

Roberts stopped tugging on the handle.

"You'll have to climb in from the front."

"The light doesn't work either," whispered Roberts as he wormed timidly into the rear. "The interior light isn't working."

Ettrick jumped into the driver's seat and turned the ignition key. The engine spluttered and died. He tried again, with the same result.

"Why haven't you turned on the headlights?" Roberts asked, in a small voice.

"In this car!" Ettrick twisted the key once more. "I don't dare switch them on 'till we're up and rolling properly. Battery goes flat every ten minutes, I swear. Doesn't even start half the time."

"No. Engines don't work that way..." Roberts began. The vehicle gave a throaty roar and cut him off.

"I'll put the lights on when we reach the street." Ettrick comforted as the car crawled through the void. "I always have to do this."

The Packard crept around the corner. Before them lay the big, filthy mouth of a car elevator.

"Aint this thing great?" the detective winked. The Packard jolted over the grated surface and lurched to a halt. "They took all the vehicle elevators out of Austin garages about ten years back, cause of health and safety issues, or some shit like that. I reckon this is the only one left in Texas."

He looked round.

"Everything fine back there, Mr. Roberts?"

There was silence. Eventually, Des Robert's voice skulked, trembling and muted, from the midnight hole of the back seat.

"I don't much like closed spaces," he croaked.

Ettrick got out of the car and hauled the iron gate shut. Echoes collided around them and the whole elevator shuddered. He pressed the 'up' button, teeth gleaming in the darkness, then squeezed back in the car. The elevator began to ascend, a mass of groans and strained metal murmurs. Occasionally the whole edifice quivered, as its flanks ground against the encasing brick shaft.

Suddenly it stopped.

"What the hell?" the detective said. "It's never done that before."

The monstrous structure - car elevator, car and passengers – dangled, motionless, in utter blackness. There were no lights in the lift or the shaft. Only searing heat, stored in the bricks all day and now re-leased. It felt like a hot towel over Ettrick's face.

"What the fuck is going on!" Robert's voice rasped, betraying barely-contained panic.

"No need to use bad language, sir." Ettrick opened the door again. "The elevator has broken down, is all. Just stay in the car."

He heard an invisible sob from the interior of the vehicle. The de-tective stretched his arm out and stepped into the blackness, lost as soon as he let go of the Packard's handle.

He stood stock-still, listening.

There. A barely perceived sibilance to his right. It was R.D. crawl-ing from his hiding place under a stack of rags, where he had been well placed to push the stop button. Eyes accustomed to the dark, the analyst pinched Ettrick's butt and the detective had to stifle a snigger. He crouched quickly as the shape slid past and dragged open the Packard's door.

"Can you fix it? Is it fixable?" Robert's voice was ruptured and hoarse. His fingers began to drum a frantic pattern on the cracked leather of the seat. Then a deeper sound. His fists.

"Please let me out," he whimpered. "I can't stand it in here. I can't, I can't, I can't."

R.D. rose up over the seat. The terrified Roberts was just able to make out the murky contours of a face that wasn't Ettrick's. An out-line, horribly familiar, of a moustache and battered fedora.

They were the same style as his long-dead father used to sport.

"Stop! Stop!" Roberts shrieked. "Oh fuck! Oh, fuck!"

"Don't you sweer at me, boy," R.D. snarled in a perfect Irish ac-cent. "Yer know what oi'll do to yer."

Des Roberts' father had been Irish.

Ettrick heard a shuddering intake of breath from the rear seat.

"Ye've been bad, son," the analyst hissed. "Ye'll have to be pun-ished."

Roberts began to scream. Ettrick scrambled away from the car, hackles standing on end. He slammed both hands over his ears, totally unprepared for the teacher's soul-shredding cries.

The screeching stopped as immediately as it began. Ettrick held his breath. In its place a came a childlike whimper, thin and utterly forlorn.

"Take me out of the dark, Poppy," Des Roberts pleaded. "Please, please, please... I won't ever be bad again."

"I will, boy. I will." Ettrick heard the click of R.D.'s dictaphone. "You just tell yer Poppy what you did. Oil forgive you and we'll get out of this place together."

R.D.'s voice was gentler than the detective had ever heard it.

He might have been talking to his own son.

About the Authors

Looking For Soul Food and a Place to Eat

Jan-Andrew Henderson is a Scottish author of 38 childrens, teen, YA and adult fiction and non-fiction books. His novels have been shortlisted for 13 literary awards and he is the winner of the Royal Mail Award, the Doncaster Book Prize, plus an Aurealis Award. He now lives in Brisbane.

www.janandrewhenderson.com

Life, Apathy and Extraterrestrials

Justin Zipprich is a freelance writer living in Los Angeles and has been writing ever since he was a kid. He has had work published in *Necrology Shorts, Foliate Oak Literary Magazine, Fiction and Verse, Whisperings Magazine* and *Luscious.*

He has had an honorable mention in *Allegory* as well as a Best Screenplay nomination at the Action on Film Festival, for his script *One Moment.*

Dread Circus

Pamela Jeffs is an Australian speculative fiction author with a love for writing short fiction. Pamela has published four short story collections, co-authored an anthology with Aiki Flinthart (*The Zookeeper's Takes of Interstellar Oddities*) and published 70+ short stories in various national and international magazines and anthologies.

Winner of the Aurealis Award, she has been shortlisted for many others, including a Ditmar Award.

www.pamelajeffs.com

This Ghost Needs to Fuck Off

Curtis McIntyre is a full-time landscaper who pretends to be a writer on weekends. His short fiction has appeared in the anthology *Howls From Hell* under the pseudonym B.O.B. Jenkin.

A Lovely Little Catch Up

Russ Carlton is a 40-something copywriter living in Manchester, England. He has been writing fiction for fun for many years. A fringe theatre addict, he is always looking for the strange, unexpected, and off-kilter. He hopes to gradually turn marketing words into real, new stories.

www.RussCarlton.co.uk

My Mom Ate My Dad and Here's Why

Casey Campbell is a librarian in New Zealand. She has published seven full-length novels and many short stories for horror anthologies. You can find her mostly on Instagram

@caseycampbellwrites

If You Go Down to the Zoo Today

Mark Locke is an MA educated graduate of Drama and stand-up comic, performing on the stand-up circuit in London. He has worked and trained as an actor with Phillipe Gaulier and completed courses in clown and fooltime with Jonathan Kay and his Nomadic Fool Academy. His parody song *Stand by Saddam* was banned from Radio 1.

He is currently rewriting *Hamlet* as a John Hughes teen comedy and trying to stage the sinking of the Titanic in a bathtub.

Woke Up Like This

Donald McCarthy has published fiction in many venues, including *Nightmare Magazine, Akashic Books, The Baltimore Review*, and *The Manhattanville Review*, while his non-fiction has appeared in *The*

Huffington Post, Undark, Salon, Paste Magazine, The Irish Times, and *Alternet.*

He was an honorable mention in *Glimmer Train's* New Writer contest and his essays have appeared in the books *It's Happening Again: 25 Years of Twin Peaks* and *The Man in the High Castle and Philosophy.*

www.donaldmccarthy.com/writings.html

Wade Hunter has appeared in *Coffin Blossoms, Little Demon Digest, Scare Street, Night Terrors Vol. 10*, and *Executive Dread*. He also writes young adult and children's stories under the name Aaron Buterbaugh.

Ophelia

Rob Smith is a Scottish writer, although stranded in the United States through work. He is winner of the *Black Springs Crime Fiction Prize* and *The Scotsman Orange Short Story Prize.*

His more literary and noir fiction has shown up in places like *Manchester Review, Barcelona Review, Gutter* and *Warwick Review.*

www.robmccluresmith.com

The Killing Pen

Pauline Yates lives in Queensland, Australia and her horror and dark speculative fiction has appeared in numerous anthologies.

Winner of the Australian Horror Writers Association Short Story Competition, an Australian Shadows Awards short fiction finalist and her short story *The Best Medicine* was translated for the *Mondi Incantati* series produced by Riflessi di Luce Lunare in Italy.

When not writing, she enjoys enticing native wildlife into her garden, arguing with her cat about his 3.00 am breakfast routine and taking photos of the sunrise, if she wakes up in time

https://paulineyates.com

The Swallow

Mark Wheaton is a screenwriter (*Friday the 113th, The Messengers, Voice from the Stone* and more) and novelist (*Quake Cities, Fr. Chavez Trilogy, Emily Eternal*). *Emily Eternal* was named one of the 5 Best Sci-Fi Novels of the Year by the Financial Times. He has also published stories in Dark Peninsula Press, Macabre Ladies Publishing, 18th Wall, Sentinel Creatives, Bag of Bones Press, Blood Song Books, Hellbound Books and others.

He worked as a genre reporter with bylines at *Fangoria, SFX, Total Film, Shivers* and elsewhere. He is also a writer of video games (F.E.A.R. franchise) and comics (Dark Horse's *The Cleaners*).

www.mark-wheaton.com

Dragon Rufus Interrupts Class

Justin Hunter has twelve published novels and over forty short stories in anthologies. He is also an award-winning screenwriter (Crown Wood International Film Festival, WPRN.TV Screenplay Competition, 13 Horror.com Film and Screenplay).

His drama *Cast Away Stones* was a finalist at the TMFF and Oaxaca Film Festivals. His horror-comedy *Chet & Floyd vs. the Apocalypse* was a finalist at the Austin Comedy Film Festival and the Portland Comedy Film Festival. He lives with his wife and four boys in Missouri, USA.

https://www.facebook.com/profile.php?id=100060328726586

The Tit-Haunted Man

Adam Breckenridge is an overseas traveling faculty member for the University of Maryland Global Campus. He travels the world teaching American military stationed overseas and is currently based in South Korea. He currently has twenty-four short story publications and most recently appeared in *Clockwork, Curses and Coal, Mystery Weekly*, Horror Addicts Press and *Beneath Ceaseless Skies*.

How To Read A Woman

SJ Townend has been writing evil dark fiction in Bristol for two years and has work published with Ghost Orchid Press, Gravestone Press, and a few other e-zines, lit mags and presses. She was also shortlisted for the HG Wells Short Story writing prize.

She's putting together her first collection of speculative, dark fiction and horror stories, working title: *Sick Girl Screams*. SJ has two children and a cat named Mr. Bradbury, none of whom are old enough to listen to her stories, all of whom enjoy licking peanut butter from plates. Twitter: @SJTownend -

Moonlighting

Mark Watson is from Winnipeg, Manitoba. He is of fiery Scottish descent and complacent Canadian temperament. The father of three, Mark truly knows what horror is. He has a number of books available on Kindle Direct Publishing. You can find out more on his Amazon Author Central page by using the following link.

www.amazon.com/author/writes_0-60

Something To Do On a Rainy Day When You're Dead

David Wesley Hill is the winner of the Golden Bridge Award. He has written about forty stories and a couple of novels, including the award-winning nautical adventure *At Drake's Command*. He studied under Joseph Heller and Jack Cady and received a Masters in creative writing from the City University of New York. Currently, he lives in rural North Carolina.

https://temurlonepress.com/category/our-authors

Never Give Up

Geoff Hart works as a scientific editor, specializing in helping scientists who have English as their second language publish their research works. He has published 54 stories, included in Darrell

Schweitzer's Lovecraft anthologies *Mountains of Madness* and *Shadows Out of Time* from PS Publishing, *Analog*, *After Dinner Conversation*, *Allegory*, *Andromeda Spaceways Inflight Magazine*, *OnSpec*, *The Tesseracts* anthology series, *Jayhenge* anthologies, *Paper Butterfly* and *Polar Borealis*.

Visit him online at www.geoff-hart.com

Pity the Penguins

M.S. Gardner moves between the worlds of fabulism and realism and draws inspiration from the curious, bizarre, and absurd nature of life. She has perfected her impersonation of a normal human being well enough to hold a job. While her physical body resides on the Gulf Coast, she mostly lives in her head.

www.thecuriousauthor.com

Sugar Mice

Ishbelle Bee is a writer of poetry, comedy horror and dark fantasy. Her novels *The Singular and Extraordinary Tale of Mirror and Goliath* and *The Contrary Tale of the Butterfly Girl* were published by Angry Robot and she was shortlisted for the Funny Women Writing Awards with her radio play series about a psychotic Victorian butler. She hopes, one day, someone will be daft enough to produce it.

https://www.ishbellebee.com

Cherry Bomb

Oh no. It's Jan Andrew Henderson again. And he gets the longest story cause he's the editor. This is actually a subplot in his novel *Hide* but he felt it made a decent stand-alone story. It's not cheating, cause nobody ever read the damned book.

www.janandrewhenderson.com

ABOUT THE EDITOR

Jan-Andrew Henderson is a professional member of the Institute of Professional Editors, an industry assessor/mentor for the Queensland Writers Centre, an ambassador for Australia Reads, a peer assessor for the Australian Council for The Arts and a convenor for the Aurealis Awards. He runs the Green Light Literary Rescue Service, offering advice and editing to writers.

He has been published in the UK, USA, Australia, Canada and Europe by Oxford University Press, Collins, Hardcourt Press, Amberley Books, Oetinger Publishing, Mainstream Books, Black and White Publishers, Mlada Fontana, Black Hart and Floris Books.

www.janandrewhenderson.com
www.greenlightliteraryrescueservice.com

www.ingramcontent.com/pod-product-compliance
Lightning Source LLC
Chambersburg PA
CBHW020401120726
47904CB00002B/662